I0532641

THE CAPTIVE SHIFTER

(MAGIC OF CLADDARE BOOK 1)

VERONICA SCOTT

Copyright 2017 by Jean D. Walker

This book is a work of fiction. The names, places, characters and incidents are products of the writer's imagination or have been used fictitiously and are not to be construed as real. Any resemblance to persons, living or dead, actual events, locales or organizations is entirely coincidental.

All rights reserved. No part of this book may be reproduced, scanned or distributed in any manner whatsoever without written permission from the author except in the case of brief quotation embodied in critical articles and reviews.

Cover Art by Fiona Jayde

To my daughters Valerie and Elizabeth, my brother David and my best friend Daniel for all their encouragement and support!

ACKNOWLEDGMENTS

Julie C and The E-book Formatting Fairies!

CHAPTER ONE

Caitlyn let the caravan master do the arguing on her behalf, although she wanted to reach through the bars of the city gate, grab the officious man standing in her way and shake him. Such a simple request—open the gate, glance at her papers and let her go on my way. It lacked but half an hour till sunset and the captain of the guard at the ancient city's portal wasn't inclined to allow a long caravan to pass so late in the day.

Lazy bastard. She eyed him, tempted to use some of her magic to influence him but inner caution held her back. This was the city of witches and magic. She needed to go slowly displaying her abilities. *Calm down, breathe. None of this will go as I hope if I let myself show anger.* Caitlyn sucked in a deep breath of the damp air and stood straighter, adjusting her hood to keep the autumn drizzle off her face.

"Camp on the meadow across the river," the captain said from the other side of the gate, addressing the caravan master. "Return in the morning."

Glancing at Caitlyn, the old man shook his head. "I've told you, one of my passengers is an applicant, identified by the queen's Searchers. She must be at the palace tonight, for the welcoming ceremony. She can't wait until morning or risk losing her place in this year's Trial."

As she edged closer to the arched entryway to get out of the increasing rain, impatience burned along Caitlyn's nerves. Why did a petty tyrant have to be her final obstacle after the long journey? The caravan master was right; she did have to be at the palace tonight. After three weeks of slow travel from her home in the South it was especially galling to be so close to missing the deadline. To literally stand on the threshold of her destination and be refused entry was unbelievably frustrating. *All right, honeyed words first, then there's nothing for it but to unleash a taste of magic on him.* Pasting a smile on her lips, she stepped forward, allowing her cape to fall open, deliberately swaying her hips a bit. "Please, captain, I'm sure the Witch Queen would appreciate your extra efforts to let me arrive on time. The Searchers told me every woman with power is greatly needed this year," Caitlyn said, in an effort to cajole him. "How about permitting me past the gate by myself tonight? Admit the entire caravan tomorrow?"

Grinning like a cat toying with a mouse, the officer shook his head emphatically, shaking a finger at her. "Against the rules. We do the entire group or none. Now come back in the morning!"

The caravan master took her elbow, probably to escort her to the waiting wagons. Caitlyn jerked her arm free, ready to summon energy to bespell the officer into giving her entry. Folly to risk using power so soon in this place but he left her no choice. She pushed aside the next worry, about finding her way through the unknown city to the castle.

A new voice entered the conversation. "Is there a problem here?"

Behind the blustering captain, the other soldiers had snapped to respectful attention and were saluting two newcomers. The first gentleman walked forward into the torchlight at the gate proper. He was older than she, dressed in black and burgundy garments projecting a subtle message of wealth and power. Attractive, if one was looking for a bedmate, which she wasn't. As the second man came into the light Caitlyn took a step back, blinking.

She'd never seen his like before. A shapeshifter? Why would such a rare creature of magic be here? The power surrounding him was palpable to one with her gifts, yet didn't flare in her second sight as it should. As if the magic was restrained but how could such a thing be possible? Dressed in a uniform similar to the officious gatekeeper's, this man was clearly a warrior – muscular, handsome, high cheekbones, piercing green eyes, long, unbound sandy blond hair. But why would a shapeshifter be in this dank, gray city? His people ran in the massive forests of the North, where their kind ruled and humans walked at their peril. A city, much less a Court with all its ritual and routine, would be the last place to find such a wild and free spirit.

He returned her gaze with open appreciation. Caitlyn lowered her eyes first.

The captain lost his self-importance as he faced the nobleman who'd spoken. "Begging your pardon, your grace, I didn't see you there. No problem worthy of your grace's attention. I've told this caravan master he has to wait till morning to clear the gate. It's too late to check them in today."

"I see. Captain Nedd, is it?" The Duke's voice was deceptively soft. He looked at Caitlyn and her companion. "But you believe otherwise, good caravan master?"

"Aye, sir, I do. This lady here has traveled from the south, from Ordlathus, to present herself at Court tonight." He gestured at Caitlyn.

She pushed her hood back and curtseyed. "If it pleases your grace, my name is Caitlyn and I was chosen by the Queen's Searchers. I asked the captain if he could permit me to enter the gate alone this evening, if there's no time to inspect the whole caravan."

"A reasonable enough request, I should think." The Duke raised his eyebrows and slapped his riding gloves against his hand as he looked at the captain. Focusing his attention once again on Caitlyn, he said, "First, welcome to our city." He gestured at the nearest guard. "Raise the gate." As the man complied and the heavy iron bars creaked upward, his companion leaned forward, speaking to the duke, although his words carried to Caitlyn.

"While you sort this out, Aerrol, I'd best go ahead. Her Majesty isn't forgiving of those who arrive late."

"So you can be on time, while I face her wrath." The noble laughed and punched the shapeshifter in the arm. "Well I'm her kinsman, which will take some of her displeasure away. You go ahead then."

Bowing, the warrior shot another glance at Caitlyn before striding away.

It was a relief not to have the power of his magic lapping around her ankles like a curious cat any more. Caitlyn gave herself a mental shake and focused on the Duke. She sensed he had a small gift of power but it was buried so deep inside him, she doubted if he even knew it existed. No risk of discovery from him.

"Please, do step inside, where it's dry," Aerrol was saying, gesturing for her to enter the now open gate. "As it happens my sister was chosen by Searchers this year as well. I'm taking her to the Palace now in fact. Would you care to ride with us?"

Safely out of the rain, she pushed back the hood of her cloak and curtseyed, unable to believe her good luck. "It's kind of you to offer, sir, thank you."

"Then the arrangements are settled." Aerrol smiled at Caitlyn. "If the captain could bestir himself to glance at your papers, we can be on our way. As my friend Kyler said before deserting us, it's not advisable to arrive late to an event at the palace."

"Thank you, your grace," Caitlyn said. She handed her papers to the fuming captain. While he made a show of leafing through the dog eared file, she shook the caravan master's hand warmly. "Thank you for your courtesy these past few weeks, sir."

"We owe you gratitude, mistress, for curing the blight on our oxen after they ate the poison weeds a week ago. I'll send your horse and trunk to the castle tomorrow, as soon as I can." The caravan master glared at the captain. "We'll be lined up at the gate at dawn."

"There's at least a half hour till full dark," the Duke said, frowning. "Captain, proceed with checking the entire caravan. No good reason for making them camp in a soggy meadow. They already crossed the river once, no need to force the poor beasts to make the effort twice more on our account. After all, this is your last night on duty at my gates, Captain Nedd, correct? Aren't you planning on entering the service of Princess Bradana tomorrow? I'd hate to see your transfer delayed on account of early morning gate traffic. I do have to sign your orders, releasing you from my guards, you know. It could take me weeks if the transfer doesn't go as planned tomorrow." He yawned, as if bored by thhe topic. "So many other important matters demand my attention."

The captain ground his teeth audibly at the thinly veiled threat but handed Caitlyn's papers to her. He saluted the Duke and without missing a beat berated his soldiers, yelling at them to start the caravan clearance as if they'd been the problem, not him.

The Duke offered his arm to Caitlyn, who was suppressing a grin with an effort. "I was to meet my sister here, to continue our journey to the castle together. She'll be waiting in the carriage, this way."

"Thank you, your grace. I was in some despair what to try next when you arrived," Caitlyn said as they walked away from the gate. "I can't miss the ceremony."

"Thinking of climbing the wall perhaps?" he said with a twinkle

She laughed. Little did he know the mad notion crossed her mind at least once in the last half hour. The feat would have required too much expenditure of magic, given other tests she might face tonight at the palace.

"I'm sorry there's no time for you to change or even wash the dust of travel off. The welcoming ceremony is beginning in a few minutes. I'll leave word with the castle seneschal to have your baggage directed to the headmistress of applicants though." The duke steered her around a puddle.

Holding her skirts out of the muck as best she could, Caitlyn regretted having to appear before the queen and her court in bedraggled condition, but there was nothing to be done. At least she'd beat the deadline, thanks to this man. Returning a year from now to try again wasn't an option. "I'd no idea people in the city were so welcoming."

"Not all are, I fear. I do my best to set the tone. And here's the carriage."

The ride to the palace was short. Caitlyn had to admit she enjoyed walking into the throne room with the Duke of the City, his mother and sister Susana. Being in such exalted company was much more pleasant than trying to find her own way in this sprawling complex. All doors were opened hurriedly for the

Duke's party. Aerrol and his mother, the Dowager Duchess, left the two women in the appointed gathering spot for applicants and then Caitlyn had only to wait her turn to meet the Witch Queen.

The line of young women moved ever so slowly toward their individual moment under the queen's gaze. Caitlyn's bones ached with tiredness from her long journey to reach this place in time, and her head pounded with stress over nearly being refused entry to the city. She studied the throne room as the line inched forward, noting with surprise the tattered and worn state of the tapestries covering the walls. In far too many places the mortar appeared to be crumbling between the great stones making up the wall. A ten times larger than life sized, golden figure of an eagle had been cunningly set into the wall above the throne as if it was hovering over the occupant. The effect would have been more impressive without the obvious spots where the gilt was worn off or tarnishing to an ugly green. *Why doesn't anyone pay attention to these things in such a mighty palace? The Queen certainly has enough staff.*

A sharp tug on her sleeve recalled Caitlyn from her speculations. "Don't fidget so," Susana said in a hissing whisper. "We're nearly there."

A moment later Susana mounted the twelve gleaming black marble stairs, curtseyed in front of the throne and answered low voiced questions from the Queen. Caitlyn watched closely, seeking to learn how this ritual was supposed to go so she wouldn't embarrass herself more than necessary. Two women sat in slightly smaller thrones on either side, interjecting remarks as the discussion continued. They must be the princesses, Bradana and Ylain.

Caitlyn eyed the guards ranged behind and beside the throne. Most were watching the guests milling about in the crowded room, probably bored with this endless ceremony. One man was staring directly at her, however, and she hastily lowered her eyes. The shapeshifter again. Was she to run into him at every turn? Furious with herself, she realized she was blushing over the obvious appreciation of her form he'd displayed.

She risked a furtive glance at the dais. He continued to study her. Worry threaded itself through her nerves. What if he could sense the many secrets she was hiding? What if he could read her thoughts? Who really knew what powers his kind commanded? Would he say something to the queen? She touched the amulet around her neck and prayed to her goddess for calm. The next few minutes were critical. She had to make a good impression on the Queen. No matter how handsome or unusual the guard was, she couldn't allow him to distract her. Too much was at stake for her people in the South.

Then the page beckoned her forward as the duke's sister exited the dais on the other side.

Consulting the tablet he cradled in the crook of his arm, the page squinted and pronounced her name a bit awkwardly. "Caity Lyn of Ordlathus."

She proceeded up the stairs as gracefully as she could, terrified of slipping on the slick stone, hoping she wasn't leaving muddy footprints, and then curtseyed. "It's Caitlyn, your majesty."

"From Ordlathus? How unusual," the Witch Queen said, her voice low and melodic. She leaned forward on her throne, looking Caitlyn over from the top of her neatly braided hair to the tip of her scuffed, stained shoes. "We've not had an applicant from there in a long time, have we, Ylain?"

"Perhaps never, in fact," agreed her sister, sitting to the right. She seemed amused by the idea, round, pleasant face dimpling with mirth. "I can't recall another."

"Ordlathus doesn't breed magic," said the other sister, Bradana, flatly, drumming her fingers on the padded arm of her throne.

"Forgive me, your majesty, but the Searchers did clear me to make the journey," Caitlyn reminded them. "I passed the basic test."

"Much remains to be done before you earn a place at this Court, access to this training, bumpkin." Frowning, Bradana shook a finger at her. Her obvious distaste for Caitlyn's appearance made her angular face even more harsh and forbidding. "Don't get above yourself so soon."

"I'm sorry, your highness." Caitlyn apologized immediately, dropping another curtsey for good measure. "I'm so happy to be here, it's all so grand and glorious for a country girl." She kept her eyes on the eagle mosaic inlay in front of the thrones. The words felt false and wooden on her tongue, probably because they were. She hoped these women are so used to flattery and sycophancy they wouldn't notice anything amiss about her tone.

"You're somewhat older than our usual candidate, by at least ten years, I'd judge." Bradana assessed Caitlyn more closely. Caitlyn made herself stand straight, shoulders back. The Queen's sister saw entirely too much. Surely it would be unheard of to reject a properly Searched candidate before the testing? She strengthened her mental shields, reinforced her glamourie, and checked her protective spells closely, even as she fended off a push at the edges of her mind, a probe clearly launched by Bradana.

"Don't scare the poor girl," Ylain admonished, laying a hand on her sister's arm. The mental probe snapped off as suddenly as it had begun and Caitlyn pressed her lips together to smother a telltale sigh of relief. Ylain smiled warmly in her direction, apparently unconscious of the byplay on the magical plane. "I'm sure there's an interesting story here, some compelling reason the Searchers selected her, despite the uh age disparity with our usual requirements. We're glad to have you here, Caitlyn."

"Welcome to the Court and to the testing," the Witch Queen said, apparently satisfied for now or else bored with the topic. "I'll be interested to see how you progress." She fished a badge out of the large crystal bowl on the table next to her, handing the brooch to the herald. Stepping forward, he pinned the medallion to the shoulder seam of Caitlyn's plain green dress.

"You can go," he whispered. "Curtsey again and exit to the right."

Heaving a sigh of relief as she backed away, Caitlyn did as she as told. On the way to the stairs at the edge of the dais, she had to pass directly in front of the shapeshifter guard. She dared to glance one more time at him, to find him gazing at her with an odd expression on his handsome face.

Does he pity me for my success in persuading them to let me stay? Before Caitlyn could ponder the guard's unusual reaction, Susana was grabbing her by the wrist.

"Thank goodness the smile and curtsey ritual is over. What a bore." The duke's sister drew Caitlyn headlong into the crush of nobility and other guests, weaving around the small chattering groups with skill. "Come on, we have to meet with the headmistress and we shouldn't dawdle. She's going to discuss tomorrow's trial of power."

"We certainly need to hear any details she's ready to share." Relief flooded over Caitlyn in a cool wave as they left the hot, crowded audience room and walked through a side hallway. The first hurdle in her quest had been cleared. She breathed a quick prayer of thanks to her goddess.

"I know how the trial goes already," Susana giggled. "I've been practicing with the crystals for months. Hasn't everyone?"

Caitlyn tripped on a loose seam in the carpet, keeping herself from falling by grabbing at her companion. So much for relief, the next challenge appeared already. *No one mentioned crystals to me.* She licked her lips, swallowing hard. "Crystals?"

"Yes, you know, the crystals." As if stirring the air, Susan waved her hand. "You manipulate the gems and depending on the patterns you throw, the Queen and her sisters decide what training you're best suited for." Eyes wide, Susana stopped dead. Caitlyn had to stutter step not to run into her. "You've never worked the crystals? Never?"

Caitlyn shook her head.

"How did the Searchers know to select you?"

The poor Searchers probably wondered themselves. There had been quite a few witches of Ordlathus sitting in the pub that night, bending the will of the visitors from the North to influence them to see Caitlyn as a wonderful choice for further training. Not something she was planning to explain to anyone. Genuine amusement curved her lips at the memory. "How do they know to select anyone?" she said. "The answer is the Searchers' mystery."

"Never mind, I'm sure it will all come right in the morning." Susana started off toward the meeting room again and Caitlyn followed dutifully. "You're here and that's what counts. So many women hope to achieve this and so few are actually selected."

Caitlyn decided to give in to the curiosity pricking at her. "Who was the guard to the far right of the throne?"

Smiling Susana said, "His name is Kyler. Handsome isn't he? Why do you ask?"

"He was with your brother at the gate so I was surprised to see him in the throne room," Caitlyn lied. "I was merely curious." Her true questions remained unasked—is he a shifter and what role does he play at Court?

Shaking her head, the other girl said, "Don't waste your time thinking about him."

"Why not? He was staring at me."

Susana stopped again, checked to see who might be near them, then spoke quietly in Caitlyn's ear. "He's not human. He's a shapeshifter, under the Witch Queen's spell. Some of the guards have an eye for the women of the Court, even for us, the applicants. It's not forbidden to have a little discreet fun as long as consent is mutual." Susana gave a trilling shriek of laughter and patted Caitlyn's shoulder. "Don't be shocked, you're at Court now, not out in the southern hinterlands. I'm sure the customs are looser here than where you come from. But he's completely off limits." Barely whispering, she added, "The queen is jealous."

You've no idea what our customs might be. "I doubt I'll ever see him again, but thanks for the warning. I don't want anything to do with any man, not right now. I came to Court for one thing and one thing alone." *Which is the truth for a change today.*

"Good." Susana patted Caitlyn's arm as if she were the older, more seasoned woman. "Keep your focus on magic for now and you'll do fine. And here we are."

After greeting the stern, elderly woman who'd be in charge of her days as an applicant, Caitlyn found a seat at the rear of the room, while Susana joined a crowd of girls and younger women she apparently knew well. Gathering her energies to meet the next test in the morning, Caitlyn paid scant attention to anything said during the rest of the interminable evening. The morning's trial would determine if she succeeded in her quest at the Court of the Witch Queen Margred. Success or hung on the results of the mysterious test and Caitlyn couldn't spare a moment for reflection on anything else.

Eventually the lecture on house rules and decorum was over and she was finally free to find her dormitory room. Her baggage was waiting, as the Duke had promised. Gratefully, she changed out of her damp travel dress and into a warm nightgown before crawling into bed. Her dreams were restless, disturbed by visions of prowling wild animals and eagles soaring ominously overhead.

CHAPTER TWO

Dawn found Caitlyn as tired as she'd been the night before. Dressing in the plain gray skirt and tunic of a candidate, she pinned her badge to the shoulder and followed Susana to breakfast in the big common room. Confronted with platters of bacon, heaping piles of scrambled eggs, and baskets of fruit, she realized she wasn't hungry. She was actually a bit nauseous, which sometimes happened to her when she was preparing for a big event. There'd be time enough to eat later. The other girls were quiet as well today. The Queen had welcomed them yesterday but each knew earning her spot at Court remained an open question.

There was some time to fill before the testing began. The good natured chatter of the other applicants in their stilted northern accents rubbed Caitlyn's nerves raw, like sandpaper. She required peace and quiet to gather her powers for the upcoming test. Remembering a glimpse of a small garden outside the commons room, she took a buttered roll, slipped away from the others, and found an unlocked door leading into the manicured landscape.

Caitlyn followed the winding path to the end of the first set of well-manicured flowerbeds, slipped nimbly through a small break in the towering hedge and strolled to the far end of the next segment. Facing to the south, where Ordlathus lay, she raised her face to the sun, enjoying the warmth. Caitlyn stretched lifted her palms to the sky, and sang her morning devotions to the Lady Tiermalleia, patron goddess of her people. Keeping her voice low was challenging but she was afraid the sound might carry. As she sang, she absorbed strength, the power flowing along the sun's rays, passing into the core of her being, where magic dwells. The song and the sun bolstered her will to succeed in this mission. After the final note, she lowered her hand, shut her eyes and prayed for a moment.

"A beautiful song," said a deep voice behind her.

Startled, annoyed, Caitlyn spun on her heel to see the shapeshifter standing a few feet away. Closer inspection confirmed her impressions from the day before—he was just as handsome, well-muscled and imposing as he'd seemed on the dais, in the throne room.

He bowed respectfully. "Apologies, I didn't mean to eavesdrop or intrude. Your voice drew me."

"Drew you?" Dismay sat in her gut like a stone. She didn't need extra attention from anyone, least of all from the bespelled guard who was the queen's alone.

"I use this garden as a shortcut sometimes. I prefer it to the crowded halls," he said. "I heard the singing and detoured to see who had so much pure joy this early in the day. In Azrimar music tends to be associated with the working of spells, never shared for sheer pleasure." Head slightly tilted, he studied her for a moment, green eyes catlike. "Forgive me if I've distressed you. I didn't understand the words, if that's any comfort. "

"I wanted to be alone." Caitlyn realized she sounded petulant and ungracious.

"To prepare for the test. I know. I'll leave you." He wheeled, paused, turned back, scarlet cloak swirling in a flash of color. "Do you really desire a place at this Court?" he asked curiously. "Are you sure this claustrophobic, ancient City built of stone is the right home for one who sings eloquently to the air and the earth?"

"My future is none of your concern," Caitlyn said. "I thought you didn't understand the words."

He shook his head, long, shining sandy brown hair swinging loose to his shoulders. "The words, no. The soul of the song, yes. You won't be happy here, mistress, I assure you. You have my pity." He left her alone, striding across the dew tipped grass with undeniable feline grace, even in his human form.

Forcing herself to look away, Caitlyn took a shaky breath and went the other direction, retracing her path to the building.

She found the headmistress standing in the common room, presiding over the drawing of lots for the order of testing. Despite arriving late, Caitlyn drew a low number and was in the first group of fifteen women taken to the spell chamber to endure the trial of power. They waited outside in the hall as one candidate at a time was called. Of the first five tested, four emerged from the room smiling and happy, each wearing a second badge, set with an amethyst, showing they'd been accepted into training. The fifth girl burst from the doors in tears and stumbled past them. A guard intercepted her and led her away.

"Not enough power." Gretha, Caitlyn's other roommate sniffed. "The team of Searchers who found her will get no bonus. Princess Bradana hates to have her time wasted."

The headmistress checked her list. "Caitlyn of Ordlathus, you're next."

Taking a deep, cleansing breath, Caitlyn walked past the thick, studded door the guards held open for her. There was no sign of the Witch Queen herself today. *Should I be relieved or disappointed at her absence?* Ylain and Bradana waited, along with a small gathering of older adepts. The guards standing behind Bradana's gilded chair included the arrogant captain from the episode at the gate yesterday. Caitlyn clenched her fists, fighting a surge of dismay. She couldn't permit anything to shake her confidence or her focus. The captain wasn't likely to play a part in the testing. Maybe he wouldn't even recognize her.

The chamber was huge. Giant tapestries depicting larger than life-size vignettes from the city's history covered the walls. A large, circular spell altar dominated the room, glittering golden sand swept flat and bare this morning.

"Over here, Caitlyn," said Ylain, gesturing to her. "You should stand next to the table to begin the test."

She obeyed Ylain's instructions, grateful for any direction about what to do next. The table in question was waist high, eight feet of highly polished black wood, supported by legs carved into the shapes of griffins, ending in clawed golden talons. Glittering gemstone crystals lay heaped several feet high in the center.

A queen's ransom.

"Has this test been explained to you?" asked an elderly adept.

Caitlyn pointed at the table. "Something about the crystals?"

Bradana closed her eyes for a moment, brow furrowed as if she had a headache. Opening her eyes to glare at Caitlyn, the princess said, "We're wasting our time here. Apparently we fielded a team of Searchers who must have been drunk or addled." She took a goblet from one of the pages and sipped the ruby beverage delicately, keeping her eyes on Caitlyn.

Ylain frowned, the expression ill suiting her sweet, placid face. "She's here, she deserves her chance to show us what she can do."

"Thank you, your highness," Caitlyn said.

Nodding, the younger princess leaned forward on her chair. "You must use your power to levitate the crystals and cast them on the altar sands, making a picture for us. Any picture will do. We discern from how the crystals respond to your will and what you do with them where your talents manifest. Then we know how best to train you for our mutual benefit."

"Searchers should have explained all this to her," Bradana said, rubbing her forehead before draining the wine from her goblet and slamming the cup down. "We waste time, sister. There's an entire room full of more likely applicants waiting."

Ylain kept talking, as if she was accustomed to ignoring complaints from Bradana. "Your power must fit into the harmonious composition the Witch Queen uses to cast her spells or it isn't worth our time to work with you."

Pleased to see her hands weren't trembling, Caitlyn rested her fingertips lightly on the table's rim. "Thank you for the explanation, your highness. I'll do my best." The unexpected test was going to be a problem no one foresaw at home when the plans were laid. Caitlyn's power spoke to and worked through the energies of living things. Suppressing a shudder, she ran one hand through the closest haphazard stack of faceted gemstones. Cold, dead, no spark of life. They might as well be pebbles in the road for all the use they were to her. The sparkling stones were primarily in red and purple hues although she noticed some flashes of green and yellow. Those maybe she could influence.

"We don't have all day to await your pleasure, bumpkin." Bradana's voice was icy and several of her ladies in waiting tittered behind their fans.

Closing her eyes, Caitlyn visualized a flower garden, with purple iris and red roses, lush green grass underfoot and golden sunlight illuminating the entire scene. *The best I can do with this material.* Holding the picture of the garden in the center of her mind's eye, she opened her physical eyes and stared at the pile of gems. As if there'd been a mild earthquake, vibrations ran through the gleaming heap. The stones slipped apart from each other, rising to float an inch or two above the table. She held them suspended with her power and attempted to move them as a group from the table to the waiting altar sand a few feet away. The mass of gems flowed sluggishly through the air, stones dropping out here and there, crashing on the floor as she failed to maintain her hold on all of them. Caitlyn's whole body felt rigid, stress thrumming in her nerves and pounding behind her temples as she battled self-doubt and fear of failure. Never before had the use of magic been an ordeal.

The door creaked open and then crashed shut behind her, the unexpected noise making her flinch. All the stones fell to the ground in a rainbow shower accompanied by discordant musical notes.

To keep herself from falling, Caitlyn locked her knees and slumped against the table, nausea rising in her gut. Have she failed so early in her quest? *What thrice damned servant of the Shadow interrupted me?*

The new arrival was the Witch Queen herself, walking to the empty throne, flanked by ladies in waiting and guards, trailed by the shapeshifter. "I've come to watch your trial, woman from Ordlathus," she said.

"Too late, sister, she failed most spectacularly. As might have been foretold." Bradana's face bore a look of satisfaction like a cat who'd devoured a succulent songbird.

The triumph on the princess's face spurred Caitlyn to protest. "I—I was distracted by the slamming of the door, your majesty."

Scowling, Bradana shook a finger at her. "A true adept, even untrained, would never be taken off task by noise. You failed." She handed the empty goblet to the smirking captain, who refilled it to the brim from a nearby carafe.

"I wasn't finished." Caitlyn dug her nails into the varnished wood under her hands. Her mission couldn't end in this dismal fashion – there was too much at stake for Ordlathus. She opened her mouth to beg for a second chance but Princess Ylain was already speaking for her.

"She was in the middle of moving the crystals after all. I propose we let her complete the effort and then we'll know beyond a doubt." Nibbling at a frosted pink pastry, the royal brushed crumbs from her lap.

"Fair enough." Apparently the Witch Queen was pleased to agree. She sat on the throne, her guards and ladies arranging themselves in a grouping according to rank. Caitlyn couldn't help but notice the shapeshifter stayed aloof from the group, leaning against the wall, a bit removed from where the Queen sat. He crossed his arms as if bored.

Queen Margred inclined her head regally. "You may take a moment to gather yourself, before you start again."

"Thank you, your majesty." Caitlyn half curtseyed and then shut her eyes, trying to calm her mind and body before calling the energies she'd been harnessing. Magic doesn't flow without both in harmony. If only so much didn't depend on this one ridiculous task. Staring at the jumbled crystals all over the floor place was depressing, threatening to bring tears to her eyes. The gems were on the table, in the sand, on the bare floor. She visualized a straw broom sweeping them together and the crystals obligingly moved into a heap, all on the floor. Encouraged, she commanded the stones to rise into the air, which they did, in twos and threes, until all had united and become a swirling kaleidoscope. Caitlyn tried to hold them while focusing on the garden picture she'd attempted to create. The next step was to separate and rearrange the different colors. Closing her eyes to diagram the picture she was creating, she heard stones falling to the floor again. Forcing herself to draw a deep, calming breath, she took comfort in the fact she only had to do a good enough job to pass. Commanding the stones to create her picture, she willed them to go and imitate her favorite flowers from Ordlathus. Needing to see the pattern, she opened her eyes, only to be confronted by a misshapen mess, colors in the wrong places.

At least the crystals were still moving. She clung to a tiny flicker of hope. Caitlyn was at the edge of losing the spell, the picture was nowhere near complete, when suddenly she was jolted by a wild, nearly uncontrollable energy adding itself to hers. The surge lasted for a heartbeat. She hung onto the new magic, channeled the unruly power, wove it firmly into her own pattern. The extra boost was enough to shake the picture into a recognizable, fairly well done portrait of a spring garden.

The final stone, an iridescent green, slipped with a clinking sound into its spot as the tip of an iris leaf.

Caitlyn gripped the edge of the table hard to keep from falling. Her legs trembled and her head swam from the sustained effort required to manipulate materials so alien to her gifts. Numbly she waited for the verdict.

Bradana and Ylain walked along the edge of the spell altar.

"Flowers? You use the magic crystals to create flowers? When others have spent the day drawing intricate symbols of power, awesome creatures of magic – you're not fit to be here," Bradana said, contempt tingeing her voice. "You're done, Caitlyn of Ordlathus."

"Now wait." Apparently always cast in the role of the reasonable one, searching for the positive, Ylain raised her hand. "These are beautiful flowers. I wish we could preserve the design for a stained glass window. What magic have you done in your own home?"

Thinking fast, Caitlyn settled on an answer crafted to win favor from the younger princess, who was a renowned healer. "I do spells with herbs and plants, your highness. Small potions. Minor healing. I was hoping I could learn to do more impressive magic here. The higher order spells your highness can manipulate." *I'll fawn all over you, if it helps me win my place.*

Ylain smiled, acknowledging the obsequious compliments to her skill. "Who taught you?"

"There was an old wise woman in our village, your highness. She said I had a gift." Not entirely lies. Was there enough truth to entice Ylain into taking Caitlyn as an apprentice?

"I fail to see any significance in knowing who taught her tricks such as this," Bradana said, waving at the sprawling garden picture. Hands on her hips, the older princess made a mute appeal to the queen, raising her eyebrows practically to her hairline.

Unfazed, Ylain went on questioning Caitlyn. "What is root of the gilded pansy used for?"

"Healing the thinning of the blood in the elderly, your highness, but only the tip of the root, not the entire thing."

Ylain continued her quizzing. "Extract of brown tarelli mushroom?"

Caitlyn damped down a wave of triumph. This factual interrogation she could handle. "Stopping the runs."

"Drum flower?" The princess was firing the names of medicinal plants at her faster now.

"Easing pain in childbirth."

Ylain tilted her head, gesturing as if to pull forth more details. "In what proportion? Mixed with what?"

Caitlyn answered with ease, adding the correct dosage for resolving two other womanly complaints for good measure. The rapid-fire inquisition continued but she had no problem answering all of Ylain's questions. The princess was obviously surprised once or twice by Caitlyn's suggestions of alternate uses for the more rare herbs. Rocking on her heels, Ylain pursed her lips as she considered the ramifications of Caitlyn's answers.

Finally the princess had asked enough questions and addressed the Witch Queen, ignoring the fuming Bradana. "I agree with my sister's assessment. Caitlyn doesn't have true magic powers at anything above a borderline level, but as she's so knowledgeable about the use of herbs for healing, I'll take her as my apprentice. I'm in desperate need of another assistant since my last one got married and left the City."

"I'm disappointed but not surprised the woman lacks the ability to do more than minor tricks with our crystals," the queen said, speaking as if Caitlyn wasn't standing in front of her. "She may continue to take basic training for a time, until we're absolutely sure no latent power exists to be tapped. The Searchers must have seen something, after all. She may consider herself at your command for matters of herb craft and healing."

"Gracious of you, your majesty," said Caitlyn. "I'm honored and grateful."

"Give her an apprentice's badge and a badge for your Household, Ylain, and let us move on to more likely candidates. This is a waste of time." Bradana was clearly done with the whole subject. She pointed to the herald. "Send in the next applicant. Surely no one can do a worse job today than what we've just seen."

The herald pinned two more badges onto the bodice of Caitlyn's dress. She curtseyed and left the room, never once daring to glance at the shapeshifter guard but extremely conscious of his presence. The extra power had to have come from him. It was rich with life, ferocious, hard to handle, like a wild beast. Curious warmth lingered deep inside her. Why would he help her eke past the test? The Witch Queen's Court doesn't strike Caitlyn as a place where anyone extended help to another without some selfish benefit. Dangerous for her to owe favors to anyone here.

Why did I take such a risk? Kyler watched the door close behind Caitlyn. He'd surprised himself, instinctively pushing a bit of power at her as she was obviously about to fail the test with the crystals. What did he care if she succeeded or failed?

Of course, making the choice to give someone assistance without it being demanded or commanded was a rare pleasure.

As the acolytes raked up the crystals he glanced at the remnants of the flower garden she'd created and found himself smiling. There had to be more to this unusual impulse on his part. He'd never felt any slightest desire to help anyone else in this palace in all his years here. This woman from the south captured his attention in the first moment yesterday, at the welcoming ceremony, without any exertion on her part to draw his eye. Kyler allowed himself a wry smile. Quite the opposite. His scrutiny annoyed her. Accepting a goblet of wine from a passing servant, he pondered the difference between the newest apprentice witch and the others. With her sun kissed skin, luxuriant brown curls, soft brown eyes and petite curves, she stood out among the thin, pale city dwellers. She was equally different from the females of his kind, who tended to be tall and rippling with muscles. Her figure was right sized for a man's satisfaction. And something about her pleased the leopard. Yesterday's green dress, although shabby and travel stained, had hugged her lush breasts nicely and shown off the womanly shape of her hips. Pity her curves were undistinguishable under the shapeless gray gown of an applicant today.

Kyler eyed the candidate effortlessly swirling the crystals in midair now, an assured city girl, crisp in her magic. Bradana was already nodding in approval. No wonder she favored this apprentice – the girl could be Bradana herself, only younger.

Bored, he amused himself in contemplation of his two public encounters with Caitlyn, the most unusual person to come his way in all the long years here. There was a hint of some other magic about her, as if she was shielding her true self. Yet there was no scent of the Shadow or outright lies about her. Unquestionably hiding something, however. His skin tingled as the cat became intrigued.

Watching her last night in the throne room, knowing she was aware of him, amused by her obvious annoyance, pondering what her true agenda might be, had certainly passed the time during the interminable ceremony. The City people so loved their rituals and protocol. It drove his leopard crazy to do so much standing and waiting.

He'd never expected her to pass the test, much less to see her again after she exited the throne room, so he'd observed her without reservation. What harm could there be in indulging himself on one occasion? Neither the queen nor Bradana was likely to take note of any special interest he was taking. Ah, but Caitlyn's effect on him was like rain to a parched desert. They wouldn't like that.

Then, when Margred decided on the spur of the moment this morning to watch Caitlyn's test, Kyler's nerves tingled with an anticipation all out of reason. But this girl who fascinated him last night had been stressed today, her magic nearly exhausted by the effort she was making. Kyler felt sorry for her the minute he entered the room and beheld crystals falling willy-nilly, out of control. He admired her bravery, speaking up in her own defense and then taking the test over again, in the teeth of Princess Bradana's hostility. When she was reaching her abilities' end, something had twisted in his heart. *I pushed power at her as I'd have done for a Packmate locked in desperate battle with enemies.* He stroked his chin as he considered the events. She'd known what to do with his magic too. Caitlyn's no novice, even if she couldn't manipulate the crystals of Azrimar any better than a child.

For better or worse, she was going to be at Court after all. He'd have to keep an eye on her, satisfy his curiosity about her motives. Buoyant, as if he was about to embark on a hunt, Kyler embraced the idea of a mystery embodied in one small woman. Learning her secrets might make the boredom of his servitude recede for a time and he was grateful. He owed her for providing a welcome diversion. But he wouldn't allow her to become anything more to him. Too dangerous for them both.

CHAPTER THREE

She wasn't to have an answer about the shapeshifter's odd generosity any time soon, Caitlyn realized. Waking hours at the palace passed rapidly, with mornings devoted to classes in witchcraft, using the crystals for every spell. Caitlyn fumbled time after time, till the headmistress tore her hair and screamed imprecations about Searchers who sent her unqualified applicants.

On the third day the much besieged woman told Caitlyn to report to Ylain instead of cursing the entire class and the instructors with her clumsy presence. "I vow your being in the room inhibits the crystals from working smoothly for any other apprentice," she said with a sniff.

Not bothering to reply, Caitlyn followed the sketchy directions to the princess's suite. She knocked before entering through the half open door, belatedly remembering to curtsey a moment after walking into the room.

"It'll be nice to have an assistant again," Ylain said, sipping her morning tea. "Are you hungry? Thirsty? Help yourself." She gestured at the heaping plate of muffins and pastries.

"The staff feed us well in the applicant hall, thank you, ma'am." Caitlyn wasn't tempted by the sweet treats, after her hearty breakfast.

"You may sit, since neither of my sisters is here." Ylain pointed to a chair. "I'm not much of a stickler for all the protocol."

Caitlyn tried not fidget while the princess devoured another muffin and a second cup of tea. Having a good relationship with this woman would aid her quest.

Finally Ylain stood, dusting crumbs from her lap. "All right, we may as well get this over with."

"Beg pardon, my lady?" Scrambling to her own feet, Caitlyn made room for the princess to pass.

Walking to a gold-and-white painted desk with spindly legs and an outsize mirror, Ylain pulled a ring of keys from the middle drawer. "I'm going to show you the still room, but I'm afraid it's quite a mess."

"So many keys, are they all for the healing supplies?" Caitlyn took in a deep breath, hoping to sound a bit simple and overawed. *And if you tell me which ones open what rooms, my task will be all the simpler. Steal your keys, find what I'm searching for and be gone.*

Shaking the key ring for a moment as she might a tambourine, Ylain only laughed. "Of course not. I don't even know what half of these are for any more, no one does. The castle has dozens of corridors and hundreds of rooms no one uses any more. My family's ancestors loved to build new spaces and let the old areas fall into disuse. I'll give you a duplicate key for the still room, never fear."

As Caitlyn allowed the princess to precede her into the drafty corridor, she asked a question to satisfy her genuine curiosity. "I'm grateful to be added to your staff, my lady, but what need have people here got for herbs and remedies? I thought the witches of Azrimar could heal with their powers. Or so it's said in the south."

Ylain glanced over her shoulder, frowning a little. "We can, yes, but Margred's opinion is magic must be reserved for more lofty purposes. I can't remember the last time we—any of us— did a major healing chant for the city."

Caitlyn decided not to pursue the topic, but concentrated on memorizing the labyrinthine corridors leading to the stillroom. The minute the door swung open to Ylain's key, Caitlyn's mouth fell open and she gasped. "What a mess!"

The room was a disaster. All the surfaces and pieces of distillation equipment were dusty from disuse. Many of the shelves behind the elaborately incised glass doors were empty. Caitlyn followed Ylain into the center of the room, stooping to retrieve a cracked mixing bowl from the floor and setting it on the scarred work table. She opened a bottle standing forlornly and needed only a sniff to tell the potion was well past potency. Walking along the cupboards, she observed the flagons contained useless hard, dry flakes where silken, fragrant lotions and nostrums should have been. A squeaking mouse scuttled away, disappearing into a hole in the wall. Wordlessly, she spread her hands and appealed to Ylain for explanation of the disorder.

"My last assistant left nearly six months ago," the princess said, blushing in apparent embarrassment as she walked from cabinet to cabinet. "She was in charge of this. I knew her mind wasn't on her work but I didn't realize things had gotten so neglected before she departed."

"Where do you grow the herbs and spices, your highness?"

Ylain raised her eyebrows in surprise. "Grow them? We don't grub in the dirt ourselves, we never have. We buy some from caravan traders. Did you see the Abbey compound outside the City gates? Off to the east?"

Dimly Caitlyn recalled seeing a collection of buildings in that direction as the caravan toiled to the city gates.

"Well, the sisters grow many things in the Abbey gardens and they also send us supplies when we request," Ylain said. "The sisters actually run the clinic in the City. I'm in charge as a member of the royal family but Senior Sister runs things day to day."

"So we don't grow anything ourselves here in the Palace? And the witches don't do healing chants or spells." Caitlyn paused, shaking her head. "Do we perform any actual Healing, your highness?"

Ylain took no offense. "Yes, actually we do. I do at any rate. I'm in charge of all the healing required within the palace. Margred doesn't object to my personal choice about using my own magic. I use my crystal primarily." She held out the glittering, goose egg sized stone on its golden chain. "I'm learned in the use of herbs and potions, however. Crystal magic isn't the first choice for some ailments and problems, you know."

Healing was too serious and sacred to be handled in such a slapdash manner. Caitlyn rested her hands on the table and regarded Ylain as she might confront an equal at home in Ordlathus. "Forgive me but I need to be blunt. If I'm going to be involved, I must have free rein to run the stillroom. I must have a garden here at the palace where I can grow my own herbs. I'll need a budget to buy the remedies we can't grow. I'll need to meet with the Abbey staff to discuss what they raise as crops and how they blend their remedies."

Ylain nibbled at her lower lip, fingers toying with the keys. "In short, you wish to be in charge."

The princess didn't sound upset so Caitlyn pressed a bit more. "Yes, your highness, when it comes to the herbs, remedies and potions. I can't bring myself to do less than a thorough job on something as important as healcraft. There's nothing worse than being confronted with an illness or ailment calling for a simple cure, yet the cure is unavailable through some oversight. I may not have your abilities with the crystals of Azrimar, but I'm well taught in everyday remedies. Obviously such an exalted person as yourself doesn't have time to do all the mundane tasks associated with keeping a proper dispensary." Caitlyn ended on a conciliatory note as she realized how agitated she'd gotten. Bit late to be tactful.

"You've made your case quite eloquently. I declare you mistress of the stillroom and all matters pertaining thereto." As if granting a title of ennoblement, Ylain made a sweeping gesture with the largest key. "In my name. Oh, Bradana was right; you will be trouble, won't you?" She giggled.

"I'll undertake not to be disruptive, my lady," Caitlyn said. "I'm grateful to you for making it possible for me to stay in the palace at all." Which was true.

"In a gesture of my gratitude, here's my key to stillroom." Ylain worked the key off the ring and handed it to her with a flourish. "I'll give orders for the head gardener to report to you about establishing a suitable garden patch. Tomorrow we'll go into the City, to do rounds at the clinic. You can talk to the Sister about how the Abbey does things. Actually, I'm glad to discover such a depth of pride and devotion in you for healcraft. I think we'll work together well."

After her meeting with Ylain, Caitlyn's routine changed and she reported to the younger princess in the afternoons. Some days they went on rounds, examining and healing sick people all over the City and at Court. Those activities were satisfying and she could do some good, although judiciously. It wouldn't do to arouse Ylain's suspicions whether her assistant could do more than perform a weak spell or two in addition to blending herbs and spices. It wasn't what she was here to accomplish but suspicions had to be well and truly lulled before Caitlyn took the next step toward her actual goal. The new assignment provided excellent reasons for her to roam more freely inside the palace than most commoners were allowed to, and covered for periods of time when she pursued her own reasons for being in Azrimar.

After a few weeks of this routine, the headmistress made it plain she was glad when Caitlyn began skipping classes in the mornings. The austere woman asked no questions. Caitlyn let it be assumed she was always working in her new herb garden in a far part of the palace grounds, mixing remedies in the stillroom or running errands for Princess Ylain. And sometimes she did all those activities, to maintain the veneer of truth.

When she wasn't methodically exploring the sprawling palace with grim determination, Caitlyn escaped the city, leaving by a hidden gate she'd uncovered in the mostly unused wing of the palace where the stillroom was located. She'd venture into the fringes of the dense forest growing beyond Azrimar. This close to the city, the old growth trees had been harvested long ago, which saddened Caitlyn, but the meadows and groves were pleasant enough to wander in.

Streams ran through the woods, feeding into the river flowing by the city. Caitlyn had a favorite spot now, deep in the new growth forest, overlooking one of these small streams. A flat stone ledge above a deep pool made an excellent place to sit and think and relax. Maintaining her guard constantly at the palace and in the city was strenuous and stressful, so letting her shields slip a bit was a relief. And to be totally honest, she was more than a little homesick and the forest reminded her of her home to the South.

This particular day Caitlyn was especially anxious to reach her spot by the stream. It had been a trying morning, with Bradana coming to watch the class, whereupon Caitlyn immediately did worse than usual and received a number of scathing comments. She was tense and worn out with the necessity to play her part. She had to hold her shields strong against the princess while not alerting the woman to the fact she even had something to hide.

"If I fail, it's going to be Bradana who trips me up," she said under her breath as she stepped into the small clearing and stopped in her tracks.

Facing away from her, a man was standing on the ledge, preparing to dive into the deep pool below. Caitlyn allowed herself one admiring glance before she turned her head. Today's occupant of her favorite retreat was the shapeshifter, nude, save for the curious golden torque he always wore around his neck. Even from behind he was glorious to contemplate, all smooth tanned skin, strong thighs, and sculptured muscles. There were intricate tattoos on his shoulders but she was too far away to make out what they signified.

Caitlyn heard the splash as he dove into the water far below. *I should retreat before he climbs to the ledge again but he must have known I was here.* Sheer stubbornness, with a healthy curiosity about the shapeshifter, held her in place. Anticipation tingled along her nerves as she waited, facing the stream.

Kyler climbed into view a minute later, treading the treacherous narrow path along the small cliff as sure footedly as the cat he was. He stopped when he realized she was watching, only his head and tattooed shoulders in view.

"Never tell me this is your favorite spot as well?" he said, voice raised. "What a happy coincidence. You'd best turn your eyes away for a minute, while I dry off and get into my uniform."

She wished she was bold enough to disobey his suggestion. The heat in her inner core as she obediently gave him privacy to get dressed surprised her. She'd seen handsome men before. Just none who were shapeshifters. Why did it please her to find him in her favorite spot?

"Safe to peek now. I won't bite in this form." He was laughing.

Swinging around to view him, she realized he'd donned his uniform kilt and tunic. After buckling on his belt and sword, he gestured at the expanse of flat rock as if welcoming her to a banquet hall. "All yours. My duties call me to the palace."

"I have duties too, if you must know, but I'm ignoring them." She came forward, onto the stone, setting her small basket containing a snack and a book off to the side. "I've never seen you here before."

"Ah, but I've scented you, in the forest and most strongly here. Violets and iris and the fresh green of spring are the essences of your perfume, I think." Raising one eyebrow, he tilted his head, giving her a breathtaking smile.

So she was right, this encounter wasn't a coincidence. He'd tracked her here and now he wanted to flirt. She laughed. "I wear no perfume, sir. A poor girl such as myself can't afford expensive oils and lotions. Best save your elegant flattery for the Queen."

"Not flattery. Tis the truth. The leopard scents the true essence of a person." His face and voice were serious. "Yours is pleasing to the leopard and to me, intoxicating."

Caitlyn knew she was blushing under his scrutiny. He stripped her naked with his eyes and she relished the sensation entirely too much, which would never do. "I'll take the compliment, sir." She bobbed a quick curtsey. "I hoped we might meet at some point. I wanted to thank you," she said as he pulled on his left boot.

"For what?" He straightened, adopting a wary attitude, his face taking on a closed mien.

She retreated a step. "It was you, wasn't it? You sent me a bit of extra power when I was losing all those damned pieces of crystal at the test?"

Taking his time while deciding whether to confirm or deny her assumption, Kyler made a business of adjusting his right boot, shooting her a quick glance.

He sighed. "You're so intent on being here, your gods alone know why, and you were trying so hard."

"Yes, and the effort wasn't going well." The memory of the test made her angry and want to think of more pleasant moments.

"No, it wasn't," he agreed gravely.

"Bradana wanted me to fail so badly." She knew she was talking too much, too freely. But it was comforting to have a kindred soul to talk with.

He failed to answer her smile with one of his own. His face remained set, serious. "Aye, she did. She nearly always gets what she wants, be wary of her." He fastened his crimson cloak with a golden pin in the shape of the Queen's eagle crest.

"You tell me nothing I haven't already figured out, I promise you. Is this to be my answer? You wanted her to be disappointed?" *I find it disappointing, for my part, when I ought to be relieved your reason was nothing more personal.*

Making her a slight bow, he walked past her. The sunshine and promise in the day dimmed with his departure. Irritation brushed over her nerves, that he lent her power solely to annoy Princess Bradana. But honestly, what other reason could there have been? Doubtless, he could bed any woman in the Court without expending magic.

At the farthest edge of the clearing, he stopped in midstep, half hidden in shadow from the tree canopy overhead. His low voice came to her, in answer to her private thoughts. "I also wished for you to succeed at something you wanted so much. Call it an even exchange for the song you'd gifted me with earlier."

"But the song wasn't the only reason, was it?" Caitlyn challenged, sure he was holding something unsaid.

"It was good to lend my magic to someone of my own free will, rather than by command." He raised a hand in farewell and walked away.

Who controls a shifter's magic but himself? Caitlyn shook her skirts and sat, resolutely bringing her book out of the small sack, seeking to distract herself from the idea and the longings he'd stirred in her most private parts. Time to take to heart all those warnings Susana gave her, about the shifter being off limits to any woman but the queen. Caitlyn stretched, enjoying the sun's warmth on her face and remembered the picture Kyler had presented, poised for his dive. What would it be like to be held in those strong arms?

Enough dreaming, time to carry out her true reason for being here today. Sitting up, she rolled her shoulders and scanned the trees for birds. This season there weren't many who hadn't already migrated south for the winter but surely a raven or grackle might remain. A thrush? A finch? Closing her eyes, she cast a small spell, sending a single musical note questing through the nearby forest. Any suitable bird would be drawn by her lure. While she waited to see what the magic net might yield, Caitlyn took her snack out of the sack and scattered crumbs on the ledge beside her.

A fat, curious squirrel loped to the rim of the stone, fluffy tail twitching as it stared at her with wide brown eyes.

"You're not what I need," she said but tossed him a large crumb anyway.

Tweeting and trilling announced the arrival of birds, swooping through the bare tree limbs, circling above her head in a riot of color, before the informal flock settled on the ledge, pecking at her generous supply of crumbs.

Caitlyn selected a robust finch, yellow and black, with intelligent black eyes. "You'll carry my message for me, won't you, sir?" she said, holding out her hand, pointer finger extended like a perch.

The bird eyed her for a moment, pecked again at the nearest piece of bread, before hopping onto her finger, holding tight with his tiny feet. Summoning her powers, Caitlyn brought the bird to her lips, where the tip of his beak grazed her skin as she gave him the all-important status to carry to Ordlathus. *Accepted by Witch Queen. Searching palace, no luck to date, will keep looking. More complicated than we expected.* Holding her hand to the sky, she said, "Now fly south, my friend, find the great stone circle of the goddess in Ordlathus, be welcomed there and sing my words to the priestess."

Spreading his wings in a flash of yellow as intense as summer sunlight, the finch took flight and arrowed into the gray sky. Caitlyn watched his progress ever southward until even her keen eyesight failed to track the bright spot. Dusting her hands, she found the other birds had scattered as well, after picking the rock clean of crumbs. The squirrel flicked his tail in disgust and bounded up the nearest tree.

Retrieving her book and opening the pages to her favorite passage, Caitlyn welcomed some distraction. She hoped she'd have a more positive report to send next time.

It was over a week before Caitlyn saw Kyler again, from a distance, at a Court function, standing at attention to the right of the Queen's throne. The Court was welcoming the ambassador from Shang, far across the dark ocean. Caitlyn didn't care who came or went. Ceremonies took time away from things she wanted to be doing. By then she'd persuaded herself there was certainly no point in thinking about Kyler or imagining what might happen between the two of them. He'd made no effort to seek her out. But her gaze kept drifting to him as the ceremony dragged on, to the point Susana leaned over and nudged her sharply in the ribs.

"You'll get yourself in trouble if you don't watch out. Another apprentice made sheep's eyes at him, two years ago, and she came to a bad end. He never noticed her infatuation but Princess Bradana certainly did."

"What happened?" Caitlyn whispered.

Susana's eyes were wide. "The girl disappeared and was never heard from again. It was rumored Bradana had her sold into slavery far from the City."

"You're not serious?"

"Shh!" Leaning closer, the girl reinforced her admonition. "My mother told me, so tis true. The Witch Queen and Princess Bradana don't want any interference with the shapeshifter."

"Thanks for the warning." Caitlyn answered. She wasn't at the City to find a man, no matter how fascinating it was to behold a legendary being of magic at close quarters. No matter how tempting it was to contemplate lying in his arms.

The next day, frustrations in the magic lessons, as well as in her quest to find what she sought at the castle, drove Caitlyn to seek the peace and quiet of the forest. It was too soon to send another message to Ordlathus and she'd no new progress to report anyway but leaving the grim palace environment restored her energy.

As she arrived at the ledge by the stream and found Kyler there, her good intentions about avoiding temptation fled. Sunning himself on the ledge like a cat seeking the warmth of the sun on its fur, he was magnificently male in human form. Legend hinted shapeshifters were well endowed in all aspects.

She could now testify under any oath how true those legends were. Knowing he must have heard her approaching, with his shifter's heightened senses, and had chosen to remain unclothed, Caitlyn refused to regret the one rapid glance she had. Lucky girls in all those old stories, the ones about mortals falling for shapeshifters. "Are you decent yet?" she asked over her shoulder.

"Indeed." He'd wrapped his kilt slung precariously low on his hips and was waiting for her. "We find ourselves here once more together."

"No duties today?" Caitlyn teased as she walked closer, chose a smooth spot and plunked herself on the rock.

With feline grace, he sat cross legged next to her. "Later. And you?"

"I can't make myself care about studying the history of queens who ruled before Queen Margred." Shading her eyes with one hand, she watched a flock of birds chasing insects above the stream.

Eyes narrowed, he studied her face. "Yet you wish so desperately to be here. Don't all aspects of the Court fascinate you?" The question was mocking.

A slip I can't afford. I'd better shake off the effect this man has on me or put my reason for being in Azrimar at risk. She needed to focus this conversation on him, not herself. Caitlyn fished an apple out of her plain cloth sack and studied the pale red fruit, casting him a sideways glance. "I was surprised to find a shapeshifter at the Witch Queen's Court. Legend says your people never leave the forests of the North."

"We don't. Usually." Staring over the stream, his jaw clenched and the pulse beat hard in his neck.

"I wasn't trying to pry," she said. "I can see I've ventured on a touchy subject."

"My presence in Azrimar is no secret." He shrugged. "If you'd been here longer, someone would have explained it to you, no doubt thrilled to share the gossip. My Pack had need of the Witch Queen's help a long time ago. There was a price to be paid."

Astonished, she forgot the apple halfway to her mouth. "You were the price?"

"Margred wanted a shapeshifter to use in her magic." He glanced at Caitlyn briefly, unsmiling. The green eyes were flat, hard. "You've tasted a small portion of power we can add to a spell."

"I'm so sorry." What he was telling her was unheard of—Caitlyn could hardly believe it. Distressing was too mild a word for the idea of a captive shifter. She wished she'd never broached the unfortunate subject.

"The Witch Queen agreed to help my Pack in return for the services of our Alpha." He built a little pyramid from loose stones scattered on the ledge. "I'm sworn to protect him, to die for him if necessary, especially since I hold the rank of captain in the Pack. How could I allow him to waste years of his life here, functioning as nothing more than a magic talisman? My sister is his mate and they've been blessed by our gods with cubs. I have no mate, no cubs. I took his place."

Surely it's not as simple as he makes the situation sound. She detected his stress and unhappiness despite the calm words of explanation. Caitlyn found her voice. "For how long?"

Face blank, eyes hard with a hint of a golden glow, he gave her a bleak look. "Forever. There's no end to this servitude. Death will set me free someday."

She didn't know what to say. What words could possibly ease the sting of this fate?

"The Witch Queen agreed to take me instead of my Alpha." He stared into space, but Caitlyn had the impression his gaze was locked onto visions from the past. "Margred may be cold, hard, consumed with protecting her people and her lands through magic, but she's not evil."

He sounds like he's trying to convince himself. "You speak as though you admire her."

"Not especially. But I can't allow myself to regret my choice. At least I know my magic isn't used for purposes of the Shadow." He frowned at some private memory. "There is evil here though. I've cautioned you about her before—"

Caitlyn knew without a doubt that he was referring to. "Bradana."

"Yes, she walks a Shadow path. She craves the sheer power of magic and she'll do anything to further her ambition. Some of the actions I've observed during my time here—" He paused, raising his eyebrows at the outrageous memories apparently, but didn't share any specifics. "She has too much influence on the Queen, which has been the situation since they were children, or so I've been told. Margred listens to any slightest suggestion from Bradana." Kyler rested his hand on Caitlyn's arm. "You must take more care to stay out of her way. I see her watching you sometimes. She doesn't think you should have been permitted to stay. She takes your presence as a personal insult and for some reason Nedd, newest captain of her guards, is obsessed with you as well."

Caitlyn took a bite of the apple, chewed the tangy morsel slowly before answering. "Duke Aerrol forced Nedd to allow me through the gates at the last minute on the day of the welcoming ceremony." *The day I first beheld you, in fact.* "He was embarrassed as a petty tyrant in front of his men and the caravan master, and he didn't like it, that's all. He'll get over his chagrin. I avoid Bradana as much as I can. Don't worry, I'll be careful." Emboldened, Caitlyn set the half eaten fruit aside and touched the golden circlet around Kyler's neck. A collar, not a necklace or simple body adornment. She pulled her fingers away, instinctively rubbing them on her skirt. "Is this how the Queen keeps you in her service?"

"Yes." He rubbed his neck. "I can't shift, can't run as my leopard. I can't travel more than a certain distance from her side. I can't say no to the Queen's demands, within the boundaries of our agreement." After a moment, he ran both hands through his hair and blew out a frustrated breath. "Forgive me, I don't usually discuss the matter at all but today is the anniversary of my agreement to serve her." He inclined his head to Caitlyn. "You're a sympathetic listener."

There had to be a loophole, something he could do to regain his freedom. Caitlyn probed a bit more. "But you knew the terms? Before she put the collar around your neck?"

Knocking over his little tower of rocks with his fist, he captured a few of the stones and hurled the largest one into the stream below as if he had to release pent-up energy and frustration. "She explained what she wanted. I had to lock the collar myself. And give her the key."

What must such an act have cost him, a proud shapeshifter, used to running free as a great hunting cat? To be collared like a pet? Used for magic? Her stomach churned at the pact Kyler had made. No matter how noble his reasons, this situation went against everything she believed in.

Kyler's sandy brown hair fell forward and obscured Caitlyn's view of his face. "Margred said the spells requiring the use of my magic wouldn't work without the physical symbol of our agreement. She feared I might fight her even without intending to do so." Tilting his head, he gazed into Caitlyn's eyes. "She's used the collar to punish as well, a time or two, when I've displeased her. Or affronted her bitch of a sister badly enough. That I did not expect, although nothing stops me from defying them whenever I can. The punishment is worth staking a claim to my independence, reminding them I'm no tame cat."

Caitlyn reached out and took his hand, squeezing gently in silent sympathy. He slowly uncurled his fingers, to twine them with hers.

"I've never told anyone this," Kyler said. "Only the Queen and her sisters know the full details."

"You don't have to tell me any more." His obvious discomfort at his reason for being in Azrimar tore at her heart like a physical pain.

Putting a hand under her chin, he tipped her face up to his. "There's healing in telling you rather than keeping the emotion bottled inside. It's been a long time since I talked honestly to anyone. You give me a rare gift today, on my bitter anniversary and I thank you."

Sure he was going to kiss her, heat and desire pooled in her body, flowing to the sensitive area between her thighs. Her breath hitching in anticipation, Caitlyn leaned forward ever so slightly, lips slightly parted to invite the caress.

Brow furrowed, he removed his hand from her chin, an expression of regret clouding his eyes. As he stood and walked to the edge of the cliff, he said, "Though it's not included in Margred's spell, any woman who shows too much interest in me suffers a cruel fate if the queen learns of it. She has spies everywhere in the palace, as does Bradana. I learned the lesson the hard way, early in my servitude when a certain lady in waiting and I—" He choked off whatever he had been going to say.

Although instant, unreasoning jealousy burned in her heart, Caitlyn pretended a cool indifference she didn't feel. "I understand the lusty nature of a cat well enough. No need to draw me a picture."

Pivoting, he studied her face for a moment. "I can't stop thinking about you, Caitlyn of Ordlathus. The leopard wants me to take you," he said bluntly. "But even were you willing, I refuse to expose you to the queen's wrath."

Fierce anger boiled in her heart at the arrogance of the Queen. "Does Margred demand you warm her bed then? Does Bradana?"

"No." His denial was instantaneous. "Bradana hinted often enough – nay, demanded – I become her lover in the early days. I'm under no such spell, never would have agreed to such terms, so I refused her as rudely as I could, no matter the punishment. I pity any man she takes to her bed." His face was set in lines of disgust, his jaw clenched. His voice held the undertone of a leopard's growl. "I'd as soon sleep with a venomous snake. And so I told her."

"I've never heard of such things, except maybe in old legends." Caitlyn's voice shook a little. "Magic— at least the kind I know—should never be subverted in such a way. I wish there was something I could do."

He shook his head. "There's no help for me. I didn't share my story to ask for anything. It was selfish of me to burden you with my troubles."

She rose, took a deep breath as she smoothed her skirt and then walked to his side, her hand out. "What are friends for? Surely we can at least be comrades in temporary exile from our homes. Agreed?"

He met her eyes for a minute, his own hard and feral, cat's eyes. Flaring magic surrounded him in the sunlight, dazzling Caitlyn's vision. He might not be able to shift because of the spell but the leopard was close to the surface at this moment. She kept her emotions firmly in check, seeking to remain calm, not wanting to unsettle the predator any further.

Taking her hand, he shook with a firm grip. "Agreed."

Caitlyn couldn't endure any more of this conversation. She needed to get away from him before she acted on the tremendous attraction the stalwart shifter aroused in her, or she spoke too much of the pity she felt for his predicament. Neither would be welcome. "I have to be going. Princess Ylain and I are doing healing this afternoon for the sick children in town. We probably won't return until late in the evening. This is going to be a busy week and I won't be able to get away again until who knows when." She bit her lip as she heard herself babbling.

Kyler released her hand. "I understand."

He probably did understand but she'd had all the emotional storms she could deal with for one day. Giving him a meaningless social smile, Caitlyn fled the clearing, remembering later she'd left her half eaten apple and the book.

Mixed emotions churning in his heart, Kyler watched her walk away, moving rapidly along the path, not glancing back once although he stood there till she was out of sight. Why did he distress her with his problems? The temptation to unburden himself to a friendly ear grew too great. He scooped a handful of the pebbles into his hand and hurled them over the cliff into the water far below. How long had it been since he was able to sit and talk freely, share the simple pleasure of someone's company? To be seen as himself —Kyler—not merely a source of power to be plundered for the purposes of others?

Although he detected Caitlyn was concealing some truths of her own, her interest in him was genuine. He could scent the truth.

He could also her body's response to him, her arousal from the first moment she stepped out of the trees to behold him lying in the sun. The subtle perfume had been unmistakable. Breathing it in, knowing she wanted him, had made him fiercely satisfied for a moment, even as his heart and the leopard proclaimed this woman was the one, the true mate every shifter craved and so few actually found. *Attracted to me though she is, she's no idea of being my mate, even if I'd been foolish enough to utter the words. At least I didn't endanger her life in Azrimar by giving in to rash temptation and bedding her.*

The leopard wanted to go after her, to give chase, to claim her as their mate. The cat inside didn't understand their submission to the restraints of the Queen's spell and the collar. Kyler rubbed the smooth, cold band at his neck. Margred was right—she did need this cursed collar to enforce the bargain. He was a man of his word but the leopard was another matter altogether. There were valid reasons leopards weren't kept as house pets. Since the moment he'd accepted the collar, the cat fought to be free. Now it clawed at him, under his skin, demanding he shift so they could be set loose, to run, to claim the mate it believed Caitlyn to be. Another battle he must constantly fight, to retain sanity, when half of his soul knew no peace.

Kyler curled his fingers into a fist till the knuckles went white. He prayed to the gods today's conversation wouldn't cost him her friendship, which is all he could hope for under the circumstances. If only he could take back what he said. But no, leaving Caitlyn in ignorance of the harsh sentence under which he lived out his life in the City violated his sense of honor. Better she understand the whole situation.

Releasing his kilt and tossing the fabric aside, he reclined on the ledge, reveling in the comforting heat trapped in the stone as it warmed his spine, while the sun continued to toast the rest of him. Soothed, the leopard settled.

Great Lord Belinu willing, he'd be Caitlyn's friend, for as long as he was blessed with her company. He'd protect her in this cursed city and get to the bottom of the mysteries she keeps. *I'll do anything left in my power to help her succeed at whatever brought her to Court.*

CHAPTER FOUR

A week after their bittersweet encounter at the riverbank, Caitlyn thought she'd managed to shield herself against temptation to deepen her relationship with Kyler. She concentrated the majority of her time on her private reason for being in the city, spending hours in the castle's library and roaming the more deserted corridors. When not busy with those pursuits, she poured her energies into working with Princess Ylain to stem an epidemic of itching fever afflicting many in the poorer sections of the City. Kyler always lingering on the edge of her mind and filling her dreams.

Walking into the dining room after a long day of healing, her thoughts turned yet again to the mysterious shifter. She was unaccountably attracted to him but there's nothing to be done about his situation. *I can't invite discovery of my own purpose for being here, by giving in to the temptation to share intimacy— and my secrets— with a shifter.* Kyler was an attractive distraction she couldn't afford. The task in Azrimar was already taking longer than she'd expected. Maybe the goddess had known how challenging the *geas* was to be, since she'd set a year's time for the accomplishment of the task. Finding that a grim thought, given how much she disliked life in Azrimar, Caitlyn moved to the serving table.

She took a plate of ham and greens from the maid, added a roll and sought out Susana, needing a friendly face and perhaps some light hearted conversation as distraction.

"Ceremony tonight," Susana said, moving over to make room for Caitlyn to sit beside her on the bench. "Are they going to let you come?"

Caitlyn buttered the roll. "Ceremony?"

"Spell casting. The Witch Queen has some major spell she wants to lay out and she needs all of us – the adepts and the apprentices – to provide energy. The headmistress is going to teach us the chant we're to sing before the ceremony starts."

Chewing slowly while she considered the pros and cons of attending this gathering, Caitlyn decided it might be wise to see how the Queen did her magic. "No one said I can't attend. So I guess I'll be there."

"Better eat fast then, we're leaving for the ceremony in a few minutes." Susana pushed her plate away and rose, after gulping the rest of her wine.

Grabbing the roll and abandoning her full plate, Caitlyn followed Susana. Unsure what to expect as she and the younger girls filed into the large spell chamber, she took her assigned place with the other apprentices on the raised tiers arranged at the edges of the room. Caitlyn took as a bad omen the fact the ceremony was occurring in the same trial chamber where she'd been less than successful. Her own magic flowed restlessly within her body, raising her pulse and making her wary, ready to flee unseen danger.

Already busily conferring with the senior adepts, Margred and her sisters paid no attention to the women filing into the room. Susana exchanged waves with her mother as she and Caitlyn sat on the hard stone bench in an upper tier.

An intricate design had been drawn on the spell altar, laid out with many colors of sand and pulverized gemstones. Caitlyn studied the whorls of the complex pattern for a moment before blinking hard and shaking her head to clear the foreign magic from her mind. If that represented what she'd been expected to create with the crystals during the test, she now understood the overwhelming consensus she'd fail. Regarding the lines too long caused her vision to blur so she focused on the tapestries on the far wall when she wasn't watching the room fill with people.

Of Kyler, there was no sign. There were no men in the chamber tonight at all, not even male guards. All the soldiers on duty were female.

Caitlyn was relieved to note his absence, both for herself and for him.

A few minutes later, after the headmistress was satisfied the girls had learned their simple chant, the spell casting commenced. The Witch Queen and her sisters sang the required words. The apprentices sang or chanted as required, directed by the headmistress or one of the senior adepts. Margred and her sisters wore flowing purple gowns, accented with golden breastplates. Their head dresses were encrusted with the powerful amethyst crystals set in patterns repeating the central design on the sand. As power accumulated in the room, the amethysts flashed and glowed, gaining brilliance as spell built upon spell.

A headache pounded in Caitlyn's head like the angry ocean waves. The powers being summoned here tonight, while not exactly of the Shadow, were alien to the clean, nature-based spells she herself worked. When would this ordeal end? When could she escape to seek find fresh air, peace and quiet? Rubbing her temples in a futile attempt to soothe the headache, she was distracted by movement at the far door.

Bradana escorted Kyler into the room.

He wore a black robe, which fell open as he walked, revealing his nearly naked body, clothed in nothing but a scant black loincloth which did little to conceal his impressive manhood. Despite his muscular build, predator's instincts and proud bearing, in his current state he appeared vulnerable, the Witch Queen and her sisters so pitiless. Caitlyn had no idea how shapeshifters viewed nudity but she didn't like the way the apprentices stared at Kyler, the whispered lascivious comments falling on her ears as he marched beside Princess Bradana, until he stood in front of the Witch Queen.

Even if how he was treated didn't bother him, it bothered Caitlyn on his behalf.

Her anger growing hotter, she wanted to shout her objections to the assembled women. *He's a person. He has rights; he has feelings, treat him with some decency.* But she could only think the thoughts in the quiet of her own mind—uttering such heresy in front of the Witch Queen and her Court would get her exiled or worse, and fail to help Kyler.

The longer she watched him, the more Caitlyn realized Kyler might be under a secondary spell, or drugged. Certainly there was no emotion showing on his face and he moved stiffly, without his normal feline grace and elegance. He had eyes only for the Witch Queen, to such a degree he stumbled over a rough flagstone and Bradana took his arm to steady him.

Margred held out what had to be the key to his collar, gesturing with it as she might have wielded a wand, pointing to the spell altar. Bradana removed his robe and then Kyler marched to the edge of the altar. Carefully he stepped barefoot onto the sand, walked a few paces before lying down, positioning himself on his back in the exact center of the intricate design drawn in the colored sands. Plucking a thick black candle from its ornate holder, the queen went to the altar herself, the taper sprouting a smoky maroon flame as she moved. She stepped onto the sands, circling Kyler, dripping the black wax onto his bare chest as she paced in time with the song chanted by the witches in the room. Margred drew yet another mystical design on his skin. The wax glowed, lines of maroon light rising from the markings on his body, creating a new, visible pattern of power in the air. Kyler tensed visibly but uttered no sound, made no movement, only closed his eyes.

Skin crawling, Caitlyn wanted to stop watching, cover her eyes with her hands, but found she couldn't. The web of magic held her motionless.

Finished with her task, the Witch Queen strolled to the throne, setting the candle into the candelabra next to her as she sat.

"Proceed," she said to her sisters, waving one hand negligently.

The princesses began a new chant, slowly dancing around the altar counter-clockwise. Power sparked and flared, spewing purple and red starbursts in the air. The apprentices sang a capella, weaving a counterpoint to the song. Caitlyn mouthed the words, not giving them voice, certainly adding no magic. Hot anger suffused her entire body, watching Kyler used as a source of power for the purposes of others. Her heart hammered in her chest so hard she was amazed no one heard the pounding.

Fists tightly clenched, she closed her eyes, launching a mental search for him in the dreamspace, almost without realizing she'd done it.

The room, the smells and the overpowering chants faded from her consciousness. Silence.

She was standing in a small forest clearing. Long tail thrashing side to side, an agitated leopard paced at the far side of the glade. The huge cat raised its head and yowled, then resumed patrolling the tree line. Apparently scenting her arrival, the leopard spun, hunkering close to the ground, snarling, the great green eyes locked on her.

Caitlyn retreated one instinctive step as the cat stalked her, belly low to the ground.

"Kyler," she said barely above a whisper. The cat paused for a moment, ears twitching before creeping closer. Trying to master her fear, Caitlyn shut her eyes, despite the predator stalking her. *I don't need to be afraid of Kyler.* Having gotten her emotions under control, she opened her eyes to find the leopard crouched at her feet, gazing at her. She reached out with one shaking hand and the cat pushed to meet her fingers, positioning its head for her to rub. She scratched behind one black velvet ear and under the chin, rewarded by a rumbling purr.

A storm raged in the forest and lightning flashed in the skies. Winds howled through the trees over her head but no breeze wafted through the clearing, no rain fell. The ground shook with a particularly loud blast of thunder. Ears flattened, the leopard snarled at the sky, prowling away from Caitlyn as if seeking escape, yet always circling to her side sooner or later. Finally, the beast flung itself on the mossy earth, panting.

She knelt beside him, stroking the velvet ears. Caitlyn murmured comforting words while the leopard closed its eyes and burrowed closer to her, laying his head in her lap, wrapping the great forepaws around her, deadly claws sheathed.

She realized he was shivering. Small growls worked their way from his throat.

"You're not alone, I'm here," she said quietly. She continued to stroke the cat's plush fur, admiring the velvet spots in the pale gray coat, tracing them with her fingertip. She kept one eye on the lightning and the swirls of power filling the air. After each crash of thunder the edge of the clearing shrunk closer.

"Margred takes too much," Caitlyn said, enraged beyond all reason on his behalf. "You'll die if she keeps this up." She gazed into the leopard's glowing emerald eyes. The cat blinked first. "No spell of hers is worth your death."

There was an iridescent shimmer in the air, like a thousand dragonfly wings, and vibration under her hands. She watched as the leopard faded, shifted, changed—until the man lay on his side, with his head in her lap and his arms curled to hold her in a tight embrace.

"I don't care if she kills me," he said, flat, cold. "At least then my captivity will end. Death equals freedom."

Caitlyn didn't know what to say to such despair. There was no answer now, just as there'd been no answer during their conversation at the river's edge when he first explained the terms of his service to her. The entire arrangement was wrong—she knew that to the core of her being—but there seemed to be no way to right the wrong. He'd given his oath freely, with full disclosure of the terms of his servitude and the practice of magic known to her held no way to undo the bondage.

Kyler sat up abruptly, as if only now realizing they were together in the dream-space. "What are you doing here? Did she command you somehow?"

"I'm not sure what happened." Caitlyn glanced at the forest clearing surrounding them. "I was watching the spell casting and increasingly angry to see how you were treated. I—I wished you could know there was one person there for you. You seemed to be deeply entranced when they brought you in the room. Does some additional spell help you endure their rituals?"

His face blank, eyes sparkling with strong emotion, he rolled his shoulders. "They drug me, to enhance whatever spell they're trying to work. I don't usually remember the full details of the ceremony."

Probably a good thing under the circumstances. A mental image of the hot wax dripping onto his naked chest flashed into her mind's eye.

Wearing only the loincloth, he stood, pacing away from her with angry feline grace, to the end of the confining glade. "Always the space grows smaller and the dead forest encroaches." He gestured at the nearest tangled, lifeless trees. Snatching a dry branch from the closest trunk, Kyler broke it in half, the wood crumbling through his fingers. "Each time there's less room left to me. Which means there's less time remaining of my life." He glanced at her over his shoulder. "The cat is desperate to break free, to run."

"I know. I've witnessed the cat's despair." She'd never be able to forget.

"But I can't run." Kyler's hand went to his bare neck and he rubbed the skin hard. "At least here, in the privacy of my own mind there's no collar to bind me. Yet, I can't avoid her will."

Could there be a weakness in Margred's spell? Caitlyn pondered. "Are you sure? Have you tried pushing back against her demands for magic?"

Facing into the forest, he shook his head. "I gave my word, freely. There's no escape from such stupidity, no end but death."

Caitlyn rose and went to him, resting one hand on his arm tentatively. He laid his hand over hers as she spoke. "You did this for good cause, or so you told me. But an oath of perpetual servitude, till death, is wrong, no matter why you gave it." Hearing the quiver in her voice, she took a deep breath. "The queen shouldn't have demanded it and you shouldn't have given your word. Your Alpha has to take a full measure of the blame for permitting this."

"So fierce." Half smile on his face, Kyler tucked a loose curl behind her ear as if he couldn't resist touching her more intimately. "It's a luxury to have a champion after all these years alone."

Unable to face the raw emotion in his eyes now, she blinked.

The next minute his lips brushed her forehead. "You must go. The spell casting is nearly complete. I can sense it. I don't know what will happen if you're here with me when the Witch Queen ends her work."

She looked into his green eyes, the fierce eyes of the leopard. "I'll go, if you promise me you won't give up."

Kyler's expression was yearning, before he gave her a small nod. "I promise, since I can deny you nothing."

The next moment she realized she was lying on the cold stone floor of the spell chamber, her head pillowed in Susana's lap. Girls clustered in small groups, whispering and staring. The chanting had stopped. The air stank of smoke and incense.

"What happened?" Caitlyn could hardly hear her own voice.

"You fainted." Susana brushed Caitlyn's hair off her face and patted her shoulder. "I think. The spell song came to a crescendo and you moaned and collapsed like one struck dead."

"Make way, make way, move aside," commanded a harsh voice.

In a flurry, the apprentices vacated the aisle as the headmistress toiled up the steps toward them. Bradana and Ylain came behind her. All three women stared at Caitlyn as she got to her feet with Susana's help.

"The magic was too much for you," Ylain said softly. "I knew it might be."

"Yes, I suppose it was." Caitlyn coughed and clutched her aching head as she swayed in Susana's hold. "I'm dizzy, the room whirls."

"Lucky for you the spell was completed," Princess Bradana told her, thin lips compressed and fire in her black eyes. "If your little outburst had broken what we've worked so hard to accomplish tonight, it would have gone badly for you."

"What were we working for tonight? What peril required such a mighty spell casting?" Caitlyn asked. "Is Azrimar at war? Are there demons at the gate? I've heard no such tidings."

Plainly taken aback to be challenged, Bradana studied Caitlyn's face with a new intensity. "This is none of your business, girl. Have a care when it comes to asking questions above your station."

Caitlyn forced herself to drop her eyes first, although she wanted to fly at Bradana and scratch her eyes out for mistreating Kyler. Clearing her throat, she said, "I'm sorry, your highness. I meant no disrespect," she lied through gritted teeth. Rubbing her forehead and pressing her hands dramatically to her stomach, she said, "I fear I'm disoriented from fainting. I feel as if I might throw up."

Bradana retreated a step, moving aside. "Get her out of here."

The headmistress pointed to Susana. "Take her to your dormitory room. She's to rest tomorrow. No duties."

"I'll send you a healing draught within the hour," Ylain said kindly, leaning around Bradana.

"I'm most appreciative, your highness." Anger and the stress of maintaining her assumed identity as a humble apprentice sent acid burning through Caitlyn's gut, making her nauseous in truth. Swallowing hard against the sour taste, she curtseyed and nearly toppled over. Susana held her upright with unexpected strength and a murmured warning for caution.

"Tomorrow we'll talk about how you can fit in here, if you still wish to stay after today's episode." Kind hearted Ylain was plainly troubled by what had happened to her apprentice.

"Oh, I do, my lady. It is all so wonderful, even if I can't truly participate in the spell casting," Caitlyn said in a rush, thanking the goddess she was under no spell of truth right now. She had to keep her place in Azrimar to accomplish the *geas*, no matter if groveling was required.

"One with the rare knowledge of herbs and potions you possess can claim a place here, even if unable to work magic," Ylain answered in soothing tones. "I know that's not what you'd hoped, not what you came to the city for, but it's something. After tonight the signs are clear you can't achieve your other dream. The magic isn't for you. Now go and rest."

Susana tugged at Caitlyn's arm and guided her down the stairs as commanded by the headmistress. Even though there was no real need to do so, Caitlyn leaned heavily on her friend and walked with a halting gait. She felt Bradana's eyes on her the whole time, until the heavy door slammed behind her and she could take a deep breath in the fresh air of the hall.

As Susana had half carried her out of the chamber, she hadn't dared take a single glance at the man who lay on the spell altar.

I'm well enough he said clearly in her mind as she left the room. *Thanks to you. Walk carefully, my friend.*

We both must. Firmly she closed her mental shields against any further sharing of minds. Princess Bradana was much too close by to risk it.

CHAPTER FIVE

Young Tabarus, the newest royal page, came to find Caitlyn first thing in the morning. He sought her out at the breakfast table in the common hall. Giving her no time to do more than gulp her hot tea, the page escorted her to the throne room. He kept a brisk pace, glancing at her curiously but asking no questions.

The Witch Queen and both sisters were waiting for Caitlyn. At first she was relieved not to find Kyler among the guards, but then worried for him. She curtseyed to the Queen and waited to find out what they'd decided to do with her. Her next moves would depend on their judgment of her.

"After last night it's clear you can't be allowed to dabble even on the fringes of the magic we practice," the Queen said. "Allowing you into the program was an interesting experiment but the fact you people of the South have no magic has been confirmed."

She actually sounded a bit regretful. Maybe Kyler was right, maybe Margred wasn't evil. But her sister Bradana certainly was far along a Shadowed path, a fact frightening to contemplate. Respectfully Caitlyn kept her eyes on the queen's face, but she knew Bradana was watching her like a bird of prey.

"It seems Bradana was correct in her assertion Ordlathus doesn't produce witches. Ylain states your skills with herbs and healing are unprecedented. She's made a persuasive case for you to remain with us at Court, to assist her. Perhaps in time to take over her duties to some extent," the Queen continued.

Only on a cold day in hell. Remaining here served Caitlyn's purpose for now but she'd no intention of becoming a lifelong resident of the City. "I'd be honored to continue to work with Her Royal Highness Ylain, your majesty."

"The matter is settled then. You may remain housed in the dormitory with the girls, as you have no family or home in the City. You'll take no more classes with them, nor will you be permitted into any gathering of the adepts or ceremonies involving spell casting. You'll be attached to Princess Ylain's household and she'll determine what perquisites and benefits you're entitled to receive." Waving a thin white hand, Margred seemed bored now as she contemplated a tray of sweetmeats offered by another page. "This audience is concluded."

Caitlyn curtseyed and retreated from the throne. Bradana's silence during the audience was odd. She was afraid to feel too much sense of relief because the princess's unusual restraint could be cause for alarm. The royal had never held her tongue before when it came to criticizing Caitlyn, so why today?

Leaving the throne room, she headed for the usually deserted service hallways, craving an escape from the palace and the City for a few hours. Deep in thought about her next moves, Caitlyn wasn't paying enough attention to where she was going and ran headlong into Kyler.

"I'm sorry," she said as they sprang apart guiltily. "What are you doing here? Are you all right today?"

"Much better than usual the day after a spell casting, thanks to you." Smiling, he stood tall. "I hoped you might be going to the stream. I've been waiting here to see if you'd be along."

Caitlyn checked to make sure the hall was empty before she continued conversing. "Waiting for me? Why?"

"I brought you something." Kyler seemed a bit sheepish as he handed her a small box, tied with a green ribbon.

"What's this for?" Dumbfounded, she stared at the package and then into his face.

He made a dismissive gesture, leaning against the wall. "A small thank you, for being a friend."

Unwrapping the gift, Caitlyn pulled out a beautifully carved statue of a leopard the size of her hand. Burnished and satin smooth to the touch, the wood displayed a grain mimicking the leopard's spots. "Stunning artistry." She ran her fingers along the figurine's arched back.

"So you'll remember me," he said. "I made it small so you could easily take it when you return home."

Setting the leopard upright on her palm, she did a double take, surprised. "You carved this?"

"Indeed." Eyes glowing, he was obviously pleased by her admiration of his skill. "My grandfather taught me to whittle when I was a boy. During these years of captivity I'm constantly faced with boredom so I pursued wood carving in earnest. A man can only drill and train so much when he's never allowed to actually fight. Margred won't risk me in any battle or skirmish."

"I want to see the rest of the pieces you've made," she said, examining the leopard from different angles, noting the perfection of the many details. "You possess amazing talent."

"I only kept a few finished pieces," he told her with a tinge of regret in his voice. "I gave some away and I've sold others, which yielded me a handful of coins I keep stashed in my quarters, in case I somehow manage to gain my freedom. If Margred dies before I do, her spell would die with her. Although as she's a young woman, her early demise isn't likely."

Relief at his more optimistic tone today lightened her mood. "You haven't totally abandoned hope, have you? I'm glad. Something has to happen, to get the Witch Queen to free you."

"Maybe." Plainly ready to abandon the subject, he lapsed into silence.

To break the awkward pause, she asked the only banal thing that came to mind. "Who do you train with?"

"I assigned myself to the queen's elite guards, the Crimson Shields. I'd rather fight with fangs and claws." He gave her a small wistful smile. "But the Shields are a tough unit. I respect them."

"What do they think of you?"

He laughed. "They were standoffish at first. Can't blame them. Once I proved my skills as a two legged warrior, defeated six of their best men in hand to hand combat, they accepted me. I also spar and fence with Duke Aerrol, who's become a genuine friend over the years." He paused for a second, swallowing hard. "But it's not like my Pack."

Conscious they were lingering too long and a servant or other commoner was likely to pass by and see them talking, she held up the wooden leopard. "I'll treasure this, thank you."

"When do you go?" he asked.

"Go?" Confusion made her shake her head.

"I was told you collapsed last night. Nearly disrupted the spell casting. Surely they're sending you home now?" Reaching out, he clamped a hand on her arm, giving her a small shake for emphasis. "You have to go. This place isn't safe for you; even if Margred remains unaware we've become friends. Bradana is your enemy."

"Princess Ylain is taking me on as her fulltime assistant," she said, handing him the empty box.

"You'd stay here to work with her?" His eyebrows rose in surprise. "You linger for something more, don't you?" Wearily, Kyler passed a hand over his eyes. "I told you there can never be anything between us—"

She jerked her arm free. Trust a man to arrive at that conclusion. Even if her heart did regret the impossibility of a deeper relationship with him. "My remaining in Azrimar has nothing to do with you."

Plainly he wasn't convinced. "Caitlyn—"

Evading the hand he stretched out, she retreated. "I came to the city for a purpose you know nothing of, before I even knew you existed. My reason still compels me."

Eyes narrowed, he followed her, the movement reminding her forcibly of the way the leopard had stalked her in the dreamspace. "What reason?"

"I can't tell you." She slipped the carving into the side pocket of her apron. "I've said too much already and it's none of your business." What about this man affected her so? Loosened her tongue and made her careless? His effect on her discretion and good intentions was worse than the most potent wine.

Her refusal to answer brought a frown to his handsome face. "Is this reason worth sacrificing your life? Bradana is undoubtedly waiting for you to make a serious misstep. I'm surprised she let Ylain offer you a place in her House." Lips compressed, forehead wrinkling, he evidently pondered the many intrigues the princess could be pursuing. "Something else is going on here, some plan of Bradana's perhaps. You don't want to be involved in any game of hers."

"I can take care of myself." Caitlyn injected confidence into her tone. Now was not the time to indulge in self-doubts.

He assessed her, green eyes glowing slightly. "Yes, I've noticed flickers of power around you, magic totally removed from the spells of Azrimar. And you came to me in the dreamspace while we were in the middle of Margred's spell casting, which requires a rare level of power. You're not exactly what you seem to be, are you, Caitlyn of Ordlathus?"

Her head swam at his question, her vision blurring in shock. Too close to the truth. Time to end the conversation. Dropping him a curtsey, she made her voice cold and formal. "If you'll excuse me, I must meet Ylain for healing rounds. I'm glad to see you so well."

He bowed sardonically. "I too rejoice, to see you well, mistress, although headstrong and foolish. I don't know what powers you command but Bradana will make quick work of you if she decides the time has come."

"We'll see." Caitlyn laughed. "I might surprise you. And her."

Pivoting on her heel, she hastened to the main part of the palace. She knew he was staring after her.

I hope he leaves well enough alone and stays far away from me. His attention might bring Bradana's increased attention in its wake and despite her brave words to the contrary just now, she hoped to accomplish her mission and flee without encountering that particular princess again.

Within a few days after her change in status, freed from attending classes, Caitlyn was able to devote many more hours to her real quest. Exploring the deserted chambers on the same hall as her stillroom, she made a genuine find in a dusty, decaying workroom which must have belonged to an architect or builder. The room had a bookcase stuffed with maps of the castle and grounds, some drawn hundreds of years ago.

Studying one crumbling parchment after another, making mental notes, Caitlyn gloated. A treasure hunter such as she'd become at the goddess's command couldn't ask for a better guide to places where the lost prize might be kept. If only it wasn't so hard to get an exact fix on the location of what she sought, due to the constant swirling of power and magic in Azrimar. Her mission would be over already and she'd be on her way home. Neither she nor the others who helped to plan this raid foresaw the difficulty of sifting through various magics and the challenges the barrier would create. Rubbing her nose to prevent another bout of sneezing from the dust, she sighed. *There were a number of things we failed to anticipate.*

According to notes on the maps, the massive series of caves under the palace might present the best place to concentrate her search. The catacombs were originally the mine from which the royalty's amethyst magic crystals were cut. For the last few centuries the area had been used as for storage, crammed with cast off possessions and discarded treasures of the Witch Queens and their kings.

No time like the present. Enough daylight left for a preliminary reconnaissance anyway to see what the magic told her. Caitlyn left the maps and books and traveled along the deserted corridor to the door at the far end, which opened onto a long abandoned garden. Wishing she dared to use her magic to gently part the thicket of riotous shrubs and bushes, Caitlyn wielded her gardening shears instead, creating a narrow path to the catacombs' entrance. The access was sealed with an iron gate. Pitted with rust, the gate hung askew on hinges split from sheer passage of time. It would be easy for one as slender as Caitlyn to slip through, which was fortunate since iron presented a barrier to her magic.

The dark and cold caverns frightened her but there was no choice other than persevering. The goddess Tiermalleia had set her a task and Caitlyn could delay but couldn't avoid the next part of her quest. Standing in front of the iron gate, head bowed, eyes shut, she prayed for a few minutes.

A touch on her shoulder sent her jumping sideways, a shriek torn from her lips. Turning with hands raised, ready to defend herself, she relaxed to see Kyler.

"I didn't mean to startle you," he said. Craning his head to see the obstacle in front of her, he frowned. "What healing can be done in a dark cave under the ground?"

Hand over her heart, which was beating like a bird's wings, she was relieved he was alone. "I enjoy exploring. This is my free time and I don't answer to you, sir."

Taking a step, he slid his hand down her arm to clasp her wrist lightly, as if she might otherwise escape him. "Did you know cats are curious?"

"I've heard the nursery rhyme," she answered shortly, trying to ignore the shiver of pleasure brought by his touch. "So?"

"And did you know once my leopard has its interest piqued by something, I can't rest till the mystery is solved? You're a mystery. You come from a territory that doesn't send apprentices to the Witch Queen. At every opportunity you proclaim your desire to be here yet you don't get upset when they remove you from the training. You do have magic—" He gestured with his free hand. "The leopard's eyes can see the spirals of power, green and lavender and pure. But not magic native to this place. You can learn nothing from them. I suspect they could learn from you if their minds weren't closed against any power but their own. You steal away to the most unexpected places any chance you get—"

"Are you finished?"

"And you're my friend." He released her wrist but leaned closer. His voice dropped, lost the teasing edge. "I worry about my friend. I sense whatever you're doing is dangerous and lonely. I want to help."

Tempted to share her burden, she lowered her head. Biting her lip, knowing she was close to taking the first step to making him her confidant, she asked, "Does the Witch Queen know what you know?"

He frowned. "I'm under no spell to tell her anyone's secrets. I wouldn't betray you."

"I didn't mean it in the way you're taking the question," she said, touching his arm, realizing she'd insulted his sense of honor. "I apologize. I meant, does she read your mind?"

He shook his head. "No, when Margred crafted the spell for this damn collar, she only included what was important to her. Thankfully she didn't have any interest in my mind, in what I might be thinking." He grinned, eyes gleaming even in the shady space where they stood. As Kyler went on, Caitlyn imagined she could see the cat's fangs. "In fact, she'd probably find my thoughts quite terrifying. Especially when it comes to how I regard her and Bradana."

Realizing he wasn't going to leave her alone without an explanation, she took his hand and made a fateful decision, ignoring the little inner voice taking her to task for deciding to trust him. Even if he was a shapeshifter with magic akin to hers and no friend of the Witch Queen, she wasn't supposed to reveal her true purpose to anyone. Caitlyn shook off her misgivings. They'd met in the dreamspace, she'd seen the true heart of the man and knew he'd never lie to her. "Come then, we need to get away from prying eyes, not that anyone else comes to this place as far as I can tell. I'll explain to you once we're inside."

She slipped through the gate, leading him into a small, unfurnished foyer. The daylight seeped in to provide dull illumination for a few feet, beyond which the darkness was absolute. Snapping her fingers, Caitlyn uttered a short spell and two globes of green light sizzled into existence like caged lightning. The lights bobbed in the air next to her, one for each of them. Their lustrous glow was strong, revealing a flight of broad stairs leading to the next level below.

"Nicely done," he said, pointing at the lights. "And my explanation?"

He told me the truth about himself. Now I've decided to trust him, I owe him the same. And to be honest, I want him to see the true me. She drew herself to her full height, allowed the glamourie to slip away. Her features were the same, but somewhat older than the perception her spells created for the Court's consumption.

"Ah," he sighed, his relaxed facial expression and slight smile redolent of sheer pleasure. "Beautiful."

Caitlyn felt her cheeks warm at his open admiration and was glad they were in the gloom, until she remembered his cat eyes saw clearly in the dark. She'd feared his attraction was drawn to the glamouried version of herself but now she could set aside that worry. "I'm a hereditary priestess to Lady Tiermalleia, goddess of the Forests and Seasons, She who renews the Earth. I can also call upon her husband, the Lord Hunter Harlann if the need is strong enough. My family is among the Guardians of the Lady's great stone circle, in Duadalne."

"A hereditary priestess? No wonder I see magic associated with you." His face took on a serious cast. "Are you one of the Three Sisters?"

"A high priestess? No." Realizing what his actual question must be, she blushed hot. "I've taken no vows of chastity. I'm free to choose any man."

"If the man was free."

She touched his cheek shyly but said nothing. They'd already had this conversation by the river, and a solution still eluded her.

"So now I know who you are but not why you've come here, so far away from Duadalne," he said, raising one eyebrow. "And why we're in this cave?"

She sent the globes of light twirling. "Four generations ago, the Witch Queen's great-great-grandfather became obsessed with getting his hands on any talisman of power in the lands, major or minor. He sent squads of soldiers roaming everywhere, accompanied by the Searchers. For the first time ever they Searched for no new apprentices. Instead the troops rode far and wide and plundered shrines, temples, even homes, if the family chanced to hold a thing of power."

Frowning, Kyler seemed doubtful. "But to what end? These people work only the crystal magic. The witches barely acknowledge the existence of other power than their own."

Feeling the chill from the drafty caves below, Caitlyn rubbed her arms. She wished she'd brought a cloak. "Our legends say he was either mad or under a curse of the Shadow. There was talk of a member of the royal family gone missing, having stolen certain precious gems, set in a crown perhaps. Being to the far south, hearing the news as his plunderers rode, Ordlathus had time to prepare for the squads."

"Prepare?" Predictably, as a warrior, he fastened on that point. "Did your people do battle with them? I'd not heard of any such war."

She shook her head. "No. We prefer to stay insignificant in the City's vision. If they ever knew how powerful our spells are, they'd try to wipe us out. Our leaders say the day will come when the situation must change, but not now. So my forebears created a false altar stone, made it all things appealing to the City folk—big, encrusted with diamonds, beautifully carved. The high priestess at the time wore the actual Duadalne Stone as a necklace." Caitlyn laughed. "Although I've never seen the Stone, I've had it described to me. It's not prepossessing on the exterior."

"So your ancestors' bold strategy must have gone awry somehow or you wouldn't be here?"

"The solders took the false image as the leaders at the time planned, but the looters lingered in the area because the king's man suspected something was being concealed," she said. "He seduced the high priestess and stole the necklace before killing her."

Kyler cursed. "And he was allowed to ride away with it?"

Gratified at his reaction on her people's behalf, Caitlyn confirmed his guess. "The goddess didn't strike him dead on the spot so the other priestesses let him go, yes."

She could tell from his frown Kyler wouldn't have made the same choice, had he been present at that distant moment in time. Pleased by his support for her people, Caitlyn continued her explanation. "The Great Circle holds a store of the Lady's energy for us to draw upon. Steadily over the years, the power drains away, much as water leaks from a poorly constructed bucket. For the last four generations my people have been waiting for the right omens. For the person to be born to the task of retrieving the Stone."

Eyes opening wide, eyebrows rising, he pointed a finger at her. "You?"

Displaying a saucy smile, she curtseyed. "Ten years ago, the omens suddenly shifted. The priestesses launched a search for the woman to carry out the quest. Once I was identified, I received intense training." Memories flooded her mind for a moment, bringing a rueful smile to her lips. "I'd already decided not to pursue the path of priestess and was older than the priestesses wished by the time I was found but they—and I—were persuaded by the omens. The word of the goddess was clear."

He rubbed his jaw. "Ten years ago, you say?"

Surprised by his interest in the date, she asked, "Is there some significance for you?"

"I've been here ten years. No shifter has lived inside these walls before I came." Kyler spread his hands, palms up. "Coincidences in the high magic realm aren't likely."

Only complications and wanting and heartbreak lay in contemplating whether his presence was a coincidence or not. She swallowed hard before continuing her abbreviated tale. "After the high priestess declared my readiness, it took our adepts a year to influence the Searchers to stop in Ordlathus for a night and discover my talents by accident. Or so they thought."

A bit belatedly, Kyler protested the decision of her priestess. "But to send you alone, to deal with the Queen, with Bradana—"

"I was thoroughly trained in my magic, I passed the test of the crystals here in Azrimar—"

"With my help," he said bluntly.

"Yes, as you say. But time grows short. Rituals of power must be performed, using the Stone, during the eclipse of Samharrain next spring. We must have the Stone to focus the influx of power, or the great Circle will come asunder instead and my people will be lost. There are enemies further south and always the unknown threats of the West. I inherited the ability to sense the presence of the Stone, so here I am. And now, we've wasted enough time on the reasons for my being here."

"Let's hunt then." Kyler bowed.

"I'm following a trail, a hint of magic." Caitlyn pointed at the stairs leading to the levels below. "The signs lead there."

As they walked down the stairs deeper into the caves, Kyler had another question. "What happened to the king?"

"He died shortly after our Stone was stolen."

"So maybe he was cursed," Kyler said with satisfaction. "If not by your Lady, then by some other angry god."

Caitlyn laughed at his ferociously pleased expression. "From what I see here, no one else valued what he'd accumulated." She gestured at the piles of household goods, boxes and bins. "At some point they must have stopped bothering to carry things to this out of the way storage."

"Or forgot it existed."

Reaching the next level, Caitlyn kept walking briskly, her steps illuminated by the green globes of light. "The items on this level appear too modern. I sense no hint of power. There's nothing here for me."

At the far end of the corridor, she found a square hole in the floor and a wooden ladder disappearing into the gloom, presumably to the next level. Matter of factly Caitlyn hitched her skirts up to her hips and started her descent. "No choice. I have to follow where the magic leads."

Kyler followed her, the aged wood creaking under their combined weight. "The idea of you exploring this pit on your own, had I not sought you out today to satisfy my curiosity, is appalling. I hope your people appreciate the risks you run on their behalf."

"I only hope this place holds together long enough for me to find what I seek and get out." As she stepped off the final rung of the ladder, Caitlyn braced herself with one hand on the cold rock wall and breathed deep, trying to calm her nerves. Being in this closed in, dark cavern so far below ground sent ripples of terror through her and her chest was tight as if she wore a constricting bodice.

Kyler jumped off the ladder, landing on the hard packed dirt next to her. Circling her waist with one arm, he hugged her close for a moment, the warmth and strength of his body restoring her courage.

Grateful for his company, she allowed herself the brief luxury of being comforted before straightening and moving out of his embrace to walk along the damp corridor. "No safeguards on anything stored here."

"No one seems to care, beyond locking the rusty gate above, do they? But who would break in here anyway, other than a pair of mad fools like us?" Kyler laughed, the sound eerily amplified by the vast echoing catacomb. "Please tell me this level is our destination?"

"I hope so. I'm definitely drawn to something here." Caitlyn paced slowly past heaps of bins and boxes, her green globe of light illuminating each as she came to it. "Do you hear water?"

"I believe the river runs underground close to these caves," Kyler said. "If there were any older levels they're long gone, washed away or destroyed by water. Duke Aerrol complains frequently how Margred ignores necessary work needed upstream, to keep the river from undercutting sections of the city. She hoards even the pennies in her treasury, he says."

Caitlyn said, "Fortunately the relics and discards on this level appear to be from the right time frame." She came to an abrupt halt and gestured for the globes of light to swing above her head. "Behold the false altar stone of Duadalne!"

Standing at her shoulder, Kyler gave a low, appreciative whistle.

The decoy had been painstakingly carved from the finest white marble in the Southern quarries. Caitlyn recognized the statue as a ¾ life-size depiction of the goddess in her three guises— maid, mother and crone. As she'd been told, the figures on the stone were adorned with large, unfaceted diamonds and smaller stones of color.

Kyler stepped closer, inspecting the faces in the green light, before smiling at her. "Incredibly lifelike. They have your beautiful facial features."

She laughed. "I'm flattered, thank you, sir. Legend has it I'm descended from the priestess who was the model but I'm reasonably sure the sculptor enhanced upon reality, at least in my case."

He retreated, to stand next to her, the soles of his boots rasping on the bare rock. "What does the actual Stone look like?"

"Small, rough, about this size." She indicated the diameter of a tiny ball. "Like a large walnut maybe. It fell from the sky in a blaze of fire centuries ago, sent by the Lady to power our magic in a dire time of need. The exterior is black, cold stone but the sphere opens by command of a priestess into three pieces and then the magic flows in an endless stream of white and green and purple and red – the colors of nature. The master of the goldsmith guild set the Stone on a fine sturdy chain for the high priestess to wear."

Shaking his head, Kyler said, "I've never seen such a thing in my time at the castle. If it's here, it's not known to be an object of power. Margred and Bradana would stop at nothing to have a talisman like your Stone to bolster their own magic."

"I know the Stone is at the castle someplace," she answered. "I've sensed its power, but only as flickers, impossible to pin down. The building is too full of old magic, soaked into the walls, as well as the powers of those who walk here now." She poked him in the ribs. "Including one distracting shapeshifter."

He acknowledged her teasing remark with a chuckle. "Why didn't your ancestress simply hide the precious bauble till the king's men were gone, lugging this work of art with them?" He waved at the elaborate altar piece.

"I've no idea. Perhaps the priestess believed herself to be safer keeping the Stone in her possession." Caitlyn moved on, the lights going with her. Disappointment weighed her down and the beginning pains of a headache throbbed above her eye. The false stone was the thread calling her here. Not sure there was any other item in the vicinity drawing her, she wanted to be thorough. Finishing her search in the caves while she had Kyler's company seemed like a highly desirable idea. Kneeling beside a jumbled pile of crates and deteriorating boxes lying beyond the carving from Ordlathus, she tore into the nearest container. Kyler came to help her but the package was soon emptied of all its contents without revealing what she sought.

"I was so hoping the Stone was here." she said, sinking onto her heels.

Kyler shoved aside a pile of rotting straw. "Why would it end up in the royal catacombs?"

"I don't know. Because it has to be here?" She shook her head. "I felt a pull. It's hard to describe. Maybe the man gave it to the Searchers after they rode away from Duadalne. My people believe the Azrimarans wouldn't be able to open the Stone or detect the emanations of the power it contains, so the gem could well be here." Heartsore, Caitlyn shook her head, handling a small statue, examining the inscription. "I wish I could restore all of these to their owners but my mission is for the one thing only, for my own people."

Raising his hand for silence, Kyler swiveled his head towards the far, unseen end of the cavern level. "Do you hear anything different?"

Tilting her head, hand next to her ear as she listened, she said, "Different how?"

"The water. I hear it more strongly than when we arrived." He stood, his stance tense and on guard.

"The river will take it all eventually I suppose," she said without much concern, setting the statue aside.

"Sooner than later." Kyler grabbed her roughly to her feet. He took her wrist in a grip of steel and sprinted toward the ladder at the far end, dragging her with him by sheer force.

"Let me go, we aren't done searching! What's wrong with you?" She tried to resist, to pause in their headlong flight.

"The water isn't creeping, not today. Can't you hear it? We've got to get out of here now." Kyler tried to push her ahead of him up the ladder but she wouldn't budge.

"If it bothers you so much, then you go ahead, but I have to—" Her voice choked off as she heard a massive sound, like a huge wave crashing on a beach, accompanied by rumbling. The ladder vibrated under her hands as the solid stone it was anchored in trembled.

CHAPTER SIX

Caitlyn needed no further encouragement, scrambling up the rungs as fast as she could, Kyler hot on her heels. They'd barely cleared the ladder and were running for the next one, at the opposite end of the level, when water fountained from the passageway they'd just left.

Swearing, Kyler stopped for a second to sweep Caitlyn into his arms, before sprinting toward the next ladder. Water flowed into the cavern, but he kept his footing. Caitlyn clung to his neck, amazed at the speed Kyler was making through the tunnel, faster than a human could run. Even carrying her didn't seem to cause him distress nor impede their rapid progress. He was up to his knees in foaming water by the time he set her feet on the rungs of the ladder. "Climb for your life."

Making sure he was right behind her, she scrambled up the rungs. Fast and cold, the water rose, swirling around her legs. Caitlyn realized Kyler must be submerged but from the way he was pressed against her, he was still climbing. With only a few rungs to go she was losing sensation in her limbs, causing her to miss the next step. She slipped and the water tugged at her. Her hands came off the ladder and she was about to be swept away until Kyler made a lunge underwater, grabbing her with a grip like iron bands. Unable to breathe, she was drowning, so chilled she could do nothing but flail her arms.

A shocking blow to her chin came out of nowhere and gratefully she surrendered to the black unconsciousness.

When she awoke, she was outside in the pale afternoon sunlight, soft grass under her back, and Kyler's anxious face hovering over hers. With his strong arms he braced her as she threw up a vast quantity of metallic tasting black water. He kept her hair out of her face, then hugged her when the spasm was over.

"We had a close call," he said.

She rested her head against his chest, calmed by the steady beat of his heart. "If I'd been in the caves by myself today, I'd have died. I didn't even hear the water coming till after you did."

"Ears of a cat," he said simply.

"Thank you," she whispered. She was trembling from the cold, her clothing soaked through.

"We must get you warm, get you inside." He rubbed her arms to help the circulation. "Your people have no idea what they were asking of you, expecting of you. I can't believe they sent you to the City so blind to all the dangers."

"To be fair, I doubt if anyone could have anticipated a flooded cave." Hand to her mouth, she waited to see if there was going to be more vomiting.

Kyler didn't seem to find her weak attempt at humor amusing. "You can laugh but death was too damned close." He stopped rubbing her arms and made her meet his eyes. "I'm sorry I had to hit you. You were flailing so much I couldn't get a good grip to carry you to safety."

" I certainly forgive you under the circumstances."

Kyler was careful, solicitous in his concern as he touched her cheek, whistling between his teeth. "The bruise rises already." Leaning forward, he brushed a soft kiss at the edge of the tender skin.

Caitlyn realized she was holding her breath and exhaled when he didn't make any further advance. "If anyone asks, I'll say I slipped by the stream and fell in. The recent rains and flooding made the banks unstable. They'll believe it."

"You need to get to your room, change out of the wet clothes. I'll have to let you go the last part of the way by yourself, though it I hate to leave you alone ever again. But we can't be seen together."

He bent to lift her but she stopped him. "I need a favor."

"Having recently saved your life, I have to ask what more a friend can do in one day?" His expression was serious, brows drawn together.

Loathing the necessity to make the request she forced the words out. "I have to know if the Stone was down there. Or if it wasn't, then I have to know where in the castle it lies hidden."

His green eyes were hooded, his voice flat. "And this involves me how?"

"I need to cast a search spell. I've tried it before, as I told you, and the energies of this place confuse and confound the results." She gestured at the hulking castle looming at the end of the overgrown garden. "I need—I'd like to borrow some of your magic to give my search a boost and cancel other influences. Please?"

He was silent for so long her resolve failed.

Is he thinking I'm like the Witch Queen and Bradana, only wanting to use his magic? With reluctance, she had to admit she was following in their footsteps in this instance. "I'm sorry, forget my request," she apologized as the awkward silence stretched on. "I had no right."

"If anyone has the right to call on my power, it would be you."

A little tingle of pleasure ran through her at the vehemence of his statement. "But?"

"Margred can tell when I've tapped my magic for anything but her purposes. She questioned me closely after the incident with the crystals," he said.

"She knew you helped me?" Caitlyn was appalled.

"Fortunately, no. She apparently can't tell exactly what I use my power for, but she can definitely perceive I have, stolen from her, as she phrased the accusation." Kyler eased the collar a bit on his neck, as if the constriction continued to affect him.

Taking note of the involuntary gesture, Caitlyn's anger flared like acid in her heart. "Did she punish you?"

"That's not important," he said, not meeting her eyes, thereby confirming Caitlyn's guess. "She mustn't connect you to me. I've never used my powers for anything unless she commanded it, in all the time I've been here. Until the day of the Trial, to assist you. If I defy her again so soon, I'm afraid she'll figure out the common thread of my unusual rebellion has to be you."

"Then sit and guard me, if you will, while I make my own attempt. I don't want you risking yourself." She didn't wait for his answer. Fighting the wet skirts clinging to her legs, she made an effort to stand, his hand supporting her. Grateful to be alive, all her senses more alert than normal, she admired the azure sky, inhaled as much sweet fresh air as her lungs could hold, then exhaled and launched into a chant combining a spell and a plea to her Lady for aid. Drawn out of her body, into the dreamspace, Caitlyn flew across the palace grounds, through the walls and into the upper halls, where the Witch Queen and her sister Bradana had their chambers. Her spirit self stopped at the door to the queen's wing, halted by some barrier, a spell safeguard perhaps. Sensible for the queen to close her private chambers to spell casters. Caitlyn tried to strengthen her own spell, fighting to hold onto the seeking a few moments longer, to locate the Stone.

She was failing, being tugged back to her body, when suddenly Kyler was standing beside her in the dreamspace, his hands on hers. Together they went thru the door as if it didn't exist, stumbling into a long hallway. As they walked, doors flew open, revealing the Witch Queen's study, her library, sitting room, bedchamber, and then a similar set of rooms which had to be Bradana's. Holding Kyler's warm hand, Caitlyn pushed onward, until she came to a door which didn't budge.

The lock was ancient, huge, with the keyhole in the shape of a stylized eagle. Their combined magic curled and coiled an inch or two above the surface of the iron banded, black wood door. Even in the dreamspace Caitlyn was afraid to touch the panel.

The spell broke and in the far garden she and Kyler fell to the grass in the real world.

Hand to her forehead to ease the pounding headache she'd developed, Caitlyn spoke first. "What room can that be?" She blinked, trying to clear the jagged lines of lightning running through her vision. "I'm going to need some of my own best headache remedy and soon."

Kyler shook his head, running his hands though his hair. "No idea. I've never been to the far reaches of the Queen's wing. But clearly what you seek is there. Even I felt the echoes of some power foreign to this place. Not of my people, but akin."

Caitlyn crawled over to him but didn't touch him. "Thank you."

He sat up, unkinking his back, having fallen on a root, rather than on soft grass as she had. "I could tell you were so close to your goal but barred from what you sought. I'll think of some lie to appease the queen."

Caitlyn's heart was so full of concern for him, entwined with rage at Margred that she couldn't find the words to tell him her thoughts. Emotion choked her throat.

Taking her hand and kissing her palm, he said, "We should return to the palace before it grows any later. You can't be gone too long in case Ylain or someone else has need of you. Your absence would be remarked."

"Kyler—"

"Let us talk about it no further. The queen won't punish me too severely. She needs me. The mission was worth the risk and the consequences. I'm still my own man and I take full responsibility for my decisions." Frowning, he stared at her. "You'll have to develop a whole new set of devious plots, to get into the Witch Queen's corridor and breech the imposing door."

"Now I know the location, I'll get my hands on the Stone," she said. "I must."

He kissed her hand lightly, a courtly gesture. "I've no doubt concerning your ultimate success."

CHAPTER SEVEN

"There's to be another spell casting tonight," said Princess Ylain the next day as they made their way to the palace from an afternoon of healing rounds in the poorer quarters of the City. "You remember you're forbidden to attend?"

"Yes, your highness. I've no desire to be there," she answered with perfect truth. "I'll spend the evening in the stillroom, preparing more of the herbal medicines we'll need tomorrow for treating this new fever. I find it concerning how rapidly the malady is spreading along the river and in the most corwded sections of the City."

"Good. I appreciate your work more than I can say." Leaving on a note of praise, Ylain headed towards her own quarters in the upper levels of the palace.

Taking her dinner on a tray, Caitlyn sought refuge in the stillroom, at first trying to work on mixing medications as she'd said she would. Even when she set safeguards with her own powers, the currents of magic swirling in the palace made her restless. She sat in the small, cool space with the dried herbs and flowers, and thought about Kyler. Without a doubt the Witch Queen would have him brought to the spell casting, drawing upon his energies to support her again.

"I don't want to watch, I don't. Once was enough," Caitlyn said out loud, hearing the bitterness in her voice. Clearing a space on the scarred table to pillow her head on her crossed arms, she tried launching herself into the dreamspace, to search for Kyler. *I need to see if he's all right, if I can help him as I did the first time. It's too soon for them to be drawing on his power again.* Her quest met a solid wall. It seemed the spell casting chamber was protected from the outside and try though she might, she couldn't cross the magical barrier to reach him.

She sent a prayer to her own Lady Tiermalleia, asking for protection for Kyler, as man and leopard and then closed the stillroom, since she couldn't force herself to work. She sought her bed, traversing hallways out of her normal route, however, attempting to gain access to the floor where the Witch Queen's chambers were located. She hoped this might be the perfect time to at least examine the door she'd seen in the dreamspace, but there were guards in all the stairwells and pacing in front of every door. She didn't want to risk the men challenging her or reporting her presence where she had no business.

Tonight wasn't the night she'd succeed in her quest.

Frustrated on all counts, she proceeded to her dormitory room. Susana and Gretha had just been released from the spell casting. Neither girl seemed too happy, Gretha avoiding her entirely, rushing out to bathe.

White faced, shadows under her eyes, Susana stared at Caitlyn, shaking her head slightly. "You should be glad you weren't there."

Misgivings crowded in Caitlyn's mind, feeding her anxiety. "Why? What happened?"

Invariably cautious about being overheard, Susana flicked her gaze sideways, as if there was someone hiding in the confines of their small room, and then she came to sit next to Caitlyn on the bed. "I'm no adept yet but these spells smell wrong to me. They reek of the Shadow. No one seems to know why we're doing this magic or what the result is. Princess Bradana took a much more active role tonight than ever before, pushing the Witch Queen and Ylain to try something new. I don't know what they were doing but it made me nauseous. Drained somehow."

"You're pale," Caitlyn agreed, taking the girl's icy hand. "You're shaking." She tore the quilt from the bed and placed it on her friend's shoulders.

Trying to calm herself, her roommate took a deep breath. "A couple of girls fainted tonight, like you did the other time."

"And Kyler? Was he there?"

Susana's face was expressionless. "Of course. According to my mother, he's always a key piece of the spells the Queen and her sister cast." Licking her lips and swallowing, she averted her eyes, pleating the sheet with restless fingers. "Don't ask me about what happened, please. I want to sleep and forget."

Caitlyn had a great many more questions about the night's ceremony but clearly Susana was on the verge of nervous collapse. "Do you need something to help you sleep? I've some mild herbs in my pack."

"Can the posset keep me from dreaming?" Susana lay back on her pillow and tears fell from her bloodshot eyes. "Ghastly nightmares haunt me after these spell castings."

"Affliction with nightmares can be another sign of the Shadow," Caitlyn said reluctantly as she hauled her trunk out from under the bed and searched for the right bottle.

"Yes, I know." Rubbing her forehead, Susana curled into a ball and tucked the quilt in place more firmly. "May I have the medicine?"

Caitlyn dosed her friend and then lay on her own narrow cot. Talking to Gretha would do no good and might do harm since the apprentice was highly regarded by Bradana and loved to make trouble. Worried about Kyler and what might have been done to him, she searched the dreamspace. There was no longer a wall in her way but she couldn't find him either, not as man or leopard. Once there was a faint hint of the leopard but the trail was gone before she could follow it.

"Tomorrow I'll seek him out," she vowed quietly to herself, rolling over and punching her pillow hard.

But the shapeshifter was nowhere to be seen in the palace the next day or the day after. Princess Ylain sent word she was standing vigil at his bedside, leaving Caitlyn to do all the regular healer duties in the City. By the third day after the spell casting, Caitlyn couldn't bear not knowing what was happening to him. The worry was driving her wild, making her unable to concentrate on even the simplest tasks. Not being able to find him in the dreamspace scared her, although if Ylain was with him, he lived. Scant comfort. In the middle of the day, Caitlyn escaped outside, to a secluded spot in the farthest garden, and prayed to her Lady of the Forest for strength.

Later in the evening, long after the palace inhabitants had settled in for the night, Caitlyn made her way to the wing where Kyler's quarters were located. She tapped on the door, opening it as she did so and stuck her head into the room,

The chamber was dimly lit by candles. Caitlyn's attention was immediately drawn to Kyler, unmoving on the bed, unnaturally pale, great bruises on his arms and circles under his eyes. She crept to the bedside.

"You know you're not supposed to be here," Ylain said reluctantly as Caitlyn tiptoed past the chair she was sitting in.

"Has he been like this since the spell casting?"

"Yes. He never regained consciousness, yet he took no physical hurt during the ceremony, I assure you." The princess sounded unconcerned, yawning.

Caitlyn caged all her angry retorts. Ylain isn't the true enemy. "Has this happened to him before?" she said instead.

Wearily, Ylain shook her head. "No, although it has taken him longer recently to regain his full strength after each spell casting. Except the last one, for some reason. He recovered from that one quite rapidly. But even when he did require significant recovery time, the symptoms weren't like this episode."

"What have you tried?"

Ylain named several combinations of herbs. Caitlyn barely heard what the princess listed. The desire to touch Kyler made her hand shake but she didn't dare the familiarity in front of Ylain.

"You appear exhausted, your highness," Caitlyn said with perfect truth. "I could sit with him until dawn and you could go rest."

Ylain appeared tempted by the offer. "I'm too tired to see straight, you're right. Three days and nights of attending to him have worn me out. But Bradana specifically instructed me you weren't to be in contact with Kyler. She said his healing was too important to be left to an apprentice."

Because she wants his magic, not because she cares otherwise whether he lives or dies. With effort, Caitlyn kept her features calm and schooled her voice to remain pleasant and reasonable. "Your highness, my only interest is in helping him regain his strength, if such can be accomplished. I want to support you. Am I not a member of your household?"

"Frankly, I'm too exhausted to think twice about accepting your offer. The Queen herself didn't issue the ban regarding your help so we can stretch the boundaries a bit. I'll seek my own bed gladly. He's to have this potion after the clock strikes midnight." Ylain pointed at a small glass of clear fluid on the side table. "I'll be back at dawn, with the manservant who assists me in his care during the day. You've only to sit and watch and summon me if anything changes with his condition."

"I can handle the assignment," Caitlyn answered with only a mild trace of sarcasm, which she knew would go over the placid Ylain's head.

She waited a few minutes after the princess left before she stirred from the chair to go to the bed where Kyler lay unconscious, barely breathing. She ran her hands over his body, six inches above his skin, checking bones and muscles and blood flow while chanting a healing spell. She found no physical injuries beyond the bruises and some loss of blood. Observing the marks where Kyler's vein had been opened and he'd been bled, her heart sank. A shifter's blood must be like liquid magic but it wasn't the queen's—or her sister's—to steal. His life force definitely flickered low.

After dragging the heavy chair closer to the bed so she could sit, Caitlyn took his hand in hers, alarmed at how cold he was. As she rubbed her thumb over his palm, she reached a decision. Going to the door, Caitlyn laid a spell to alert her if anyone tried to enter. Back in the chair a moment later, she leaned forward to pillow her head on his bare chest. Although slower than normal, the steady thump of his heartbeat under her ear was reassuring. Closing her eyes, she searched for his spirit. Here, in the same room with him, touching him, she knew she couldn't be denied access.

The dreamspace clearing was even smaller this time. Gnarled, dead black trees pressed close on every side, slimy gray roots invading the grassy area. The moss and grass were dying off, dry brown spots spreading like a plague.

In leopard form, Kyler lay at the exact center. Caitlyn sat cross legged beside the great beast, which was breathing in panting gasps, tongue lolling. The eyes were glazed, unseeing.

"What have they done to you? How can you be so stricken?" She pulled the cat's head gently into her lap and stroked his fur. She rocked him as she would a sick child and she cried. Her hot tears fell onto his fur, once so glossy, now matted and dull. Tentatively he licked her hand with his rough tongue, made a sound deep in his throat that could have been an attempt at a purr. The tip of his tail twitched. The slight effort appeared to exhaust him. The situation was beyond desperate, even worse than she'd feared after Susana's minimal account of the spell casting. Kyler was going to die if she couldn't think of something. Helping him was going to take a powerful spell, beyond her abilities in the current conditions.

After maneuvering the leopard's head from her lap, to lie on the grass, Caitlyn considered how best to proceed. The cat growled deep in his throat at being moved.

I refuse to let him die, even if he thinks death is what he wants right now. I can't bear to let him die. Her heart stuttered at the mere idea and she brushed away an angry tear. While there's life, there was hope. He was a fighter, a warrior, but Margred and Bradana in their greed and arrogance had taken too much, worn him out. Even the strongest person can only battle for so long, especially alone.

"I'm going to help you," she said out loud. "Whether you want my assistance tonight or not. We made a vow of friendship, to watch each other's backs in this wretched place and I refuse to stand by and watch you die. Together we'll figure out something to break the spell of the collar after you've regained strength, I know we will."

The leopard looked at her for a moment, and then laid his head on the dying grass and slowly the glazed green eyes closed.

Using her teeth, Caitlyn tore strips from the trim on her underskirt, placing the fabric meticulously in a circle on the grass around the cat, forming a crude version of the mystic spiraling symbol of Tiermalleia, Lady of the Forests. Caitlyn had no instruments of magic here with her in Kyler's dreamspace, nothing to draw upon but herself. She took off her tiny golden amulet, with its incised Tree of Life pattern, and placed the medallion on the leopard's side, above the heart, beginning to sing the most potent healing chant she knew.

The magic practiced by her people didn't normally involve blood sacrifice of any type, but Kyler's life force was so depleted Caitlyn knew she had to transfer some of her own to him. Such an act required a gift of blood. Kneeling in front of the cat, she took one massive paw in both hands and kneaded the pads carefully, pushing the tips of the lethal claws to unsheathe. She drew one claw across her wrist, making a shallow cut immediately welling with red. Caitlyn held her wrist above the amulet where it lay on the matted fur and watched her life's blood drip slowly onto the necklace and the cat's fur. Twenty five drops exactly, she counted before wrapping her wrist firmly with another strip of cloth. The cat growled weakly. Dizzy, staggering a bit as she stood, Caitlyn circled Kyler three times, staying within the boundary of the symbol she'd created with the rags. Beseeching her Lady to grant a boon of life, she sang the song Kyler had so appreciated on her first morning in the palace.

As the final notes ended, Caitlyn glanced hopefully at the leopard.

It's not working, it's not enough. Even my blood isn't sufficient. Kneeling to pet the leopard, she considered the situation. Kyler was all male, a warrior, a creature of the forest. Perhaps his energy was closer to her Lady's godly husband, Lord Hunter Harlann. Caitlyn wasn't used to asking Harlann's intervention in anything, but she added a small prayer to him, sang a song the men of her country chanted when they marched to do battle against their enemies.

Above her head, the sky lightened, as if dawn was coming, but Caitlyn heard the low rumble of thunder and lightning forked above her. The boundaries of the tiny glade grew less confined, the invading roots retreated each time the lightning flashed. As she finished her chant, she cradled the leopard's head in her lap again. Another crash of thunder heralded the impact of a massive bolt, spiking straight down, hitting the amulet and blinding her with explosive force. The world reeled and she knew she must be blacking out.

CHAPTER EIGHT

She didn't know how long she was unconscious but as she regained awareness, she was cradled in strong, warm arms. Opening her eyes, she was relieved to see Kyler, returned to his human state, holding her close. "The spell worked, you came back to me," she said, snuggling closer, breathing in the intoxicating scent of forest and musk and man.

He crushed her to him in a fierce embrace, kissing her as if he couldn't stop. Then he held her at arm's length, gave her a gentle shake. "What were you thinking? You can't risk yourself for me."

"Do you want to die? Is death what you were hoping to accomplish? Did I petition both my Lady Tiermalleia and her husband the god Harlann for nothing? Did I spill my blood for naught? Should I have left you?" Her voice rose higher with each question. "I was so frightened of losing you." Feeling herself edging into hysteria, she took a deep breath. "I can't bear the thought of your death."

"Hush, be quiet and rest." He lifted her wrist and kissed the slash mark, which was already healing. "While there's life, there's hope—isn't that what you said to me? How could I repudiate the precious gift you gave me?"

Moving closer he kissed her with rising passion. His tongue pushed against her closed lips, seeking entry. Surprised, she gave him entry and her tongue engaged his in the warmth of her mouth. As they kissed, she met his desire measure for measure and slowly reclined on the grass, drawing him with her. He was so warm, ablaze with heat. She wanted to surround herself with his enticing warmth, lose herself in his embrace. Covering her with his naked body, Kyler impatiently pulled what remained of her skirt above her waist with one hand. The hard, impressive length of his arousal pressed against her bare thigh. Instinctively she brought him between her legs. Her hand caressed the taut muscles of his abdomen, quested lower, to grasp the hot hard cock throbbing against her skin. Her fingers couldn't circle the girth as she slowly stroked from root to tip, then brushed a drop of arousal from the sensitive head with her thumb, rubbing the fluid in a teasing motion across the skin.

Kyler lifted his lips from hers. "We could risk this in the dreamspace, beloved," he whispered. His hand cupped one breast, teasing at the nipple as he lowered his head to taste the aching bud through the fabric of her dress. Caitlyn arched against him—

The warning spell she had set on the bedroom door shrieked in her mind, jerking her away from Kyler's embrace. Caitlyn sat bolt upright in the chair, realizing she was in the physical space of the room. Balancing a tray, seeming as startled as she was, a young page stood on the threshold.

"What do you want?" she asked, risking a quick glance at Kyler, who remained unconscious but seemed less bruised and shadowed. Her blood stained Tree of Life pendant lay around his neck, atop the spell collar. Swiftly she moved to unfasten her amulet, tucking it into her pocket for now.

"It's his breakfast, my lady," Tabarus said. "I was ordered to bring the meal at this hour."

"In the middle of the night?" Remembering the potion she was supposed to have given Kyler, Caitlyn swept the glass off the table, going to spill the liquid into the fire.

"It's an hour past dawn." Yawning, the page came closer to the bed and set the tray on the table. "How is he?"

She was touched to learn anyone else shared even a little of her concern for Kyler. "I think he's a bit improved today. What do you think?"

Leaning closer the page eyed Kyler's face. "Maybe. The big bruise isn't so purple anyway. I'm glad."

"You like him, don't you?"

"Yes, my lady. He doesn't yell at me and he doesn't box my ears. Like some people, like Bradana." Tabarus gave her a sideways glance, apparently worried he'd said too much.

Caitlyn ruffled his hair. "Don't worry, I won't tell anyone."

"Kyler carved me three horses and some soldiers," he said, brushing his hair into place. "I didn't have any toys after they brought me to the palace last year. They aren't allowed for the pages. But he said I could tell the seneschal I was conducting war games, practicing to be a warrior, if anyone caught me."

"So what did you bring him for breakfast?" Caitlyn lifted the covers from the dishes. She frowned, her displeasure immediate. "Gruel? Toast? For a shapeshifter?"

"It's what was ordered." The page retreated toward the door. "I'm sorry, my lady."

"No, it's not your fault. I didn't mean to snap at you."

Princess Ylain came in then. "How is our patient this morning?"

"He seems to be resting easier," Caitlyn said as the page bowed and left the chamber.

Eyebrows drawn together in a frown, Ylain gave her a stern look. "What did you do to your wrist, child?"

Suppressing a guilty start, Caitlyn hid her arm behind her skirts. "I got scratched by rose thorns in the garden yesterday." She dropped a curtsey. "With your permission, your highness, I'm going to the kitchen to order a more suitable breakfast for him."

"More suitable? Didn't the kitchen send what was ordered?"

Caitlyn barely suppressed an angry retort. These women had no concept of what they were dealing with. "He's a leopard, your highness. A predator, a meat eater. He can't regain strength on a diet of gruel and toast."

"Oh yes, I suppose he is. I forget, it's been so long since he was allowed to shift. Not since he entered my sister's service actually."

Since she made him a slave. Caitlyn bit her tongue, hard.

"Go ahead and get him a different breakfast. We'll try it today and see how a new menu affects his recovery." Dismissing her, the princess threw back the heavy red quilt covering Kyler and examined him, checking his reflexes and pulse.

Caitlyn clenched her fists in her pockets, hating the other woman's touch on Kyler's skin. She'd never seen any sign Ylain was sexually attracted to Kyler but plainly he wasn't a person to Ylain, she didn't care whether he lived or died except for the inconvenience his death would cause her sister.

Ylain glanced at her, forehead wrinkling in a frown. "I gave you leave to go. Why are you still standing there watching me?"

"Sorry, your highness." Caitlyn curtseyed before leaving the room. She made her way through the palace, navigating the interminable halls beginning to stir with daily activity, descending multiple flights of stairs to the vast kitchens. Activity there had been at a fever pitch for several hours already, she knew, the staff working to prepare and distribute the hundreds of breakfast meals for the Queen and her Court.

Not even the Witch Queen herself ventured into the kitchens. The Cook was absolute ruler in this area and no one ever risked her displeasure. Caitlyn, however, walked into the kitchen fearlessly. She'd been here before. Undercooks and kitchen maids bobbed their heads and spoke greetings as she passed. She made her way through the supply shelves, through the preparation stations, past the plating area, into the heart of the kitchen, where its undisputed monarch, the Cook, held court in the glow of the ovens and stoves.

"What brings you here, my friend? Come, have a hug." Nadelma, the head cook herself, smiled at the intruder and beckoned her close. Nadelma was substantial, with a proud bearing and a serene face. Her glossy black hair was neatly dressed in a giant braided bun, woven through with colorful beads. A long angry scar slashed across her cheek, disappearing below the collar of her dress, where a pot of boiling sauce had spilled on her many decades before, according the kitchen lore, when Nadelma had been a kitchen maid. Caitlyn had secretly worked healing magic on the cook's scar for weeks, carefully reducing the impact a bit at a time, making the mark less prominent, less red and twisted. She liked Nadelma.

Early in her time at the palace, Caitlyn had applied to the Cook for permission to prepare healing potions and ointments in the kitchen, during the off hours. She'd stated she'd use her own utensils and clean her station thoroughly. Properly flattered by her carefully deferential approach, Cook had been pleased to agree. Caitlyn made herself useful by healing small accidents that occurred inevitably in a kitchen and also brought Nadelma rare herbs and spices from time to time.

"I need a favor, ma'am," Caitlyn said.

Nadelma raised her tea cup. "A favor from me? You know you have but to ask. We here in the kitchen are grateful for your help and we repay our debts, unlike some of our betters."

"The request is actually for Kyler, the shapeshifter. They've ordered him food totally unfit for what he needs to recuperate from the last spell casting. He needs meat, ma'am, and fortifying soup, not the child's pap they've been feeding him."

Eyebrows raised, lips pursed, Nadelma studied her for a moment. "Aye, I did wonder at the orders relayed from Princess Bradana. Not my place to question. In the past, when he was less stricken, he ordered much the same as what you mention. Certainly I've never known him to eat what she listed."

"Bradana put Princess Ylain officially in charge of his care and she gave me permission to try the altered diet," Caitlyn said, choosing her words carefully. Even Nadelma would have to think twice before defying Bradana, so it was necessary to give her a loophole. "He's not doing well, ma'am."

The cook shook her head. "A pity, the way the royals treat him. One of my kitchen maids developed abilities with the magic crystals a few years ago, after she got her womanly courses. I arranged for her to be tested and admitted to the training. She's a junior adept now and we stay in touch as best we can. She told me about this last spell casting because the way the ceremony was conducted greatly troubles her. Did you know Margred spilled his blood?"

"Yes." Caitlyn couldn't utter more than one terse syllable, anger closing her throat.

"My girl tells me there's a lot of talk and unrest among the adepts today." Nadelma eyed Caitlyn. "Some think the Witch Queen goes too far. They don't want to be associated with these rituals."

"One of my roommates, Susana, said much the same thing," Caitlyn told her. "Susana's mother is a great lady of the Court—"

"Aye, high born herself." Nadelma smiled. "A good person, powerful with the magic."

"Well, Susana said this morning her mother walked out of the ceremony when they took Kyler's blood. She resigned from Court over this last spell casting, in fact. Susana's worried about her. I think she fears the Witch Queen will take some revenge on her mother."

Nadelma reached over to pat her hand. "Don't waste your worries for Susana's family. The Duke is next in line for the throne, after Princess Ylain. Neither the Queen nor Bradana can touch the likes of them." The cook finished her tea. "Aerrol's a good man. He'd rule the City well and his mother would practice appropriate magic until the duke marries his own witch."

"I'm relieved for Susana's sake to know they're beyond the Queen's vengeance," Caitlyn said. "But Kyler's my true concern."

"Strange times we're in, with the poor shifter caught in the middle. He carved me a special wooden spoon last year for the winter festival, you know—all my favorite flowers and fruits on the handle." Nadelma pointed at the far wall, where the spoon was hung carefully on display. "It's far too beautiful to cook with and so I told him."

Purring, the kitchen cat rubbed against Caitlyn's ankles. Bending over, she stroked the soft gray fur, thinking sadly how dull and matted the leopard's coat had been. "So you'll allow me to make something proper for Kyler to eat?"

Nadelma pointed one large hand at the chair. "You sit here, at my table, and eat a bite yourself. Been up all night worrying over him, have you?"

"Is nothing a secret from you, ma'am?" Caitlyn asked, sinking onto the designated seat.

"In a word, no." Nadelma hoisted herself from her chair with an alarming amount of effort and said, "I'll fix him a breakfast suitable for a warrior with my own hands and we'll see if my food doesn't do him more good than what the high and mighty ordered. They do their magic, I do mine."

She gave rapid orders and a gigantic breakfast was soon set in front of Caitlyn by a beaming undercook. She ate more of it than she thought possible.

The occasions were so rare nowadays when Nadelma deigned to cook that the kitchen staff gathered to spectate. The cook was clearly enjoying the sensation she created as she prepared multiple dishes to a chorus of appreciative murmurs, moving from one stove to the next and back, adding a spice here, checking the flavor there. She deftly plated her offering to a chorus of laudatory oohs and aahs. Caitlyn pushed away the remnants of her meal, curious to survey the tray for herself.

"If I hadn't just eaten, I'd be challenging Kyler for this, ma'am," she said truthfully. Nadelma had prepared a breakfast to tempt the palate of the hungriest carnivore. The offering included a rare steak, an omelet bursting with cheese, crisp bacon piled high, country potatoes and freshly baked bread for dunking in steaming fish chowder.

"One thing missing." Nadelma pointed at the nearest kitchen maid, "Fetch me a glass of the fresh milk."

"Milk?" Caitlyn laughed. "For Kyler? He's a grown man, not a boy."

Nadelma winked at her. "He once told me he runs as a cat. Or am I wrong?"

Caitlyn looked over to where the kitchen cat was lapping her bowl of milk beside the stove. As a vivid mental picture of the ferocious leopard with milk dotting its muzzle came to her, she grinned. "You're right, I wouldn't have made the connection."

"Which is why I'm head cook in this palace." As Caitlyn reached for the tray, Nadelma stretched out her hand. "I'll have the kitchen boy take it. He knows how to conduct himself among his betters, never fear."

Realizing how tired and drained she felt, after her efforts in the dreamspace on Kyler's behalf, Caitlyn was grateful to accept the offer. "Thank you. Princess Ylain did say I wasn't to return to Kyler's chambers until this evening. Will you send him a noon meal and a dinner along similar lines?"

"Of course. I like a challenge. And he's a good man, for all that he's part cat."

Caitlyn watched the breakfast carried away and then she thanked Nadelma again. They briefly discussed whether Caitlyn needed help with the herb garden. Nadelma offered her the services of the kitchen tweeny. "Tis only fair, dear," the cook said, "Seeing as we benefit from what you grow. I've gotten spoiled, having the exotic fresh herbs and spices to liven up my cooking."

"All right then," Caitlyn said, thinking she had a duty to train someone to take over the garden by the time she had to leave. "I don't care to have the royal gardeners touch the herbs. They don't understand what's a weed to them might be a valuable cure to me. We've had a few bouts of sharp words."

"Millie, the tweeny, comes from a farm family, out in the river valley. She'll take to the work just fine," Nadelma promised.

"We'll figure out a schedule then. Thank you." Caitlyn gave the cook a hug before leaving the kitchen. She was debating whether she could get a quick nap before she had to start on the healing rounds, when she stepped out of the stairway and into one of the main corridors of the palace. She stopped in her tracks, much to the annoyance of people swerving to avoid bumping into her.

She felt a shift in the air, a perturbation in the currents of magic swirling through the Witch Queen's palace. Seized by a compulsion to hurry, she followed the invisible thread to the throne room. Standing on the threshold of the deserted chamber, Caitlyn furrowed her brow. Why had her instincts brought her here? But the otherness of the magic that had called to her echoed in the room.

CHAPTER NINE

"The audience is done," said a gruff voice behind her. "If you wanted to see them, they're already gone. A fine sight they were though, I must say."

Startled, she bumped into Quarl, sergeant of the guards, for whom she'd cured a minor but embarrassing rash not long ago. "See who? Who was here?"

Leaning on his spear, he whispered, "Shapeshifters, from the North."

"You can't be serious?"

He nodded.

Impatience sent her adrenaline spiking and she felt ready for any challenge. "Truly? Where are they now?"

He pointed down the hall with his chin. "Going to the stables. Better hurry if you want to see them. They were sent about their business fast enough by Her Majesty. Rode hundreds of miles from the North for nothing. She barely even listened to them."

"Thank you." She walked rapidly in the direction he'd indicated.

"Be careful." He said it just loudly enough to be heard.

As soon as she'd rounded the corner, Caitlyn broke into a run. Hearing footsteps in the hall ahead of her, she skidded on her soft slippers around yet another corner, literally running into the men she sought.

Steadying her with one hand, the person she'd collided with set her not on her feet and promptly released her. The man was already following his companions out the door to the stable courtyard. She tugged at his arm. "Wait, I have to speak to you, please."

The group wheeled in a loose formation, five tall, well-muscled soldiers, grim faced. They were dressed in green and brown uniforms, long swirling cloaks at the shoulders, swords belted. All five were incredibly handsome in the same way as Kyler, with brilliant green or golden eyes and long, unbound hair brushing their wide shoulders. Caitlyn was riveted by the tattoos outlining the heavy muscles of their upper arms. Did they all run as leopards?

"Well? Have you gawked enough, woman?" said the man who'd kept her from falling. "What can a servant of the Witch Queen have to say to us?"

"More insults, no doubt," said the man next to him, voice nearly a growl. "'Tis all they know here."

"It's a trick," said the one beside him. He scowled at Caitlyn.

"I'm no servant of the Witch Queen. I'm from the South, from Ordlathus." She glanced nervously up and down the corridor. "This isn't a good spot. Normally this hall is much traveled and we mustn't be seen talking."

"Where then?" asked the leader.

She drew them into a small side chamber a bit further along the passageway, easing the door shut, leaning on the panel and staring at them. "Did you come about Kyler?"

The warriors exchanged hard looks and then the leader advanced on her. "What do you know of this?"

Too much was at stake today to waste a moment on fear so Caitlyn didn't give any ground as the man came near. "Does your visit have to do with Kyler?" she repeated impatiently.

"Yes, we've come to this place for the fourth time in as many years, with the same bitter result," he said.

Appalled and fascinated by his response, she probed further. "What did the Witch Queen tell you?"

The man threw his heavy riding gloves onto the table. "She knew the time of indenture was only to be five years, she agreed, yet now that the date is long past she won't release him, claiming no term was ever set. We can't prove it and she only laughs. She won't even let us see him."

"Kyler told me the agreement would end only upon his death," Caitlyn whispered.

The shifter walked to her, clamping his hand on her arm as if she might flee, and pulled her close. "You know him? You've seen him?"

"Is he well?" demanded another fiercely.

They crowded her, firing questions.

The leader abruptly released her and made a shushing motion to his men, gesturing them to spread out and give her room. "Kildar, stand watch in the hall. We can't be interrupted, nor can we be taken unawares while we talk," he said, sending one of the shifters sliding silently out of the room. He gave Caitlyn a courteous half bow. "We've begun badly, my lady. My apologies. I'm Kellan. I run as a leopard. Kyler is my younger brother. And we're both pack captains under Alpha Dumaire."

She gave a slight curtsey. "I'm Caitlyn of Ordlathus. Kyler is my friend."

"He has need of a friend in this cursed place," said another man.

"But you said he was only to serve the Witch Queen for five years?" Caitlyn asked.

"Five years was the agreement, but now she claims no term was ever set. We expected Kyler home five years ago. When at first he didn't arrive, we weren't worried." Kellan fidgeted with his gloves as he recited the bare facts for Caitlyn. "But then the following year, we rode to claim him. Our request was rejected. Every year since it's been the same treatment. Today she told us not to return on pain of our own deaths."

The man to the left flexed his hands and long wicked claws slashed out, scoring the table. His face took on the appearance of the hunting cat, deadly fangs lengthening. Sheathed in the cat's snarl, his words were barely intelligible. "Let her try to kill us, let her just try."

"Control yourself," Kellan said, his voice like a whip. "Now is not the time or place to shift."

"Kyler's endured much during his captivity here and weakens day by day now. The cat is certainly near to collapse," Caitlyn said, frowning at Kellan. "The Witch Queen doesn't let him run as a leopard, not ever."

"How can she deny him a chance to shift?" muttered one.

"It's the core of who we are, what we are," agreed another.

The other men cursed in their own tongue. Caitlyn felt power swell in the room, fueled by their anger, and her own magic flared in response.

"You speak as if you'd seen the leopard but if he can't shift, how is that possible?" Kellan asked.

"We have a connection, meeting in the dreamspace sometimes," Caitlyn said. "I met the leopard there." From the way the men exchanged surprised, surreptitious glances, she could tell the information carried unknown significance for her audience. She was curiously unwilling to discuss the topic with them. "The Witch Queen told him he has to stay as a man, to hoard the magic energies she needs for her spells. He's not to waste energy or magic on shape changing and the spell she cast over him enforces her will."

"I don't know what's wrong with her," Kellan said. "The kings and queens of Azrimar were ever honest in their dealings with my people. Hard, cold, but honest. They respected our magic and we walked carefully around theirs. And now she won't release him? And to forbid his leopard to run—" He swore again. "Can you arrange a way for us to see him?"

She shook her head. "No, I'm barely allowed to see him myself any longer. They suspect he and I might be, that we might—"

"I'm glad he has a friend in this place," Kellan said gently, interrupting her tangled sentence.

"What kind of people are you, to let him put himself into this situation? What kind of leader allows someone else to stand in his place and endure what Kyler goes through here? I believed shapeshifters had honor. I understood Pack meant everything to you." White hot anger of a kind she'd never experienced before drove her words, her emotions intense in her fury over what had been done to Kyler. "All well and good you came to claim him but why was he here in the first place?"

Kellan seemed sad, but not upset by the harsh words. "Nay, you mustn't think so ill of our Alpha. It's true he has a mate and children, while Kyler has none, but Dumaire was prepared to accept the temporary servitude the Witch Queen demanded nonetheless. The need was dire. Our forests were dying, hundreds of acres a day, devoured by some species of beetle unknown to us. Our priests divined the insects were created by a black spell from a mighty practitioner of the Shadow, dwelling in the West. Queen Margred halted the encroachment for us, reversed the spell against whoever had cast it. She brought half her staff of adepts North with her to take on the effort."

"But if your Alpha was going to honor the agreement himself, why is Kyler here instead?" Caitlyn seized on the fact concerning her most.

"We were negotiating the specific terms with the Queen's sister. Our Pack depends on having a strong Alpha at the head. To have a weak Alpha is to invite a takeover attempt by another Pack, which means death for all but the females of the defeated Pack. The warriors perish in battle and the elders and male children will be slaughtered. Do you understand?"

"Not exactly," she admitted, "But I get the general idea."

"Dumaire and his senior captains, including me, were establishing a structure to keep the Pack intact and our home safe while he was gone. We were negotiating how long he would be here, how he was to be treated, a provision for two of our soldiers to accompany him as bodyguards, stipulating terms about yearly visits from his mate—"

Kellan studied his hands. "We were trying to ensure the indenture would be fair for both sides, although Princess Bradana was pushing for as many concessions as she could get. We're not afraid of the likes of her, particularly not in our own homeland. But we owed a great debt to Azrimar and we knew it."

"Wouldn't surprise me if Bradana set the forest blight loose in the first place," Caitlyn said.

"There was no taint of the Shadow about her. Not then at any rate. And the Shadow practitioner who cast the blight spell was killed in the backlash of the Witch Queen's spells. Our priests confirmed the facts. Give us some credit, Caitlyn of Ordlathus. We wouldn't agree to relinquish our Alpha, even temporarily, if we hadn't been positive we owed a debt of honor." Kellan shook his head. "I will say today when Princess Bradana came into the throne room, I caught the stench of something rotten, something of the Shadow creeping about her."

"I'll take your word for it. I try to stay away from her." Caitlyn concentrated on the aspect of all this history she cared most about. "But if negotiations for a proper treaty were underway, how did Kyler end up here enslaved with no protective agreements?"

"We took a break for the noon meal. In the midafternoon, as the documents were being copied out for Dumaire and the Witch Queen to sign and seal in blood, word came to Dumaire that Kyler'd given himself to Margred in the Alpha's place and the debt was satisfied, " Kellan said. "She and her people left our woods and we've not seen him since."

"So technically, the Witch Queen didn't agree to the five year limit or anything else when she accepted Kyler's offer. And he didn't know what had been settled with her by your Alpha." Caitlyn frowned as her hopes sank. Kyler's impetuous but generous gesture to save his leader had indeed cost him much.

"That's right. My brother always was a bit hotheaded." Kellan smiled before his face grew grim again. "But nonetheless, honorable beings would have applied the negotiated terms, no matter who the shapeshifter was."

"Queen Margred and Princess Bradana are far from honorable. At least not now. Maybe they were ten years ago," Caitlyn said. "I tend to doubt it myself."

"Can you help him?" asked one of the other shapeshifters hopefully. "You have the strong scent of power about you."

"Yes," Kellan said slowly. "I've seldom felt as much power from a human who wasn't a witch of the City. You've weren't here on any of our previous visits."

Caitlyn shook her head. "I'm recently come from the South, as I told you," she said with deliberate vagueness. "I've thought and prayed to my Lady Tiermalleia and I receive the same answer no matter how I pose the question—he voluntarily submitted to the Witch Queen and his oath can't be undone by anyone, not here in the City. Margred has too much power here. Only the Queen herself can end the spell inside the borders of Azrimar."

"It goes hard against my heart to leave him here, but as you say, even five of us can't hold against her power in her own home. Not to the extent we could hope to rescue him and win free." Kellan's voice was full of frustration.

"She'd kill him with the collar before she'd let him go," Caitlyn told them. No need to repeat exactly what Kyler shared with her. These men clearly got the idea.

She and Kellan regarded each other without speaking for a long moment.

"We'd better take our leave of you. We were supposed to have ridden out the gate some time past and Margred's flunkies will no doubt report we linger." Kellan retrieved his gloves. Leaning over, he kissed her forehead. "At least you give me a flicker of hope for my brother."

"I'll do all I can to help him," she said. "I know it's not an impressive vow, not when five shapeshifter warriors can't do anything, but I'll try. And the next time I'm allowed to see him, I'll let him know you haven't forgotten him."

"We can ask no more, my lady. I hope we meet again in a better time and place. If you have need of us, or if anything changes, send word to the North, to me or the Alpha. We'll come, I swear." Kellan bowed. "We owe you a debt for trying to help Kyler."

It was a relief to be surrounded by such strong men, to feel she had allies. Protected, even if only for a moment. To savor their magic in the room, curling around her, adding power to her own. She let herself bask in the fleeting warmth and then firmly pushed it away. They had to go—Kellan was right. She was still alone with her mission. There was no help to be had, even from these men.

"I'll remember," she said.

"My brother is fortunate in this one thing at least." Kellan put a huge hand on her shoulder, squeezed once and moved to leave the room.

"Wait," Caitlyn said, struck by a new thought.

They paused, puzzled but obedient.

"I can't think of any way to get you a chance to see him here in the palace. But there might be a possibility outside the palace."

Kellan retraced his steps, an eager expression on his face. "I'll take the chance. Where? When?"

"He and I have a favorite spot deep in the forest to the south of the palace. It's a big flat ledge by the stream. He likes to sun himself there," she said, the memory bringing warmth to her as well.

"If you and Kyler have been there in the last few months, we'll find it. Our leopards track prey by scent, you know." Kellan tapped his nose.

"He wasn't even conscious this morning, although he was improved, so it may be a few days before we can sneak out there."

"What was done to him? Why is he unconscious?" Kellan demanded harshly. "Our kind doesn't fall ill. Did he suffer some injury?"

"It was a spell casting. I wasn't there but I was told by several people Queen Margred and Bradana used Kyler's blood to strengthen their spell," Caitlyn said.

Kellan snarled and Caitlyn could see the leopard fighting to come to the surface. After a long minute, the captain got control but clearly only through great self-discipline. His eyes flamed golden and green, but the claws and fangs receded.

"We'll find this place by the river and we'll wait until he comes, or until you send word it's impossible to meet. Agreed?" Kellan said.

Knowing the difficulties facing her but determined, Caitlyn nodded. "I'll do my best. I think it would do him good to see you, to know he isn't forgotten by his Pack. Margred must shield him against your magic when you're inside the palace or he would've known you were here. The traces of shifter magic are unmistakable to me."

"This is what they tell him? His Pack has forgotten him?" Kellan's voice was low and deadly, more than a hint of a growl in the tones. "Seems the Queen and her sister are full of lies."

"Can you remain unseen in the woods, if this takes a few days to arrange? I don't mean to be insulting," she hastened to add, as several of the men appeared ready to take offense at her question. "I understand you're experienced scouts and warriors. But we can't let Margred or Bradana realize you've chosen to stay in the area. They'd never allow Kyler out of the palace again."

Kellan extended his hand to shake Caitlyn's. Then he raised her hand to his lips and kissed it. "We owe you much already, Caitlyn of Ordlathus. Bring Kyler to us and our debt will be a hundred fold greater."

Retrieving her hand, Caitlyn shook a finger at him while laughing. "I see dangerous charm runs in the family, sir."

He bowed and then he and his men filed carefully out of the room

Lingering a few moments until she thought the coast would be clear, she took herself off to conduct medical rounds in the city.

Somehow Caitlyn filled the hours of the day until she could safely enter Kyler's quarters without being refused entry by Ylain. It was dinnertime and she was delighted to see him sitting up in bed, working his way through a thick steak, so rare the juices ran red.

I owe you much, he thought to her as she entered, *Not only for the steak.*

I need to tell you something, she answered.

Ylain was watching her, a strange expression on her face, brow wrinkled, eyebrows lifted.

Belatedly Caitlyn remembered to curtsey. "Forgive me, your highness. I was so pleased to see our patient much improved."

"Yes, I told you he recovers rapidly from these spell castings. I'll grant you the change in food seems to have hastened the process." Ylain rose. "You and I need to talk, Caitlyn. Not here. Come."

"But shouldn't one of us sit with him?"

Ylain shook her head. "He's fine. He needs no further nursing."

"I'm grateful to you both," Kyler said, his voice sounding a bit rusty. *Don't fight her. You must go.*

"Well then, I bid you good evening, sir." Frustration made her want to bite her nails but Kyler was right. She couldn't linger when the princess was so anxious to take her away for a private conversation.

Ylain made a bit of business of gathering the stitchery she had been working on.

I have to tell you something important. I'll try to return later. Caitlyn thought rapidly in Kyler's direction.

And then Ylain was drawing her out of the room and if Kyler had any answer for her, she was unable to hear it. The door shut firmly behind her.

CHAPTER TEN

Ylain led her rapidly towards the wing of the palace where the two princesses were housed but didn't utter another word until they were safely in her bedroom with the door shut.

"I'm leaving the City," she announced as she closed the door.

Whatever Caitlyn expected her to say, this certainly wasn't it. After a moment of shock, she collected her wits and asked, "Leaving? What do you mean?"

Ylain paced through the room, picking up items of clothing from the floor and the chairs and dropping them aimlessly on the bed or the bureau, seemingly unable to keep still. "My sister gave my hand in marriage to the emperor of Shang."

Blinking, Caitlyn had to allow the news to sink in. Shang was many days' sail away, across the deepest ocean. "You can't be serious."

"Deadly serious. Margred didn't even consult me. She's been negotiating a treaty behind my back for months apparently. Do you remember the welcoming ceremony a few weeks ago when the Emperor's ambassador arrived? Negotiations were completed today. There's to be a marriage by proxy in two weeks' time and then I sail. Do you want to hear the cream of the jest?" Ylain leaned close to Caitlyn and whispered. "I've been traded for another magic talisman. Margred wanted a certain red jade tablet of ancient spells the Emperor owned and I was the price."

A flicker of pity rose in Caitlyn's heart for the princess but the emotion was overridden by the memory of Kyler lying near death last night. Maybe now Ylain could better understand part of what he felt about being a pawn.

"This is all Bradana's doing," Ylain said, seeming distraught, wringing her hands together. Caitlyn brought her a glass of water. "I'm not naïve, I knew as a member of the royal family, I'd have to marry for statecraft, not love. But I expected to be consulted. I expected my husband to be from a neighboring kingdom on this side of the ocean at least. There are several royals I wouldn't mind marrying and so I've told her. Little did I dream my sister would force me into anything of this nature. I tell you, Margred's changed over the years and not for the better. Bradana has too much influence over her. Did you know Bradana's not even our full sister? She's the daughter of my father's mistress. She doesn't belong at Court—she ought to have been sent away at birth, adopted out."

"But yet she's treated as your equal. I certainly thought she was your legitimate older sister." *No one ever explained this information to the authorities in Ordlathus. But what would we have done differently if we had known?* Probably nothing. Court intrigues in Azrimar didn't affect daily life in the south.

Ylain sipped the water before setting the glass down hard enough to crack the stem. "Older, yes. I'm told our father loved his mistress far more than my mother, the Queen. Their marriage was strictly political, exactly the same as my fate. No love lost between the royal partners. There was a romantic bard's tale about Bradana's mother, how the king was out hunting one day and came upon her wandering in the woods, apparently the only survivor of a caravan that had been attacked by bandits." Ylain leaned close. "It's said she was from the West."

Touching the amulet at her throat, Caitlyn was shocked as she considered the news. "No one dwells in the West, only demons and sorcerers."

Ylain toyed with her cracked water glass. "Makes you think doesn't it? My mother told me the whole court thought Father had fallen under a sorceress's spell but his councilors and courtiers were afraid to talk to him about it. My mother was already pregnant with Margred so Father refused to set aside the marriage to wed this new woman, although I'm sure she schemed to become his wife. My maternal grandparents sent their own guards and hired witches privately to cast spells to safeguard Mother and the unborn baby. Bradana was born two days after Margred." The princess shuddered. "If Bradana had been a boy, Father might have declared such a child the Heir, illegitimate or not."

Quite a tale. Caitlyn could hardly take in all the details Ylain was sharing but the information certainly shed interesting light on the Azrimaran court politics. "And Bradana's mother?"

"Died in childbirth. Bradana was wrested from the womb by the attending witches. She was the apple of Father's eye, his pet. Starting when they were barely out of the cradle, Bradana exerted all her wiles to make Margred loyal to her. My old nanny used to tell me tales." Ylain closed her eyes and rocked in her chair for a moment. Pained by her obvious distress, Caitlyn patted her hand. "I wasn't included in their tight circle of two. And now I'm being disposed of. No chance I'll ever sit on the throne now. But neither will Bradana, if that's her long term aim. The nobles and the adepts won't accept a baseborn bastard Queen."

They might if the magic was powerful enough. Could wearing the crown be what Bradana was working toward? The idea of Bradana commanding Azrimar's forces left Caitlyn nauseous. And only Aerrol and his sister Susana stood in her way.

But Ylain had more to impart, this time in the form of a warning for Caitlyn. "You should leave the City yourself. When I'm not here to shield you, it'll be easy for Bradana to have you killed, or given to her loathsome captain Nedd—he fancies you—or even sold into slavery. Don't expect Margred to save you. Your novelty is long past for her."

Flinching at the thought of Nedd laying a hand on her, Caitlyn pressed her knees together reflexively. "I appreciate the caution, your highness. Did you ask me to come here today in order to warn me?"

Ylain shook her head. "I know you have more power than you let on. I've watched you all this time, while we've been out and about, doing healing. You use your strange magic carefully, clandestinely, but you do possess gifts."

Upset with herself at having misjudged Ylain's degree of naiveté, Caitlyn's thoughts raced. Lifting her chin, she challenged the princess. "Are you going to tell your sisters?"

Ylain shook her head. "It's not my concern any longer. I won't be here." She took Caitlyn's hands in hers and clasped them tight. "Can you do foreseeing? I've heard the women of the South have the talent. I want to know what waits for me in Shang. Will I be happy?"

Caitlyn took a breath and opened her mouth to answer.

Ylain forestalled her with an upraised hand. "Never mind—I ask too much," she said with a bitter laugh. "Can you at least tell me if my marriage will be bearable?"

Caitlyn was torn. On the one hand, it was important to hide the true depth of her abilities from these people. On the other hand, pity for Ylain suffused her heart. "I can do a small amount of foreseeing, your highness. I need something to focus on."

Ylain jumped from her chair and ran to search through a stack of lacquered boxes, tossing items on the floor until she located what she sought. "The Emperor sent a portrait." Unrolling a small scroll, the princess came to show Caitlyn her bridegroom-to-be.

Staring at the face gave Caitlyn the sensation of confronting a deadly snake. What was Margred sending her sister into? The Emperor was handsome enough, in the manner of his people—dark hair, brown eyes, thin lips—but after a moment of gazing at him, Caitlyn felt fire licking at her feet so strongly she expected the carpet to be ablaze. Thick gray smoke streamed off the painted parchment and coiled threateningly above the Princess. As if paralyzed, Caitlyn fell to the floor, unable to breath, pain racing across her back.

"What is it? What's the matter?"

Ylain dropped the scroll, moving rapidly to support Caitlyn. As the princess's hands touched Caitlyn, another man's face took the central position in her vision and the new arrival brought with him tremendous cold, dousing the flames, banishing the smoke and soothing the painful sensations. Caitlyn blacked out.

When she awoke, Ylain was weeping next to her. "Was my fate so awful then?"

Caitlyn sat up, searching her heart as she moved to a chair, trying to understand the strange set of images she'd received. It had been such a powerful foretelling the room still spun. "Your highness, the vision was jumbled, confused. I'm not positive what meanings the omens carry. I think perhaps the future has several possibilities, once you reach Shang. I saw one path leading to—to great pain and troubles." She shivered, remembering the agony accompanying the impression of being burned alive. "Yet another path leads to the happiness you've been hoping for." Caitlyn rubbed her temples. "Neither may be a true foreseeing, I warn you. The emperor is powerful so my advice is walk carefully in all things, keep your own counsel, be true to yourself."

Ylain wiped away tears with a heavily embroidered handkerchief. "Thank you for trying. I'm sorry it was painful to do. I had no idea what I was asking of you." She plucked the scroll from the floor and went to restore the portrait to safekeeping in the lacquer box.

Happy to see the painting removed from proximity to her, Caitlyn felt as if Ylain had carried a poisonous spider away. Wiping her brow in relief, she said, "No lasting damage, your highness."

"I told my sister you'd continue to do the healing until she can find an adept to take over. She needs to have someone handle those duties, which will keep you safe for a time but you must get away from the City. I don't know why you came, or why you stay, but it will be your death to remain after my ship sails." Rising, Ylain straightened her gown, frowning at some dust marks from sitting on the floor.

Caitlyn was thinking rapidly. This wedding might provide an opportunity to gain access to that closed chamber on the Queen's corridor. "What time is the ceremony to be then?"

"At midafternoon on the fourteenth day." Ylain flushed in obvious embarrassment and looked anywhere but at Caitlyn. "I know you're a member of my household, but you won't be invited. Only members of the court."

"Don't distress yourself, your highness. I'll wish you well now." Caitlyn left her chair, smoothing the wrinkles from her skirt and ran a hand through her hair. "Did you have any special instructions for me, as regards the healing duties for the next two weeks?"

Steepling her fingers together, Ylain cocked her head. "I intend to continue to exercise my healing powers, whether here or in Shang. This emperor will have to accept my wishes as far as using my magic. Please assemble an assortment of our finest remedies for me to take with me. A small chest of our best potions and the rarest dried herbs would be perfect."

Pleased to see the princess trying to so hard to be positive and determined to make the best of things, Caitlyn smiled. "The task will be my pleasure, your highness."

They shared an awkward hug and then Caitlyn curtseyed and walked out of the room. As she strode down the halls, she was deep in thought about the best way to retrieve the Stone of Duadalne while everyone of higher rank attended the wedding ceremony two weeks hence.

She forced herself to wait until well after midnight before she ventured to see Kyler. Fortunately he was alone and awake when she scratched at his door. Seated at his desk, surrounded by blazing oil lamps, he made intricate cuts on a new sculpture.

"No one sits to keep watch on you tonight?" she teased him as she came into the room.

"I appreciate small mercies." He set aside his knife and the block of wood. "It's too risky for you to come here. What if the queen or Bradana find out?"

She picked up a length of wood he'd rejected for some reason, passing the rough branch under her nose and sniffing the pine scent appreciatively. "What I have to relate is important enough to take a risk or two."

Stretching his long legs and rolling his shoulders, he snorted derisively. "Important enough to risk your life?"

"I think so." Setting the wood on the desk, she walked to the nearest chair and sat, afraid to touch him. One touch led to another, and that road led nowhere. "Your brother was here today, along with four other shapeshifters."

Speechless, eyes wide, Kyler was as taken aback as if she'd shifted into a cat herself.

Pleased with his reaction, Caitlyn went on with her news. "Kellan told me this is the fourth year in a row they've ridden from the North, trying to get you released from the Witch Queen's spell."

He stabbed the carving knife into the desk and pushed his chair back, rising to pace the floor. "You've met my brother? You talked to Kellan? I can hardly believe this. The Pack actually came on my behalf?"

"Four years in a row," Caitlyn repeated patiently. "Margred sends them away. Today she threatened to kill them if they venture south again."

"Let her try," Kyler said roughly. "Unlike me, they're under no spell that would keep her safe from claws and fangs."

Caitlyn laughed. "Yes, Kellan said the same thing. At any rate, I had a chance to talk to him briefly, once I convinced him I wasn't a servant of Margred's. We arranged for them to camp at our ledge by the stream, in hopes you can slip away and meet them there in the next day or two."

Kyler didn't instantly agree, which surprised Caitlyn. Instead he paced the room for several minutes, finally stopping in front of her. "I'm not sure I want to meet them," he said.

"Why not?" She couldn't keep herself from doing a double take at this unexpected answer. She'd thought he'd be thrilled.

He raised one hand to the golden collar but didn't quite touch it, fingers trembling ever so slightly. "My packmates never saw me like this. I can't bear to see contempt, or worse—pity—in their eyes."

Immediate understanding brought a prickling to her eyes and she rushed into her answer. He wouldn't welcome pity from her either. "Your brother loves you. His emotion was plain today when we were talking. He wants to see you; to be sure you're doing all right. Being in their presence would be good for you, might help restore your energy." The solemn expression on his face told her Kyler wasn't convinced. Time for more arguments in favor of the plan she and Kellan hatched. "They rode all this way, four years in a row, and you won't give them even a few moments?" She caught his sleeve. "They know what you sacrificed to save your Alpha. They won't think less of you, I'm sure."

He captured her hand, held it tight. "Come with me?"

Although surprised, she agreed without hesitation. "If you want me to, of course I will."

"We'll go tomorrow morning. No one cares if I resume active duty with the guards so I'll be free to slip away. Can you meet me at the edge of the forest path, say at midmorning?"

"Yes, Princess Ylain gives me wide latitude these days. I set my own schedule of duties. Especially now." Deliberately she dropped the last tidbit, knowing he'd be curious.

Head tilted, eyebrows raised, he looked a question at her.

"She's been given in marriage to the emperor of Shang, in exchange for some ancient tablet of spells Princess Bradana coveted," Caitlyn explained. "The wedding by proxy is in two weeks. Ylain has my sympathy." *Especially after the terrible foreseeing I did for her.*

"Of course she does, with your tender heart." When Kyler smiled, his whole face lit up and he seemed ten years younger. She caught a glimpse of the man he must have been before his life changed, when he was a free ranging shifter, in control of his own destiny. Caitlyn's heart thumped in response.

Taking her by the hand, he drew her from the chair and led her to the door. Cracking the portal open an inch or two, he checked the hallway before whispering over his shoulder. "Clear. You have to go, much as I long for you to linger." Hugging her close for a moment, he kissed her forehead. "We can't drift into spending too much time together. The risks to you are too high. If Ylain won't be the cover for your activities any longer, you'll have to leave the city, you know."

Without answering, she stood on her tiptoes and pressed a kiss on his cheek, then moved away.

CHAPTER ELEVEN

After bidding Caitlyn goodnight, he couldn't summon any interest in the carving and he'd slept so much in the last three days, returning to bed was out of the question. Lost in thought, making what plans he could, he sat by the window in his room watching the fog create eerie patterns in the gardens until the appointed hour to meet her.

Together they hiked through the woods until they reached what he thought of as "their" rock ledge by the stream.

Kellan stood there alone, facing the trail, waiting. His brother appeared unchanged to Kyler, unaffected by the passage of time since they last met.

For a moment there was silence between them. Kyler's throat choked with emotion at seeing Kellan—seeing anyone from his Pack again. A moment later the shifter magic of the pack reached out to him. The power curled around him, calling to his leopard and the effect nearly took him to his knees, as the trapped beast inside fought to be free and welcome their brother properly. An emotion akin to panic threaded through his nerves and he had to fight the impulse to retreat. This was the worst moment of his entire captivity, being confronted with who and what he used to be. Why had he listened to Caitlyn's pleas? Better to have stayed away. But even as the bitter thoughts swirled in his mind, Kyler clung tight to the one reason he'd agreed to meet with his packmates.

"It's good to see you, brother," Kellan said, reaching out to enfold him in a hug, pounding his back, while Caitlyn stood aside and watched, a pleased expression on her face.

Pleasing her is no small thing to me. Kyler scented the approach of his other packmates and broke free from Kellan, placing himself between Caitlyn and the warriors, which took her by surprise. Four huge leopards paced out of the forest and shifted to men in a blur of iridescent shimmers between one step and the next. His leopard relaxed somewhat since they'd chosen to shift into the clothed state, garbed in their customary uniforms in deference to Caitlyn. Shifters could be pretty casual about nudity when resuming human form.

He heard Kellan smother a laugh at his protective, jealous stance but he didn't care. *She's mine and I'll take no chances with her safety.* From deep inside, he heard the leopard's answering snarl of agreement.

There was a backslapping reunion with the four newcomers, all men he'd known well in the Pack. He appreciated their coming into the dangers of Azrimar on his behalf. His former comrades seemed unsure what to say to him and Kyler had few words in response to their questions. Normally he was dominant to all of them except Kellan but the restraints imposed on him by the collar and the spell confused their leopards, made the men edgy. Apparently sensing the problem as well, Kellen allowed the general conversation to go on for only a few moments before ordering his men out on patrol. They strode away, shifting into cats as they proceeded into the forest. The power of their changing tore at Kyler with physical pain, as his leopard struggled to do the same, making his bones ache and his head swim.

Caitlyn came to take his arm, evidently concerned by what she read in his face. Swallowing hard, hunched over somewhat against the agony the magic flare stabbed into him, he leaned on her more than he wanted to. Grateful Kellan didn't make any remark about his display of vulnerability, Kyler uttered the first inane thing that came into his head to break the awkward silence. "You've met my brother then?"

"Indeed, I was fortunate enough to meet her at the palace," Kellan said before Caitlyn could answer, with a graceful bow over her hand. "A rare flower in blooming in a grim Court."

Barely restraining himself from tackling his brother to keep him from touching Caitlyn, Kyler fought with his snarling leopard and managed to speak words rather than growl a challenge. "I saw her first."

Glancing from him to his brother, Caitlyn was plainly confused and troubled by the hostile tone of his voice. Brow furrowed, she took a step away. "I'll leave you two to talk," she said. "We don't have much time and you undoubtedly have a lot to say to each other."

Kyler watched her go before giving his attention to Kellan. His older brother spoke first.

"You're too thin. You look exhausted. I understand Margred bars you from shifting?"

Kyler didn't bother denying his brother's claim.

"Caitlyn told us they steal your blood for their rituals now. Margred has no right to such service." Kellan's jaw was clenched, his brows drawn into a vee of anger.

Unable to shake off the lingering effects of being caught in ripples of shifter power, Kyler staggered to the nearest small boulder and sat. "I agreed to it."

Coming after him, boots scraping on the granite, Kellan shook his head. "The Queen pushes your service beyond the bounds of the Light."

"Oath breaking is a serious thing, brother, not something our kind does." Kyler answered warily.

Resting one hand on his shoulder, Kellan launched into the plea Kyler had been expecting, nay dreading. "Leave this cursed place, come home with us today. Dumaire would gather the entire Pack, I'm sure, and we'd petition Lord Belinu of the Sun to declare you a free man. If the god grants, then together, the Pack would have enough power in our homeland to break the spell, set aside this damnable thing." He pointed at the collar.

"I can't." Kyler answered simply.

"You owe that bitch nothing more," his brother said, making an obvious effort to hold onto his temper, although his cheeks grew red and his claws broke through on both hands. "You've more than fulfilled any obligation Alpha Dumaire himself was prepared to accept. Our people's debt has been repaid many times over."

Time for the first piece of news. Kyler took a deep breath, the fresh air of the forest clearing the tightness in his chest to some extent. "The spell has an invisible leash, brother. I can't get beyond a certain distance from the Witch Queen." With one hand he indicated the trees surrounding the clearing round them. "This is about the limit, in fact."

Frowning, Kellan eyed him for a moment, clearly pondering this, trying to solve the problem. "What if you were unconscious? Between us, my four men and I could subdue and restrain you, exile your consciousness into the dreamspace for as long as it took to get you home, perform the ceremony and break the spell."

Kyler shook his head. "It might work. It might not. I don't know." He checked on Caitlyn, who gave him a cheery little wave although her face was set in serious lines, obviously curious how his conversation with his brother was proceeding. Time for Kellan to understand the most important barrier, much more meaningful than Margred's spell. Addressing his brother, he said, "It doesn't matter because I can't leave."

"Damn it, you're being hot headed and stubborn, which is what got you into this trap in the first place." Hands on his hips, Kellan seemed ready to do physical battle with his younger brother to get him to change his mind.

"If you calm down, pacify your leopard for a moment so you can reason clearly, you'll know my primary reason for not accepting your offer today." Kyler pointed toward Caitlyn with his chin.

"No." Making a slashing gesture of denial, Kellan shook his head vehemently. He didn't even glance in Caitlyn's direction. "I refuse to accept this. A human woman, no matter how exceptional, can't be allowed to stand between you and freedom."

"I can't leave her. I won't even try. She's my mate." How bittersweet to say the words, utter the claim.

"You haven't taken her. Your claim is unfinished, there's no scent of a bond." Kellan argued as Kyler'd known he would.

Shaking his head, Kyler brought out the counter arguments he'd been considering all night, in the lonely privacy of his chambers. "Don't try to deny the reality of what I'm telling you. You know I'm right—she's my mate, whether we've been together or not. How could you be in her presence above five minutes and not realize what a rare soul she is? My leopard and I were drawn to Caitlyn from the first moment we beheld her."

Rubbing the stubble on his chin, Kellan thought hard for a moment. "All right, fine, then we kidnap her too and take her north with us."

"She has her own reason to be here in the City. I've no right to interfere with her task, which she does in the service of the forest goddess Tiermalleia." Deliberately Kyler invoked the name of the deity. Although his people owed her no allegiance, Kellan would think twice before interfering with someone acting under her command. His brother blinked and swallowed whatever he'd planned to say next. Kyler offered a bit more explanation. "Caitlyn has to stay until her task is completed. I need to be here to protect her, as much as it's in my power to do so."

"Then we're at an impasse." In apparent frustration, Kellan smacked his fist into his other hand.

"I was reluctant to come here today," Kyler said. "I didn't think you'd understand. I expected you to try kidnapping me for my own good. But she persuaded me I should meet you."

"Of course I understand," Kellan shouted, flinging his arms out. He lowered his voice as Caitlyn half rose, a distressed look on her face. "Finding a true mate is the one thing we all long for, live for." Running his hands through his hair, Kellan said, "I curse Fate for bringing love to you here and now, where nothing can come of it. Particularly when the woman's presence keeps you from grabbing at a chance to escape."

Kyler sat straighter. "Now we're at the crux of the matter, why I agreed to come here. I need you to do something for me."

"Anything." Kellan leaned forward, an eager light in his eyes.

"I want Caitlyn's name entered into the Pack membership as my officially recognized mate. I need to know she can call upon the Pack for protection."

Frowning, Kellan paced the length of the ledge and back. "An unprecedented request where you haven't actually taken her. Dumaire may refuse."

"Dumaire can go to the Shadow and rot then," Kyler said with considerable heat, anger burning in his heart. "He owes me."

"Our Alpha's a fair man and he knows what he owes you, trust me, but your demand is highly unusual." Kellan shook his head as Kyler opened his mouth to protest. "I'm the alpha of our family and if I recognize her status as your mate, then Dumaire won't refuse. I'll do it, for you and for her. She's an unusual woman, I grant you. She may be only human but she has power—"

"She has a true and good heart and she's all I live for now," Kyler said. "She shed her own blood to bring me from the brink of death two nights ago. This is the only thing I can do to try to protect her." Now he left his perch on the boulder and paced himself, unable to remain seated with so much anger and frustration pent up inside. "My leopard claws at me every waking moment and in my dreams." He laughed. "Or should I say my nightmares? The cat wants to run free, to take her, to watch over her, to cherish her. All impossible. The Witch Queen and her sister demonstrate a keen eye for punishing any woman I show more than casual interest in. I can't put Caitlyn in additional danger by allowing my claim, my love, to be plain, much less by bedding her. The castle is full of spies and gossips. "

Kellan laid a hand on his arm, stopping his restless movement along the ledge. "Easy, brother. She'll be recorded as a member of our family and therefore a member of the Pack."

"My acknowledged mate," Kyler repeated. "Nothing less."

His brother put one hand over his heart. "From this moment she stands as my responsibility to honor and protect to the death, in recognition of her mating bond with you," he said formally. "I personally pledge anything in our power she might need, will be done."

"Thank you." The brothers shook hands. Kyler glanced at the position of the sun in the sky. "We have to return to the palace. She has duties, I have duties and it must not ever be remarked upon that we're both missing at the same time."

"After I make my report to Dumaire, he'll march to Azrimar at full Pack strength and demand your freedom from these witches," Kellan said.

Kyler shook his head. "Talk him out of it, brother. It's not worth risking the Pack for one man. I chose my path freely although I fear Margred and her sister move toward the Shadow now in their spells and their schemes."

"The Queen may not be in the Shadow yet but the sister is definitely across the line. How can you fail to smell the stench?" Kellan's lips curled and his nose wrinkled, showing as much distaste as if he was breathing the rotten odor of evil magic this very moment.

With difficulty, Kyler kept himself from rubbing the collar, which was chafing his neck. "I don't let myself. I can't. Unfortunately the oath I swore to Margred in return for the assurances she gave me didn't specifically rule out using my power for spells in the Shadow. Who would have dreamt a Witch Queen of Azrimar would contemplate such blasphemy?"

"It's the sister's influence, no doubt." Kellan's voice was emphatic.

"Tell Dumaire from me the Pack needs to forget me, leave me to serve out my oath." Kyler shook his head. "No good will come of any further involvement with Azrimar under these conditions."

Kellan leaned closer to Kyler. "There's something else. If you and Caitlyn often come to this place, you need to exercise great caution."

Kyler surveyed the forest, trying to detect any hidden dangers. The way the spell blunted his natural abilities enraged him. Kellan shouldn't have to tell him of dangers, especially where Caitlyn was involved. "Why? What have you scented?"

"Strange currents of magic in the woods, and on the outskirts of the city, reminiscent of the odor of the great curse our forest suffered under, the one from the

West," Kellan said, frowning. "Traces of someone or something making incursions into Margred's territory. She's not maintaining her borders well in any respect. We were barely challenged as we came south and our arrival has taken her by surprise each year instead of being reported from the borders long before we arrived at the City. The military has grown lax."

"My friend, Duke Aerrol, often complains bitterly how Margred and Bradana channel all their energy and resources into the magic, and neglect the physical infrastructure a city and an army must maintain," Kyler said. "Over the past few years I've witnessed many an argument between them over this issue."

"He's her heir?"

"If there's anything left to inherit and rule over." Kyler said with a short laugh. "The longer I'm here, the more I see the wisdom of the original founders of Azrimar, dividing the throne between a King with little or no magic and a Witch Queen. If only Margred had taken a strong husband, Bradana's influence would have been nullified. Magic and practicality need to be held in balance."

Kellan grunted. "Well the issue is Azrimar's problem, not mine. If only you were well out of it."

Shaking his head to stop the discussion, Kyler said, "I'm grateful to know the Pack hasn't forgotten me. We need to leave it there."

Raising his hands as if to ward off a blow, chuckling under his breath, Kellan said, "All right, I know when I've lost a battle." His eyes brightened as he made a new suggestion. "I could station a man here, to assist you and Caitlyn. Kildar, maybe. He's the most senior soldier, steady. He could stay out of sight in these woods and stand ready if needed."

Momentarily tempted by the offer, Kyler paused, but then he shook his head. "Caitlyn needs protection inside the palace, where no shapeshifter but myself can walk. I appreciate the offer though."

Kellan didn't seem too surprised. "We'll be away to the North then. Take care of yourself, little brother."

"And you."

The two men hugged with more back slapping, and then Kellan bowed to Caitlyn and walked into the woods without so much as a backward glance.

She came to Kyler, studying his face as he gallantly took her hand. "Thank you for making me come to meet them today," he said simply.

"You're welcome. Was the conversation helpful?"

He nodded. "Yes, but we'd better go. I'm on duty later today and you have healing rounds to do in the city, right?"

"I don't know what they'll do when I'm gone but if I can get my hands on the Stone of Duadalne while Ylain's wedding is being celebrated, then I'll have to leave you too, like Kellan and the others did." Sorrow played over her expressive face, unshed tears in her eyes at the thought of leaving him alone at Court.

"I know." He squeezed her hand as they walked in the general direction of the Palace. "I'll be fine, sweetheart."

And we both know I'm lying.

CHAPTER TWELVE

Caitlyn had nightmares for the next three nights running, rising each morning unrefreshed and tired. On the fourth morning, she lingered in bed, which was highly unusual for her. Susana and Gretha gave her puzzled looks as they prepared for their day of classes and finally left the room. Susana only left after being assured Caitlyn wasn't ill. Once she had the room to herself, Caitlyn got out of bed and grumpily rejected the dresses Princess Ylain had given her to wear, as a member of her staff. They were plain, serviceable, well sewn, but not what she wanted today. She took out the green dress she'd worn to travel from her home far to the south, to this City. She pulled the garment over her head and smoothed out the wrinkles, realizing she'd lost weight. Stress and worry could do that to a person. Maintaining this glamourie, searching for the Stone, worrying about Kyler...

She slipped out of the palace grounds and hiked into the woods, seeking their special place, despite the warning from Kyler's brother about unknown intruders roaming in the vicinity. Confident in her own magic, especially in an area where she could call upon the forces of nature as well, she found no reason to deny herself the peace of mind she was seeking today.

Once there, she curled up in the pale winter sunlight, pulling her new, heavy cloak closer and watched the colorful leaves falling softly. The stream babbled and gurgled below. Only a few birds called today, as most had flown south to avoid winter. Caitlyn envied them but she wasn't free to follow their path, not yet. She still had to retrieve the Stone of Duadalne.

Leaving her heart behind in Azrimar, with Kyler.

Caitlyn prayed to her goddess Tiermalleia but the Lady was well into her cycle as the Crone. The goddess wasn't viewing hopeless pleas for lovers who could never be together with any favor. Trying not to cry, Caitlyn rested her head on her knees.

"It's someone's birthday today, am I right?" Kyler asked from behind her, sounding cheerful.

Caitlyn wiped away her tears quickly, wanting to greet him with a happier demeanor. They had so few opportunities to talk, she wasn't going to waste a moment weeping. "How did you know?"

He came forward, holding a small bentwood basket, incongruous dangling from the hand of a warrior like him. His cheerful expression fading as he took in her tear stained face and red rimmed eyes, Kyler set the basket down, sat and gathered her into a comforting hug. "Why so sad, sweet? Are you missing your home? Your family?"

Throat tight with more unshed tears, she burrowed into the warmth of his embrace.

"Nadelma told me this was your birthday. Evidently you mentioned it to her at some point and she never forgets these things. I thought you might be out here, in the forest. Let's see what she put in this basket for you."

Caitlyn opened the woven top of the container and brought out a small cake on a plate, covered with a brightly colored cloth. "How thoughtful of her," she said, smiling.

"Nadelma baked it herself, I'm told. Not even the queen gets a cake baked by the cook," Kyler teased. "Nadelma has three master pastry chefs on staff. So you must rank astoundingly high in the order of things."

Caitlyn broke off a crumb to sample. The cake tasted delicious, pumpkin, raisins, nuts and spices, warm from the oven. A brown sugar glaze was melted on top. All the flavors of autumn. "Nadelma has her own form of magic. You have to taste this."

"In a minute. I've brought something else." He handed her a small cloth bag. "I made this for you."

Caitlyn loosened the green velvet braid holding the sack shut and spread the edges apart, in order to lift out the small, heart shaped wooden box. Made of rich dark wood with a high gloss, the box's lid was inlaid with mother of pearl and variegated woods, forming a mosaic of a leopard running.

She ran her thumb across the satin smooth surface, moving the box this way and that so the light caught the details of the leopard. "It's beautiful."

"I used some of the coins I told you about, to buy the mother of pearl for the inlay and mahogany wood from the far tropics," he said, obviously proud of his workmanship. "Go ahead, open it."

Caitlyn did as he requested but the box was empty. She looked at him with a puzzled frown. He leaned forward and kissed her lips before explaining. "It holds my heart, my hopes and dreams, just for you. They can't be seen, I can't act upon them but that doesn't mean they don't exist."

She wept, holding the box to her heart.

"Sweetheart, the last thing I meant to do was make you cry. I hoped my gift would please you, not upset you." Blinking rapidly, he scratched his cheek as if unsure what to do next and then took the edge of his cloak to wipe away her tears.

Raising her face to his tender ministration, she said, "The box is wonderful. Don't mind me—I'm fragile today. It's the most romantic and poetic gift I've ever received. I'll treasure the box and all it represents. Thank you."

He circled her shoulders with one arm and pulled her closer to him, wrapping his cloak to cover them both, as a chill breeze rattled the bare tree branches.

"So tell me what you'd be doing at home this day."

She closed the heart box and set it aside, then cut the cake with the small knife in the bottom of the basket, offering him the larger piece. As he munched appreciatively, Caitlyn snuggled against his side and nibbled at her slice.

"I have a large family—three sisters and two brothers, in-laws, nieces and nephews. My mother would have spent the day with my sisters, cooking a special dinner and making a cake. Not like this one, although it's delicious, but her own recipe, reserved for birthdays. And then in the evening we'd have a gathering of our relatives and friends, with music and dancing. My father and my brothers and sisters all play various instruments. Most people do, in Ordlathus. I'm no musician myself but I enjoy listening." She hummed a snatch of the tune for him, keeping time with one hand before breaking off the song with a gusty sigh. "I know I'm here of my own free will, for a compelling reason, but today I felt sorry for myself."

"My people don't celebrate birthdays particularly," Kyler said, licking some of the glaze from his fingers. "But we have other special occasions we take note of with feasts and revelry. The pangs of self-pity have tortured me more than once, being alone here in the City on a day sacred to my kind. I understand."

Nice of him to say but Kyler was the least self-pitying person she'd ever met, even with all the good reasons he might have. "People are so formal in the City, so cheerless. Even when they do celebrate a holiday, it's laden with protocol and etiquette," Caitlyn said.

"I believe the common folk, in the City at large, are freer, high spirited," Kyler told her. "In the palace itself, the atmosphere has been more somber each passing year. Princess Bradana is not one for merriment."

She popped one last, fat raisin in her mouth. "I've noticed."

Kyler finished licking the frosting from his fingers. "And she influences Queen Margred, even in small things like this."

"I'm so torn, because once I get the Stone of Duadalne in my possession, then I've carried out my mission and must leave in haste, abandoning you." Caitlyn tried to deny the sorrow her thoughts brought to her heart.

Kyler apparently agreed they should try to keep the mood lighter. "Let's not talk of the Stone today. We should be happy in the celebration of your birthday. Is there any more cake left?"

She handed him the remnants of her slice. "You and your leopard have a sweet tooth, don't you?"

"I don't deny the truth." He finished off the cake and searched out the few crumbs on the plate. His tone changed, became more serious. "Caitlyn?"

"Yes?" Watching his face, seeing the way he hesitated, she was wary.

His question was blunt. "Is there someone special waiting for you?"

She felt her cheeks warm as she blushed. "No one." Tracing the leopard on the lid of the box with her fingertip, reluctant to meet his eyes, she said, "I always wondered why I never fell in love like the other girls my age. Settling their futures was so easy—they'd meet a man, fall in love, get married, have children—but I never truly loved anyone."

With a gentle hand under her chin, he tipped her face up. Green eyes locked onto her, voice low, he asked, "Never?"

Raising her own hand to stroke his cheek, she smiled. "I was waiting for you."

He hugged her close.

"Are you sorry we met?" he asked, his voice low and quiet in her ear. "It's a hard fate we share."

She feathered kisses along the line of his jaw. "How could I be sorry?"

"I'll never regret meeting you either," he answered. "You haven't asked, but there was no special woman for me in the North. Now and forever there will only be you."

"I think, despite the circumstances, this is the best birthday I ever had," she said with a contented sigh, laying her head against his shoulder and nestling there. "Thank you."

"That's what a friend is for," he said earnestly. "And now I realize birthdays are celebrated with a cake such as the one Nadelma sent you, I'm going to select a day for my birthday and make sure she knows about it."

Caitlyn laughed at his boyish enthusiasm. "An excellent plan, but you have to stay in her good graces until the birthday if you want her cake."

"You doubt my ability to be charming?" Opening his eyes wide, she could see he strove to present the most innocent expression he was capable of assuming, before breaking into a laugh.

His good humor was infectious and Caitlyn chuckled. "Oh, no, I've seen far too much proof of your fatal charm, sir."

Still pleased with himself two days later, for having brought Caitlyn good cheer on her birthday, Kyler's mood took a sudden reversal before breakfast. Margred was going to summon him. The signs were unmistakable. The collar had been twitching against his neck since dawn broke and he had a dull, pounding headache. Together those were invariably signs she was going to call him to a spell casting. The Witch Queen couldn't be bothered to send a human servant to forewarn him when the collar's spell could be employed to remind him of his lowly status.

They'd gone through this ritual many times in his long years at Court; however Kyler wasn't prepared to be summoned in the early evening to her private suite of rooms instead of the side rooms of the spell chamber. Her chambers had been strictly off-limits to him since the day he arrived in Azrimar. And a change in her unvarying routine couldn't be a good sign. Not now, when so many omens point to growing darkness in Azrimar. He told himself to be prepared for anything, maybe even questions about Caitlyn.

Strolling unchallenged past the guards, he was disturbed to find Captain Nedd in charge of the queen's personal security as well as Bradana's. The man made Kyler's leopard wild, adrenaline racing, as if he was in the presence of a treacherous threat, another predator lurking. He could feel the talons pricking at his skin, trying to overcome the power of Margred's spell and unsheathe, ready for combat. Ignoring the cold sensation between his shoulder blades, as if he was waiting for an attack from behind, Kyler kept his outwardly casual air and sauntered through the doors to the queen's suite. The outer room was empty so he paused in the center of the swirling purple and black rug.

"Your majesty?"

Bradana appeared on the threshold leading into the next room, the queen's sleeping quarters. She beckoned to him. "We're waiting for you in here, shifter."

Senses on the alert, Kyler brushed past the princess and walked into the bedroom. Ignoring Bradana, who he loathed more each hour he spent in the City, if so much hatred was possible, he focused on the Queen. "You summoned me, your majesty?"

"Kneel to your queen, shapeshifter," Bradana said from behind him. "How many times must we tell you the proper etiquette?"

Moving so she wasn't at his back, he glared at her from his greater height. "She's not my queen. My allegiance is only to my Alpha. How many times must I tell you that?"

"Margred, I insist he pay you the proper respect." Bradana said as she walked past Kyler to stand with her hands on her hips, glaring at him. "This behavior cannot be tolerated."

Kyler wasn't surprised when the collar clenched on his neck. *Don't they ever tire of this petty game? I've never knelt to her voluntarily and I never will.* Having drawn in as much air as he could in the second before Margred commanded the golden circlet to constrict, he fought to remain standing, until his vision was blurring. Rather than pass out in front of these two women he hated, he finally sank to one knee, glaring at the Witch Queen as he did so. Margred shrugged as if to say none of this mattered to her but Bradana must be appeased and tucked the golden key into the low cut bodice of her sheer white dress.

The collar relaxed.

He took a deep breath and rose to his feet without waiting for anyone's permission, rolling his shoulders and standing tall.

"Now to the reason you've been summoned." Apparently satisfied he'd been properly reprimanded, Bradana moved to stand in front of Kyler, between him and the queen. "Her Majesty has decided she wishes to bear a child," she said. "Tonight is the first propitious night."

After one stunned moment when he thought he must have heard wrong, he threw back his head and guffawed. Amazed and appalled at her arrogance, he pointed a finger at Margred. "Oh no, neither your spell, nor our agreement holds any requirement for us to share a bed, much less for me to get you with child. It's past time for you to find a willing would-be king, your majesty, to sire your spawn. Don't look to me."

Margred winced under the effect of his cutting words. Bradana stepped closer, hand raised as if to slap him across the face. He caught her wrist in one hand, using her momentum to shove her away from him.

"Such things don't have to be arranged through use of a spell," Bradana said after she regained her balance.

"Are you her procurer now?" he said, lacing his question with contempt. Margred refused to meet his eyes, wrapping her filmy white gown more closely about her. She shrank into her chair and curled up, as if seeking warmth. "I'd rather be drawn and quartered than lay one hand on you," he said, voicing the utter revulsion he felt. Even such a bald statement didn't move Margred to look at him. She closed her eyes tight as he finished his declaration. "You've no right to share my bed, much less to bear a child of mine. No shifter—no honorable man—would ever accept such a condition. Certainly my Alpha wouldn't have accepted such a request and when I took his place to spare him, I never agreed to fuck you." Deliberately he chose the cruder term. "Not part of the bargain, Margred." Anger coursed through his veins so fiercely, he thought he might explode into flames. What is the matter with these people? How twisted had they become in the last ten years? A thought struck him, like ice water. *She must think if she has my child, she won't need to steal magic from me any longer. She can kill me during a supreme spell and still have the child's inherited shifter magic to command thereafter.* Disgust made his stomach roil.

Bradana clapped her hands in a slow, exaggerated rhythm, a mocking expression her face. "A fine defiant speech but in my experience all men have a price. What if we offered you your freedom the day a healthy baby was born?"

Disbelief and disgust warring in his mind, the leopard raging for permission to shift and kill their captors, he could hardly form words. "You'd have me trade my freedom for my child's life? What kind of people are you in Azrimar? I'd die before I abandoned any child of mine. We're done here. I may be held by the power of the oath I gave you and the spell embodied in this collar, but thank the gods certain things are beyond your power to command." Not even glancing at Margred again, he marched from the room, ignoring Bradana's shouts for him to remain. It seemed the queen was ready to be done with the conversation as well, since the collar never so much as twitched.

He vowed that as long as the collar stayed quiet and he had breath in his body, he'd put as much distance between himself and the royal sisters as possible.

Hours later, Kyler stood on the ledge overlooking the little stream, out in the forest. The moonlight glinted silvery on the frost touched trees while black water rippled over the rocks. Gray tendrils of fog crept here and there before drifting elsewhere in the chill breeze. Thinking bleak thoughts, he closed his eyes. Driven to find somewhere free of any link to the Witch Queen or her sister, he stumbled to the forest. But even here, surrounded by nature at her most peaceful, his angry leopard could not be soothed.

Not tonight.

The frustrated cat was perilously near to crossing a threshold of sanity Kyler wouldn't be able to recover from, not as man or beast. *I'd say Margred has breached our agreement with her repulsive demand, even though I have the power to refuse what she wants in this case. I've served my time, honored my oath.* He fingered the collar, cold, unyielding to the touch. Yet if his gods didn't choose to set him free of her spell, there was nothing he could do to escape Azrimar. He'd have to allow her to plunder his store of magic until he perished. He glared at the moon, sailing serenely in the cold winter sky.

"I hope my death serves some worthy purpose for you, Belinu most high, since you ignore my prayer, refuse to intervene." Lowering his head, he clenched his fists and stood, trying to soothe the leopard enough to walk the halls of the palace without wanting to lash out, playing his part.

Caitlyn stepped out of the forest behind him. He scented her, smelling sweetly of flowers and spring. There was silence between them for a moment. No doubt she was puzzled at the lack of a greeting from him. He couldn't bring himself to do so just yet, much as he longed to revel in her soft arms holding him. He required more control over himself and over the leopard caged inside. The demands placed on him in the last few hours, even though he'd refused them pointblank, re-emphasized the hopelessness of his situation.

I'd give anything to make love to Caitlyn, to have a child with her.

Caitlyn whispered his name, a question in her voice. He heard her take a step toward him, her foot crushing the moss. Unable to repress the words any longer, he said, "The queen wants to bear a child. My child."

"No!" Caitlyn's protest was soft and appalled. She took another step toward him before hating uncertainly.

"I refused her of course. There will be no child. There will never be a child," he vowed, his voice low and cold. "Nothing sexual was included in her spell and I wouldn't have agreed to such a condition, not even to save my Alpha." Now he did turn his head, unable to deny himself the comforting sight of his beautiful love. "Did you know my kind mates for life? And it's rare we find our mate. All shifters—male or female—dream of experiencing the joy, which only a lucky few obtain. My Alpha is mated, which is why I decided to come here in his place."

A faint smile on her lips, she said, "I remember. You told me."

"They have a family— three cubs the last I knew. Only with a shapeshifter's true mate will there be a child from lying together." His heart ached as he indulged himself for a brief moment in the dream of someday holding a son or daughter born of the love between Caitlyn and him.

She walked forward slowly, gazing steadily into his eyes as she came and took his hand in hers. "I could tell something was wrong—your emotions were buffeting me. Anger. Despair. I couldn't sleep," she said. "I searched but I couldn't find you in the dreamspace."

"I'm sorry." He kissed her hand. "I'll be more careful to shield my emotions against you in the future."

"Shielding me isn't the answer," she answered immediately. "My heart would break if I was barred from contact with you. I can handle whatever is going on, as long as I know we're linked, and I can be sure you're unharmed." She smiled sadly. "But harm isn't always physical, is it? As soon as I felt the impression you'd be here, in our private spot, I got dressed and came."

He gave in to temptation, gathered her close, and rested his aching head on hers. She came into his arms willingly, warm, sweet, wanting only to comfort him. "To find me," he said

"To help, if it was in my power."

"I never thought I'd be blessed with a mate," Kyler said, stroking his hand through her long, soft curly hair, grateful she'd left it loose in her hurry to find him. The motion soothed the leopard, calmed him. "To give my heart and soul to you for the rest of my life is more than I'd ever hoped for." Kyler took her face in his hands, raising her chin so their eyes met, and kissed her forehead. "You're my mate, I know it, the leopard knew it probably the first time I ever saw you, the day you arrived at Court." He swallowed hard. "I hope you feel the same."

"I love you." Caitlyn kissed him tenderly. "I'm proud to be your mate."

He savored her words even as he was shaking his head. "There's no future for us because I'll never be free of this captivity. Tonight's events reemphasize the truth. The Witch Queen and her sister won't let me go. If they had any idea what you mean to me, you'd be in grave danger."

Raising her chin and looking him directly in the eyes, she said, "Bradana hates me anyway. I'm not afraid of her."

"Bold words. " Kyler had to laugh—she sounded so ferocious, his mate, even without claws and fangs. "If Bradana had any idea how much I love you, she'd find a way to use you to force me to do her will, to do things that aren't required by the spell. She'd enjoy torturing you to break me."

"This spell of the queen's is wrong," Caitlyn said. "Whatever was intended in the beginning, she and her sister have misused it, abused you. And this new obsession with having a child goes totally against the Light."

"I asked the god Belinu to free me tonight," he said, touching the collar. "I've never prayed for that before, not even after you came into my life. I'm a man of honor."

"I know." Caitlyn squeezed his hand.

"After ten years, after what Margred wanted of me tonight, her demands so far removed from what was originally intended between us, I judge my oath is fulfilled. But the god gave me no answer. Certainly he didn't choose to release me from servitude."

Caitlyn worried at her lower lip, frowning. "I'm sure my Lady Tiermalleia would intercede, declare the shapeshifter debt paid in full, free you if we stood before her in the great stone circle at Duadalne. But how we could accomplish the journey—"

"I can't escape the spell." His voice was impatient. "My brother wanted me to go north with him, to try to get Belinu to break the spell in our place of power, where we worship. Kellan thought the god would reach the same judgment as your goddess, would grant my plea there."

"Yes, I heard your brother ask you to go."

"But I can't. And even if I could, I wouldn't leave you under any condition." Kyler gripped her tightly, hands locked on her upper arms, eyes glowing. "I made Kellan promise to enter your name in our Pack records as my mate. There's no doubt of your status, even if the pairing goes unconsummated. You'll be entitled to their protection. All you have to do is send word or go there."

"Not without you," she said stubbornly, hiding her face against his chest.

Kyler felt her shiver. The cold didn't affect him but he realized she'd come out ill prepared for the chill night air in her haste to find him. He unfastened his crimson cloak and wrapped her in it. "You're freezing. We'd better get you to the palace before anyone takes notice of your absence and says something that reaches Bradana's ears. It'll be dawn soon."

"Harder to sneak inside then," she agreed. "I go in and out the kitchen receiving gate during the day since Nadelma is my friend and her staff follow her lead. No one there will gossip about me. My roommate Susana views herself as my friend and wouldn't say anything to make trouble but you're right about Gretha—she's devoted to Bradana. I can't trust her. Carrying juicy gossip about me to Bradana would make her happy."

Hand in hand, they strolled away from the stream, through the forest. He kept reliving the scene in the queen's bedroom, even now, hours later having a hard time believing the outrageous demand Bradana had made. "You know the oddest part of the whole thing?"

Caitlyn squeezed his arm and raised her eyes to his. "What?"

"I don't think Margred herself wanted to lie with me, much less to bear a shifter's child. I think the entire scheme was Princess Bradana's idea, for some secret plan of her own. She has a frightening degree of control over the queen. Margred acted almost as bespelled tonight as I am."

"Bradana is a dangerous woman, I think," Caitlyn observed. "In many ways. Ylain shared a few stories about their childhood with me."

"She'll stop at nothing," Kyler agreed. "Unfortunately I'm a pawn in her game but I want to be sure you don't become ensnared in the schemes as well."

"I'll be careful. I have so much at stake, for my people, for my goddess."

They'd reached the edge of the palace grounds. Lingering in the cover of the trees for a moment, reluctant to part from her, especially not knowing when he might see her again, Kyler raised Caitlyn's hand to his lips, placing a tender kiss on her palm. "Being unable to openly claim you as my mate is far worse than anything I've had to endure in this wretched city. Yet if I hadn't come to Azrimar, I wouldn't have met you."

"I'll try to find some way to counteract the leashing aspect of the spell so we can get to a place of power and have the entire agreement nullified," she said. "Even if I have to leave you here once I've gotten the Stone, I'll beg the high priestesses in Ordlathus to work on the problem for us, search the archives. There has to be a solution."

"I can't allow myself to hope." He shook his head.

"I'll nurture hope for both of us, my love." Rising on her tiptoes, tugging him to meet her, she kissed him passionately, before walking away, towards the kitchen receiving gate.

He watched her, a half smile on his lips. Despite the undeniable bleakness of his situation, she did inspire hope in his wary heart. Kyler trudged off to tackle the meaningless duties of the new day.

CHAPTER THIRTEEN

Caitlyn didn't see Kyler again that day or the next, although she was aware of him through their mental link, which was reassuring. She assumed he shared her belief that things were close to tumbling out of control and the less they were together, the fewer the chances of betrayal. It was so close to the end of her time at the palace, she couldn't risk discovery of any of the various things she was concealing. The days ticked away towards the date of Ylain's wedding and what Caitlyn hoped would be the completion of her task in Azrimar.

The night before Princess Ylain's wedding, Caitlyn was surprised to find herself drifting off to sleep easily. She'd thought she'd lie awake all night, endlessly thinking about retrieving the Stone of Duadalne in the morning and all the possibilities for her search to go wrong. But her eyes grew heavy and she collapsed onto her bed at an early hour.

Sometime later, Caitlyn opened her eyes and realized she stood in the dream-space, positioned at the outer edge of the Great Lady's stone circle in her home land. It was night, still deep in winter by the position of the stars overhead. She was barefoot, wearing only a thin white nightshift, but didn't feel cold. The massive granite trilithons towering over her head were lit by the brilliant winter moon but the Circle was deserted. No torches were lit, no fires burned at any of the smaller altars, no one there but herself. A glow of pale light emanated from the center of the circle. Knowing the path through the labyrinth by heart, Caitlyn walked unerringly to source of the light. When she reached her destination, she stopped in mid step, her heart stuttering and a sinking sensation of dread in the pit of her stomach.

Draped with black cloth, as was done to honor heroes fallen in battle, a funeral bier sat in front of the altar. Kyler lay on the raised platform, eyes closed, hands at his sides. He was dressed in a uniform such as she'd seen his brother and packmates wear, a sword at his feet. The moonlight streamed harshly on him, cold as the grave. Her heart stopped beating for a moment as fear paralyzed her.

Controlling her agitated breathing, Caitlyn forced herself to take one faltering step after another until she was standing beside the waist-high bier. Hoping against hope, she touched her beloved's hand, finding it chilled, like stone. No breath of life remained, even when she tried to curl her fingers around his.

"He'll never see spring. He'll die as a human," said a raspy voice behind her. Caitlyn wheeled to see Tiermalleia the Crone, bent over and hobbling, but taller than any mere human even so. Dressed in black rags that fluttered as she leaned on her cane, the goddess had a forbidding expression on her wrinkled face.

A dream of prophecy then. Caitlyn closed her eyes against the tears threatening to fall. But was this the only possible fate, or was there something she could do to prevent his death?

"He *may* die as a human." Another voice amended Tiermalleia's bleak statement

Caitlyn opened her eyes wide and spun to seek out the speaker who offered some hope.

Stepping from the shadows was a man, taller than the Lady, handsome, save for a jagged scar down one cheek. He was cloaked from head to foot in a green and brown cape, the colors swirling slowly as he moved. A simple leather lace held his long blond hair from his face.

"Forgive me, sir, I don't know you," Caitlyn said. Clearly the newcomer was a Being of great power and she preferred what he'd said to what her goddess announced. She clung to a tiny shred of hope.

Flinging the cape aside to reveal a uniform all in tones of green, he took a position at the head of the bier, resting his hands on either side of Kyler's broad shoulders, as if he was prepared to recite a spell or perhaps a blessing. A huge ring in the shape of a golden cat on his left hand caught her attention as the emerald eyes glittered in the moonlight. "I'm Belinu, Lord and Master to Kyler's kind. Not too long ago you called to my brother Harlann for aid to this shifter."

Caitlyn dropped a curtsey. "I apologize if I was wrong to seek his support. You're not of my people so I didn't think to petition you."

"Perfectly understandable," he said, waving the hand which bore the heavy ring. "You've a good and wise heart. Others have petitioned me on his behalf as well."

"Kellan? Dumaire?" She named the only people she knew in Kyler's life.

"And more—kith, kin, friends. This shifter of mine is much beloved, not only by you, human girl."

This dreamspace encounter might be Kyler's chance for freedom, since he yet remained alive in the real world. Convinced she had to speak for him, Caitlyn swallowed and licked her lips. "I know he prayed to you to end the spell the other night. Are you aware of what the Witch Queen asked of him?"

"I am," Belinu said, his eyes fixed on her face.

"The queen seeks to go outside the requirements of his oath. He's more than served his time, paid the Pack debt with his life," Caitlyn said, stroking her hand gently across Kyler's cheek. "He doesn't deserve to die a captive in Azrimar."

"And you love him, enough to spill your own blood for him." Belinu's remark didn't carry the lilt of a question.

"I'm his mate," she said, proud to claim the title. "I'd give my life to buy his freedom."

"Be not so free with your blood, child." The Crone's admonishment as she joined the conversation was uttered in a harsh tone. Hobbling closer, she shook her bony, gnarled finger at Caitlyn. "You're under a *geas*, set to a task of mine, not yet completed. I haven't released you from obligation. In any case the two of you have yet to seal the mate bond."

"I remember my duty," Caitlyn assured her. "I hope to complete my task tomorrow and commence my journey home."

"I'm reassured to hear your report of progress. I feared you'd forgotten your own task, lost in contemplation of your shifter's plight." Tiermalleia thumped her cane on the flagstones for emphasis. "Much depends on your quest, which must be complete before the eclipse." Waving one heavily veined hand, she said, "Regaining the lost Stone is far more important than a love affair between a mortal and a shapeshifter."

"I know our love isn't important to you, my Lady, but to us the bond means more than life itself." Caitlyn smoothed Kyler's silken hair away from his face. "All we want is to be together, free to love each other, to have children, to grow old together."

"And the leopard? Not afraid of the beast? You accept that part of him?" Belinu asked. "After all, you're only human, even if gifted with magic."

Did Belinu think a mortal couldn't be worthy of one of his magical creatures? "Kyler and the cat are one," Caitlyn said. She wished she dared to ask why he was interrogating her, why the gods showed her this tragic vision of her beloved. *But as my mother always says, best to tread softly in an encounter with the gods.*

A snarl to the left drew her attention. The great leopard prowled in the next ring of the stones. Apparently the cat was being denied entry to the inner circle, where his human half lay. Swinging its head restlessly, tail beating from side to side against its flanks, the cat paced and yowled.

Belinu made a small gesture, outlined in the moonlight by a shower of green sparks from the ring's emerald eyes. A second later the hunting cat bounded forward, making a run at Caitlyn. She stood motionless. *I'll show no fear, whether this is a test or not. The leopard is Kyler and he loves me.* As if the cat heard her thought, it stopped abruptly, claws striking sparks from the flagstones, before walking the last few steps to rub its head on her legs, practically knocking her off her feet with its enthusiasm. She leaned to pet the leopard's soft fur, scratch lightly behind the tufted ears. When she gazed into the beautiful glowing green eyes, Kyler's personality and intelligence were reflected there. The leopard purred, deep in his chest.

She stood, one hand on the leopard's head as it crouched beside her, drawing strength from the fact at least this portion of Kyler's physical presence lived. And the soul of the man was held safe inside his alter. "Well?" she asked Belinu. "You said he *might* die as a human, which indicates to me the fate is not yet set. What must be done to avoid his death in Azrimar? What can I do, bearing in mind my oath to my own Lady Tiermalleia?"

Ignoring Caitlyn's questions, Belinu addressed himself to his fellow goddess, his tone as if they were continuing an ongoing conversation. "Love is a powerful force," the shifters' god said to the Crone. "Were you not wrapped in the chill of winter, my sister-by-marriage, you'd admit the validity of my point."

"I might," she said grudgingly, lips pursed. Tiermalleia hobbled closer to the bier. "I remember love, even in this withered form." With a bony, crooked hand, she rubbed her wrinkled cheek, closing her pale eyes for a moment. A smile hovered on her thin lips as she said, "Harlann gratefully warms my bed each Spring, you know, when I'm renewed by the seasons, when I regain the beauty of my youth, as Nature revives from Winter's grip."

Might she be receptive to Caitlyn's plea while thinking about her own lover? Moistening her lips, Caitlyn said, "If allowing us to be together is out of the question, is there a way I could at least save his life? Prevent this from becoming his true fate?"

"Gave him your blood in the dreamspace, didn't you?" the Crone asked.

Was she upset by the sacrifice? Trembling, Caitlyn confirmed the goddess's assertion. "I did, my lady."

Tiermalleia ran her hands in the air above Kyler's body. Twenty five small points of bright green light glowed, circling his heart in the twisting symbol representing her power. "True love." The goddess raised her eyebrows. "One of the most powerful magicks known."

"But how can I use my love to prevent his death after I've left Azrimar?" *Careful, don't let frustration slip into your voice when addressing the goddess.* Tiermalleia in Winter was notoriously short tempered. The leopard butted against her hip, as if seeking to calm and comfort her. Caitlyn scratched the cat's chin and he licked her hand with his raspy tongue when she stopped.

"Their Fates are entwined," Belinu said. "Our purposes are therefore aligned, whether we wish it or not, Tiermalleia."

"I need the Stone reinstalled in its proper place before the eclipse," the goddess said, her voice grumpy. "I've naught to do with shifters."

"And I care nothing for your circle of power," the god answered with a sardonic bow. "Yet we both answer to a higher Power than ourselves. We're required to keep balance, I in the North, you in the South, while Azrimar holds the dividing territory under their own deities. What if the fate of Azrimar threatens to overturn everything we hold dear? What if the West gains a foothold in Azrimar? What if my shifter and your priestess hold the key to prevent this catastrophe, but only by working together?"

Tiermalleia was silent under the onslaught of questions.

Caitlyn glanced from one to the other. The things they spoke of were above her head, beyond any mortal's ken. Why did Belinu think she and Kyler had anything to do with such cosmic matters? *We're a man and a woman who fell in love, no more but no less.* A tear trickled from her eye and impatiently she brushed the moisture away.

Any other time she'd be terrified to stand between two bickering gods. Having the leopard—Kyler—at her side, gave her courage. "Please, once I've completed my task and brought the Stone of Duadalne to this place where it belongs" —she gestured at the circle of stones— "Then will you, both of you, support me in rescuing him? He helped me in my quest for you, my Lady. And he's kept his honor, my Lord, although much mistreated."

Belinu laughed. "Seek you to bargain with us, human girl?"

"I'd give my life to save his. So yes, I am, sir," Caitlyn said.

"I can see why you appeal so much to my shapeshifter, why you're his mate in truth." He bowed to her ever so slightly. "And as you are his mate, you too fall somewhat under my jurisdiction."

"Go slowly, Lord of the Sun," the Crone warned, shaking her finger at him. "The mating wasn't consummated. She's my priestess, which takes precedence." Tiermalleia took a halting step toward Caitlyn. The leopard moved to a position between Caitlyn and her goddess, as if protecting her although Tiermalleia ignored the fearsome cat. "Quite a bit of Power is ranged against you. If the man was brought to this Circle of mine in the real world where you dwell, however, then I could do more."

"Don't overstep your bounds, Crone." Belinu's warning was immediate. "He serves me. I'd release him, not you."

"Not in my Circle."

"True." Belinu inclined his head in recognition of the point. "I'd have granted his prayer three nights ago, but even one such as I must regard the omens. His freedom isn't mine or yours to give, not while he stands in Azrimar."

Impasse yet again. Caitlyn exchanged glances with the leopard, sure she detected a glint of Kyler's personality in the emerald depths of its feral eyes. If the gods couldn't help them, they'd have to help themselves, but how?

"Must the two of you argue?" said a new voice. "You've been at it since Time began." A woman came forward from the shadows. She had long straight blond hair and deep blue eyes glowing like stars in the dark of the Circle. Her dress was blue as well, with a filigreed silver overskirt. She had attention only for Belinu, ignoring the Crone after her one chiding remark, and not even glancing at Caitlyn. "We gave our shifters the gift of the true mate, remember, my love?" she said to the god as she twined her arm with his. "We chose to offset the killing, the blood and violence attached to the animal nature. To give hope. To give humanity. The fact this shifter found his love in a human woman doesn't diminish the power of the bond or its gifts."

"True." Hands on her hips, Belinu drew Arduwina closer and kissed her on the lips. "Are you minded to help this pair then, wife?"

Arduwina drew away a little, gazing at Kyler's form on the bier. "I think the ruler of Shadow who dwells in the West is counting on us to argue, to insist on our separate goals, till we're divided and diminished, easier to defeat. I believe that's why we all find ourselves here tonight, in the dreamspace, contemplating our shifter's fate. The shifter may be the symbol for all of us—die by the Shadow or vanquish the evil and defeat its plots."

Caitlyn was unable to take her eyes off the new arrival, mesmerized by her unearthly beauty. She'd thought the gods brought her here, were showing her the vision. If not them, then who? Was this scene arranged by the powers in authority above the gods she herself worshipped?

Arduwina gazed at Caitlyn from her greater height, idly making braids in her flowing hair as she pondered. "I think you can help yourselves, human, and us, should you recognize the moment. Your bond has power of its own, a strange blending of sister Tiermalleia's gifts and ours. The Shadow of the West won't have seen its like before. Together perhaps you can defeat his plans for Azrimar." Arduwina pointed at Caitlyn. "I give you the gift of clear sight." She drew a symbol in the air, unfamiliar to Caitlyn, glowing with sparkling blue power. The symbol drifted slowly in the cold air, settling between her and Kyler's motionless form, dispersing in a small explosion of sparks, which fell soundlessly on both of them before winking out. "Prove yourself worthy of your mate and he won't die as a human, nor be sentenced to live as a perpetual captive of those who work in Shadow. His Fate isn't set but it does lie in your hands. And the outcome will affect all of us."

Without another word, Belinu and Arduwina walked away into the night. The leopard rubbed against Caitlyn's legs before bounding after them. She felt bereft as it vanished, wishing she could hold the cat by her side for a moment longer.

The Crone lingered. "The oath you gave me overrules all else. There should be no questioning of this, no doubt in your heart. But I do remember love, even in cold, harsh winter." Her voice trailed off.

"I'm not sure I understand, my lady. Kyler's gods appear to believe we two must stand against some threat from the West but how? When?" Caitlyn waited, not daring to hope for too much from this most stern incarnation of her goddess.

The Crone brushed one hand lightly across Kyler's forehead, a soft caress. "A handsome man, a true heart, to match yours. The blood you used for your spell provides some limited protection for him against the spell Margred cast years before."

"Because I never agreed to her oath?" Caitlyn felt chagrined that this aspect hadn't occurred to her previously, although she couldn't imagine how the fact could be used to set Kyler completely free.

Tiermalleia leaned on her staff. "I grant you both this much, if you truly perceive the moment of clear sight Arduwina promised, I'll support you. But miss the chance, fail to act when action could save all, and he will be dead, even as you see him here."

"Thank you, my lady." Caitlyn knelt and bowed her head. "I'll do my best not to fail you."

The Crone laughed. "I'm not as convinced of the omens as Belinu appears to be, however I can't deny these are strange times. But make no mistake, I must have my Stone returned to Ordlathus before the eclipse."

Caitlyn woke in her narrow bed at the Witch Queen's palace with the harsh sound of Tiermalleia's mirth ringing in her ears.

Susana threw a pillow at her, missing in the predawn gloom. "Go back to sleep, we don't have to get up for at least another hour."

"Sorry, I didn't mean to wake you," Caitlyn whispered, retrieving the pillow from the floor and tossing it to her roommate. Rolling over, she focused on the cracks in the wall, tracing the biggest one in the predawn gloom with the tip of a finger, thinking through what the gods said to her in the dreamspace, although the dream was fading in her memory. Would she recognize the moment that was her only chance to save Kyler? She had to. There was going to be one fleeting opportunity to save him and she'd seize the moment or die trying. All the talk of the West and schemes of the Shadow meant very little to her but if saving Kyler required her to challenge Bradana, she would.

One thing was clear—Tiermalleia hadn't released her from recovering the Stone of Duadalne. Pulling the blanket more tightly over her shoulders against the cold, she curled into a ball. Today would be eventful. Princess Ylain wasn't the only one who'd have a life changing twenty four hours.

CHAPTER FOURTEEN

The bells in the great tower rang, sending vibrations through the walls of the palace as the nobility, the highest ranking townspeople and the senior adepts assembled to watch Princess Ylain marry the Emperor of Shang by proxy. By mid-morning Caitlyn had delivered the requested trunk of herbs and potions to Ylain's chambers where the long suffering servants added the modest box was added to a huge pile of trunks and crates. Promptly shooed away by the hovering ladies in waiting, she had no chance to speak a word of farewell to Ylain. Caitlyn lingered in the side hall, off the great chamber. If anyone challenged her, she was prepared to say she wanted a last glimpse of her princess, in her wedding finery.

She did indeed see the less-than-happy bride march past n her way to the ceremony but in reality Ylain's exit was the signal for Caitlyn to run up the servants' stairs to the level where the Queen's rooms were located. Although she'd never been there in real life, she found the vision she and Kyler had shared was detailed enough to get her where she wanted to be

The hall was deserted, all members of the higher ranks gone to the wedding. The servants departed to the less exalted regions of the castle to take a well-deserved break after the madness of getting Ylain ready to wed. Caitlyn carried a second, small basket of dried herbs and other items from the stillroom as her excuse, in case her presence in the royal area was challenged but Ylain's rooms were empty, only a few traces of her remaining. Dresses, shawls and lingerie lay strewn on the bed and even on the floor, rejected for the journey to Shang for one reason or another. A broken bottle of perfume had been swept carelessly to the side and semiprecious baubles lay in the half open drawers of the jewelry box. Two weeks to prepare and pack and of course Ylain must have waited till the final moments to make her decisions. Feeling pity for the princess's long suffering maids, Caitlyn added the medicines to the small trunk she'd already packed, which was perched precariously on top of the stack of containers and trunks waiting to be hauled to the harbor. Dropping the empty basket into a handy chair she darted across the room to the desk.

Breathing a prayer to Lady Tiermalleia, she yanked open the middle drawer. Relief flooded her in a cool wave as she found the huge ring of keys, tossed in the corner of the drawer. Grabbing them and stuffing the collection into her apron pocket, she shut the drawer and hastened into the hall.

Empty, thank the goddess. Caitlyn hurried along the corridor, going past the doors to Bradana's chambers and then those of the Witch Queen.

One last spiral of the hallway and she was facing the heavy wooden door, barring entry to the Kings' wing of the palace. A gilded replica of Azrimar's crown was set in the wall above the door, a bit shabby, like so many other things in this castle. Odd Margred never wed when Azrimar's foundation was teamwork between a warrior king and a witch queen. Bradana probably didn't want the competition a husband for the queen would inevitably create. No king worthy of the name would allow the illegitimate sister's undue influence to continue unchecked.

The depth of silence in this area was eerie. Caitlyn stood in front of the door, fumbling for the keys, tangled in her pocket. Why was this door out of all the doors in the castle banded in iron? To keep magic out? Or to keep something in?

Thinking she heard voices in the cross corridor behind her, Caitlyn hurriedly inserted the large key with the eagle's head into the lock, taking care not to touch the ironwork. The lock was stubborn, probably undisturbed since the last king, Margred's father, died. *I should have brought linseed oil.* Fear of discovery made her hands a bit sweaty and the key slipped in her grasp, falling to the threadbare carpet and bouncing onto the stone floor beyond with a muffled clink. It was if the door didn't want to open and reveal the imprisoned secrets behind the portal.

Taking a deep breath, Caitlyn waited for her heartbeat to calm down before retrieving the keys and inserting the right one into the lock a second time. With a click the door swung open a few inches. Sliding the key into her pocket, she pushed the door open wider and slipped inside.

With a thump the door swung shut behind her. Caitlyn took a hasty step in retreat, bumping into the panel, heedless of the iron bands touching her. Hand at her throat, she closed her eyes to block the chaos she was seeing but even with her eyes reopened the same visions assaulted her senses.

The Kings' wing was riotous with pent up magic. Caitlyn couldn't see the real corridor through the overlay of magic crowding the dreamspace. Drawn by her powers, great swathes and swirls of the purple and red power wielded by the Azrimar witches came gusting through the hall to ensnare her like a net. How long had this place been walled up? Raw emotions from those who'd lived here in the past—fear, anger, arrogant power—threatened to squeeze breath from her lungs. There was more than one thread of hatred. Murders and other foul deeds had happened here. Icy fingers tried to snare her wrists and indistinguishable words beat against her ears. Caitlyn jerked her arm away from the aggressive phantom's grip, keeping a tight hold on the amulet around her neck.

I'm not here to give the dead a voice. I'm not here to right old wrongs. I'm here to find the Stone of Duadalne. But the vestige of old spells and curses and disembodied ghosts continued the assault on her senses, drawn to her life force and her magic.

Shaking with fear and loathing, she fumbled desperately behind her for the door latch, even as more and more magic of a kind alien to her people came pouring through the hallway to drown her in a tidal wave of sensations and impressions. As if she was going under the surface for the final time and he was her only salvation, she thought of her beloved. *I'll beg Kyler to walk this place with me. His shifter's power will help me keep this dreamspace maelstrom at bay long enough for me to find the Stone.* It would take a few minutes to fetch him but surely the halls would remain empty. Ylain's wedding agenda was laden with speeches and ceremony.

Kyler would never refuse her.

Enlisting him to help her was the most sensible course. And if he was at the wedding surely he could slip away, if she called him through their mental link.

The cold touch of the latch on her hand as she prepared to leave ripped through her like an ice storm.

Shuddering for a moment, she straightened and drew in another deep breath. *What am I thinking? I can't borrow any more of Kyler's waning power, even if he's willing to come to my aid.* This was her task, not his. She was sent to accomplish this on her own, for her goddess and the people of the South. She could do it if she didn't waste this one opportunity.

She had to talk herself past the panic set off by the unexpected assault of strange magic, ghosts and echoes of Azrimar's unsavory past. *None of this has to do with me. None of this can hurt me. I have to wade through it.*

Moving away from the door so the iron couldn't inhibit her power, Caitlyn called a ball of Tiermalleia's green fire into existence to light her way. The illumination repelled some of the forces surrounding her. Narrowing her eyes, she took a moment to assess her surroundings, trying to penetrate the fog of magic and see the prosaic castle below. The longer she concentrated, the more details became clear—tapestries covered in cobwebs, chairs lining the hall, statues smothered in inches of dust. A little ripple of bright green along the baseboard caught her eye, gone as soon as she blinked.

Green was the sacred color of Tiermalleia, nothing these people used. Even the green crystals in the queen's spell casting didn't employ true organic magic. So if Caitlyn was seeing green ripples, the Stone must have been here.

Excitement causing butterflies in her stomach, Caitlyn walked forward, searching in the subsiding fog of magic for more of the vivid green. She passed doors, some of which stood half open, although most were closed. The idea of entering any of these rooms didn't appeal to her but sooner or later she might have to force herself to do so. "The Stone isn't likely to be conveniently lying on a side table," she said under her breath. Another quick flicker of green ahead caught her eye and she broke into a run.

The enticing, encouraging flashes of verdant color came and went, drawing her further into the depths of the wing, but her confidence never wavered. Sure she followed the trail of the Stone, she didn't fear falling into entrapment. At last she reached a closed door, where green light flared underneath, from inside.

The Stone must be hidden there.

Hoping the room wasn't going to be locked, unsure if any of the keys she'd taken from Ylain's room would work, Caitlyn wrapped her hand around the oval doorknob, which refused to budge. Retreating a step, she pulled the key ring from her pocket and quickly leafed through them, squinting a bit in the green light from her spell globe. None matched the design on this door, but determined not to fail, she tried them all. Too small, too large, wouldn't turn, none of them were right. She chewed her lip in frustration, pondering the situation.

The trapped green light flared and then dimmed, disappearing as if moving away from the portal.

"Nothing for it, I'll have to spell the lock," she said, tucking the keys away. Taking a rapid glance at her surroundings, she was glad to observe the ambient magic had died away, leaving only a residue of thin purple fog along the carpet and ceiling. She hoped her spell didn't stir the frenzy up again. Spreading the fingers of her right hand wide and placing her palm over the keyhole, Caitlyn channeled her Lady's power and uttered a spell word followed by a short command, "Tentiramay! I must pass this barrier!"

Green sparks flew as the door split asunder, Caitlyn hopped out of the way, nearly falling. The portal was neatly cut in two, one side hanging from the hinges, the other toppling onto the carpet, raising a cloud of dust. It was as if an invisible woodsman had sundered it with his axe on her behalf. Thin smoke drifted from the blasted keyhole. Good thing no one ever came into this wing of the castle or the noise would have drawn a crowd. Caitlyn stepped across the threshold, ordering her light globe to precede her into the gloom. She added a second light globe, sure this must be her destination.

She was in a sitting room, the bedroom lying beyond. The chamber was as messy as Ylain's had been, only here furniture was toppled and broken as if there'd been a fight. As she pivoted on her heel to see the entire room, she noticed the mirror was cracked and a knife was embedded in the wall next to it. Boots and the remnants of a man's ceremonial robes lay in a heap next to the desk. There was no hint of green magic, no sign of what she'd come to find, so Caitlyn stepped forward, stumbling over an obstacle in the dust at her feet. Catching her balance by gripping the nearest chair, she bent to find out what tripped her. Grand enough to be a king's scepter, her prize was a walking cane, finely carved, with a great amethyst at the top, set in gold.

Heedlessly, she curled her fingers around the smooth wood, intending to move the cane out of her way, but icy cold flowed from her fingers into her arm, through her veins and she was caught, paralyzed by the vision playing itself out in front of her. In the scene magic recreated for her, the room was dim, lamps flickering low. She had a clear view into the bedroom through the doorway, where a man and a woman lay together on a massive bed, talking in low tones, naked bodies partially covered by furs and quilts. The sound of the opening door behind Caitlyn was startling, since she knew the panel was broken, but the couple in front of her reacted with horror. The man leaped from the bed, pushing the woman to the other side, out of Caitlyn's view.

Someone brushed past Caitlyn and she heard the echoes of outraged shouting, the words muffled by the centuries gone by since these events played themselves out in reality. Standing in front of her now was a man garbed in ceremonial robes and a crown, between her and the bedroom, sword drawn. The man from the bedroom, kilt carelessly knotted at his hips, carrying a sword at the ready, knife in his other hand, ran forward in challenge. The two fought a desperate battle, going through Caitlyn as if she wasn't there, which if course she hadn't been, hundreds of years ago.

Try as she might, Caitlyn couldn't stop the vision, couldn't leave the dream-space. Someone or something wanted her to bear witness to these events. There must be some relation to her actual purpose for being here.

The king eventually triumphed over his adversary, skillful though the man was, striking him a mortal blow and then standing in triumph, breathing hard, watching his enemy bleed out on the floor from the massive wound. With a scream of grief and rage Caitlyn heard more distinctly than she'd heard anything else since the vision began, the Witch Queen of this long ago time shoved past her husband, falling to her knees beside her dying lover.

Trying to heal him. Heart pounding, tears in her eyes at the tragedy, even though these people had been enemies of her own ancestors, Caitlyn's knees were weakened by sheer emotion. The vision held her in its grip and she couldn't stop watching.

On the tragic day this scene was reality, the king had evidently come to the same realization about his unfaithful wife's intentions. With a roar, he stepped forward and slashed at the woman's neck, nearly severing her head. With her dying breath, the witch released all her power, flinging the spell at her murderer. Powered by the hate which must have been her final thought, the magic consumed the king in a sheet of black and purple flame. He too fell, blasted and burned by the force of her emotions, toppling onto the floor next to his late wife, who breathed her last cradling her dead lover.

No wonder the people of this time left the room as it was. This tragedy had so much force and magic woven into its fabric, the scene must play out for anyone who set foot here, even those without magic.

"Have you come for me?" The deep voice was behind her.

Slowly she spun on one heel, her globes of light pivoting with her. The long dead King of Azrimar stood behind her, but not as a man. He was a corpse, a terrible blackened hulk leaning on a singed sword, shreds of cloth hanging off, jagged broken bones sticking out, black pits where eyes should have been.

"No." Able to drop the cane now the vision was over, Caitlyn did so, tossing it a few feet away while she fought her nausea. Horrifying as the ghost was, he had no power in the real world, no magic even in his lifetime. "You and your death have nothing to do with me."

"Yet you're in my chambers where none have walked since midnight of that day." The ghost pointed at the corner where he and his wife and the adversary had died, the corpses now gone from the dreamspace. "Either you're a foolish curiosity seeker, or there's a connection between us. Who are you?" His voice rang with command.

As if I was unschooled enough to give you the power of my name. Caitlyn sniffed. "I'm from Ordlathus and I've come seeking something stolen from us at your command."

"I sent my troops and Searchers to many places in my last year of life, bringing home dozens of objects of power," the ghost said. "Many of them cursed, I discovered to my cost."

"This was a small rock, on a golden chain. Your man seduced our priestess, then stole the necklace and killed her."

"Bastard seduced my wife too." The apparition pointed his sword at the corner of the room where all three had perished, as if he could still see the bodies. "He gave her the necklace you speak of. She took a fancy to it, the ugliness of the rock compared to her crystals of power. She claimed it was a puzzle to be solved."

"Not by the likes of her," Caitlyn said. Disgust had her shaking her head. Might as well see what she could learn from this troubled spirit. "Do you know where she kept the stone?"

"She wore it on her belt, said it was too awkward to be a necklace. She had on her person earlier in the day I found them together and killed them." The ghost guffawed, pieces of ash falling away from his corpse. "You'll have to search the bedroom, see if the servants left it there when they cleaned away the mess we left."

They well might have refused to touch the Stone, if the Court was aware her doomed lover had given it to her. Caitlyn walked to the open bedroom door and peered inside, the ghost drifting after her, a faint smell of wet ash and smoke assaulting her nose. It didn't appear the room had been touched since the queen and her lover had spent their time in pleasure. Her attention was drawn by a flicker of the green from under the bed. With growing excitement she entered the chamber, closing in on the green like a hunter stalking prey. No more visions assaulted her in this room. Apparently nothing taking place in this room had left an indelible impression in the dreamspace.

What had been a beautiful brocade dress and silken underthings trimmed in lace lay in a pile on the floor, testimony to the late queen's impatience to bed her lover. Caitlyn lifted the pile of rotting fabric, sneezing as a cloud of dust rose into the air. Discolored suede shoes tossed carelessly aside lay where they'd been kicked off, but no sign of the Stone. Getting on her knees, Caitlyn peered under the bed, hoping maybe the necklace had fallen there, but other than huge clumps of dust and mouse droppings, her green illumination globes revealed nothing.

Dusting her skirts off, she stood, growing more frustrated by the moment. Out of the corner of her eye, a glint of bright green flickered. Spinning toward the glimmer, she recognized the Stone of Duadalne, hanging from one of the life-size lions carved into the elaborate headboard covering the wall to the ceiling. Breathing a prayer of thanks to the goddess, praying the ancient slats would hold her weight, she reluctantly climbed onto the bed, raising more dust into the air, and snagged the chain loose. Scooting off the mattress rear-end first, Caitlyn stood breathless and trembling for a moment, marveling at what she held—the Stone in her hand at last.

Black and craggy as legend said it would be, the Stone was the size of a walnut. Caitlyn found it strangely beautiful. Little glints of light from mineral chips embedded in the exterior reflected the green of her magical globes. Faint warmth pulsed in the palm of her hand where the talisman rested. Bringing the precious relic to her lips, she blew a whisper of air to clear the dust settled in the pits and indentations in the stone's surface. Green light flared for a moment. Caitlyn looped the fine gold chain over her neck and the Stone fell to rest between her breasts, not nearly as heavy a burden as she'd expected.

Now to make her escape from this palace, out of the city and on her way home.

But when she walked to the doorway, the ghost barred her way. With a hand of scorched bone bearing a melted gold signet ring, he reached for her. "As I suspected, the necklace is a thing of power, in the right hands. "

Evading his touch, Caitlyn retreated into the bedroom, since the ghost apparently couldn't follow her there. "Let me pass."

"Not until you use your powers to bring me back to the world of the living. I died too soon, left too much undone. I want my full span of years." The ghost's voice thundered against the walls. "My wife and her lover cheated me, may their spirits rot in a pit of flames."

Heart pounding, Caitlyn shook her head. "I can't. Your body isn't even here, your majesty. It's been entombed with your ancestors for centuries now. Even if I had the power, such an act is forbidden. No one can raise the dead."

"Do you think I care about your rules, witch? I can keep you penned in the bedroom for all eternity, you know. You can't pass me." He held out his skeletal arms, gesturing. Scorched, cracked teeth showed in an obscene attempt at a grin. "This room is the extent of my kingdom right now and I'll kill any interlopers. I'll hold you in the dreamspace till you die." The voice got softer, more beguiling. "But if you do as I ask, you can be on your way. Clothe my bones with flesh again. A powerful witch like you can cast the right spells."

Caitlyn walked away from the door, retreating to the far side of the room, where the ghost couldn't see her from his spot blocking the entrance. A quick glance confirmed there was no other exit from the bedroom. She gazed into the dusty mirror. What action to take now? This angry ghost had real power in the dreamspace, having been killed before his time, in the midst of blood rage, and then confined to the place of his death for hundreds of years. The deities who held sway over Azrimar had evidently allowed the spirits of his queen and her lover to move on but he was sentenced to re-enact his crime for eternity. "How can I interfere with a justly deserved penalty from his gods?" she said out loud. "Yet I must if I'm to succeed in my own quest." Frustration made her nerves thrum. Leaning on the bureau, she drummed her fingers, keenly aware of precious time being wasted. She only had so long to get away unseen before the Queen's wing of the castle teemed with people again. She couldn't get caught now that she had the Stone. She'd have to outsmart him and win her freedom without delay.

Straightening, she folded her hand over the Stone, encouraged as the rock warmed to her touch. Should she call upon the powers locked inside? No. The rightness of the answer resounded in her bones. Her need would have to be much direr; the situation hopeless, before she'd dare unseal the Stone.

She wished Kyler was standing by her side—he'd make quick work of this ghost.

As the solution to the dilemma occurred to her, she raised an eyebrow at herself in the dingy mirror. Rolling her shoulders to release some of the tension in her muscles and nerves, she ventured to the doorway, where the king waited, a foot beyond the threshold.

"Changed your mind, have you? Seen the fruitlessness of disobeying my command?" he asked, flashing his hideous smile.

Saying nothing, Caitlyn stepped into the outer room. The king grabbed at her with bony hands, pulling her close. The odor of wet ash was overwhelming. Her lungs felt as if they were full of the stuff, unable to pull air into her body. Embracing the ghost as if they were in some macabre dance, Caitlyn exerted every ounce of her willpower and pulled them both completely out of the dreamspace.

He threw her away from him as flesh clothed his skeleton, starting at the toes and moving upward. "You've done it, witch. I live!"

But not for long. Seizing her chance while the king was exulting in his long-desired corporeality, she ran across the room to the door, squeezing past the broken half and spinning to witness the next few moments, hoping she'd guessed right in her strategy.

The king stood in the center of the room, fully reconstituted, dressed in his old fashioned brocade robes and breeches, long hair tied in a neat queue with a black ribbon, boots shiny. Handsome in a harsh featured way. A faint resemblance to Margred and Aerrol, his descendants. Only the sword remained tarnished and pitted, Caitlyn was relieved to note.

He strode toward the door. "Now I'll reclaim my throne from whatever whelp sits on it and…" He staggered, as if he'd tripped. A frown crossed his face. Regaining his balance, the man took one more step and then clutched at his heart. "What have you done to me?"

"I didn't give you the gift of life," she said. "I only pulled you from the dreamspace into the real world with me. In the dreamspace you were a ghost, here you have human form since the real world can't harbor your ghostly form. But you *are* dead, sir, centuries ago."

He made no answer, unable to utter words any longer, as the hundreds of years that had passed since he last walked in the world of men caught up with him in a violent, crashing moment, his skin wrinkling and decaying, bones splintering, eyes going filmy white with cataracts, hair falling out onto the carpet. The sword fell to the floor and the king collapsed in a heap of bones, which exploded into dust coating the walls and floor.

CHAPTER FIFTEEN

After hastily checking her dress for outward marks of the ghost's disgusting embrace in the dreamspace and thankfully finding none, Caitlyn forced herself to walk slowly, pulling the Stone's chain over her head as she went and tucking the precious talisman into her pocket. She mustn't bring any suspicion on herself at this point, not after finally getting the Stone in her possession. Two guards walked by her, belatedly sent to secure the Queen's door no doubt. She acknowledged their polite greeting with a smile, hand clenched on the Stone in her pocket.

"You there, where are you going?" The officer in charge of the detail ascended the stairs. He didn't appear inclined to ignore Caitlyn's departure as his men had.

Of course it would be Captain Nedd, the officious fool. Caitlyn kept her manner deferential. "I was ordered to bring more medicines to pack with the princess's baggage, which I've done, sir. Having no further business in the royal wing, I'm off to the stillroom."

"I believe the maid is telling the truth. She's highly trusted in the royal household, sir." Sergeant of the guard Quarl, the man she'd cured of his unsightly facial rash, spoke on her behalf.

"When I want the opinion of a common solder, I'll ask for it." Nedd surveyed Caitlyn from head to toe, his expression contemptuous. "You may go then, girl, but know I'll be watching you. Princess Bradana spoke to me about you because she has serious concerns about the liberties you take in the palace." He leaned closer. "You and I'll be getting to know each other better, once your mistress has sailed for Shang later today." Reaching out with a gloved hand, he ran his fingers over Caitlyn's cheek.

"I'll be more careful in the future, sir." Caitlyn babbled, which wasn't hard to do with her nerves wrapped as tight as a bow string. She curtseyed as if the man was the queen's equal.

He grunted. "I've no time for dalliance right now anyway. I suggest you get out of here for your own good. You've no need to watch what your betters do in the privacy of their halls. Guards, come with me."

As the squad marched down the broad stairs behind Captain Nedd, Caitlyn followed at a safe distance. She walked across the hall below in the general direction of the old wing of the palace housing the stillroom, as if obeying his order to leave, before ducking into a deserted side passage. Curious about what Nedd was doing, why he lingered in the central foyer with a squad of soldiers, she hesitated.

The queen, Bradana and Duke Aerrol entered, all of them dressed in their wedding finery. A small crowd of courtiers followed at a respectful distance.

"All well and good you have some new talismans for your rituals, cousin," Aerrol was saying with considerable heat in his voice, "But I'm telling you the western gate is in imminent danger of collapse. I need funds and men to repair it. Any number of other maintenance and infrastructure projects have priorities higher than more magic play things. All the gold you paid Shang and the value of a royal princess's hand in marriage would have been better spent on shoring up our defenses than in obtaining one more tablet covered in scribbles. There have been reports of spies from the West, probing our borders. I fear the Shadow plans to move against us."

"These issues are no longer your concern," Bradana said.

"Stay out of this." Aerrol shot her a contemptuous frown. "You're not the ruler of Azrimar, for all you give yourself airs and Margred indulges you."

Raising her thin eyebrows, Bradana gestured at Nedd, waiting off to the side.

He marched forward at the head of his small troop. Puffing out his chest, hand on his sword, the captain said, "Duke Aerrol, you're under arrest for high treason to the crown of Azrimar."

"Take your hands off me." Aerrol struggled with the soldiers attempting to strip him of his sword and bind his hands behind his back. "Margred—"

Hand to her lips to stifle a gasp of horror, Caitlyn could hardly believe her eyes as the scene played out.

Projecting a regal haughtiness, the queen walked to the stairs and ascended partway, before pausing to address the cursing duke. "You've been plotting to steal my throne, Aerrol."

"Who told you such lies? Bradana? She wants your throne for herself, cousin. You can't believe anything she tells you."

Margred reached to take Bradana's hand, pulling her onto the same stair side by side, as if they were equals. "My sister is the one person in Azrimar I can trust. I'm grateful for her support and loyalty."

"You're a deluded fool then and I pity you." Aerrol spat.

"Take this man away, lock him in a dungeon to await execution," Bradana said.

Aerrol's jaw dropped and he stopped struggling against the soldiers who held him. "I'm the heir to the throne, Margred. You can't put me to death." Voice stern and commanding, the duke made a final appeal to the queen.

She shook her head, toying nervously with her amethyst crystal. "Treason demands a death sentence, cousin. I'm sorry matters have come to this through your foolishness."

"My foolishness?" Aerrol raised his eyebrows, standing tall and regal in the hands of his captors. "When all the actions I've taken, all the improvements I've made have been to protect your city, your kingdom? In spite of your blind refusal to see the jeopardy Azrimar faces from the Shadow in the West?"

"I'll spare your mother and sister if no evidence is brought against them." Margred made a shooing motion and Captain Nedd shouted orders to his men.

As Aerrol was dragged away, cursing her, the queen and Bradana linked arms and continued to ascend the stairs, while the thoroughly frightened and confused courtiers milled in the foyer, talking amongst themselves in low tones.

Pulse pounding, Caitlyn gasped, appalled at this alarming development. Aerrol was no traitor—his arrest had to be part of Bradana's plot to further isolate the queen and gain power herself. But even as she closed her hand on the Stone, ready to call forth her magic to help Aerrol, Caitlyn hesitated. Slowly she uncurled her fingers from the talisman and walked away from the foyer, moving more and more quickly through the hall. The duke's fate wasn't her concern. His arrest didn't rise to the level of what the gods discussed in her dream. Tragic and wrong though it might be, the duke's arrest was an Azrimaran matter. She wasn't sent to do anything but retrieve the Stone and escape with it. Tiermalleia didn't expect or want her to become embroiled in royal intrigues.

She ran.

Acutely conscious of time ticking away, Caitlyn headed to Kyler's quarters. She didn't even knock but boldly entered and closed the door behind her, leaning on it, head back, breathing hard.

As if summoned by the sound of the door, he came out of the inner chamber, running his hand through his hair, frowning until he realized she was the uninvited guest. He wore only a kilt. "What are you doing here? What's the matter?"

Praise to the goddess, he's still alive. Launching herself across the room, Caitlyn sought comfort in his strong embrace for all the traumatic events of the day so far, closing her eyes and wrapping her arms tightly around his waist.

"Are you all right?" Kyler pulled back after a moment, surveying her from head to toe, anxiety written on his face. He tipped her chin up. "Talk to me."

"Bradana had Aerrol arrested," she said.

"What?" He raised his eyebrows and then frowned. "She couldn't do such a thing, she hasn't the authority. It must be a rumor."

Caitlyn shook her head. "No, I was there, in the queen's foyer, I witnessed the event myself. They'd just come from the wedding and Bradana had Captain Nedd waiting with a squad of soldiers. She arrested Aerrol for high treason. The queen was there but she confirmed Bradana's orders. He's been condemned to death."

Jaw clenched, Kyler asked, "With no trial? No evidence?"

"On Bradana's word alone." Caitlyn walked past him and sank into the bedside chair. "I wanted to intervene, to save him somehow, but I can't. This isn't my affair." She hoped he'd tell her she was correct in her conclusions because guilt at not having taken action was making her queasy.

Kyler's reassurance was immediate. "Of course you can't get involved." He sat on the edge of the bed next to her. "I'm having a hard time taking in the news, figuring out the possibilities, what Bradana plans next. Arresting the heir to the throne is huge. She must be highly confident."

"Margred said his mother and Susana would be spared, unless new evidence comes to light." Caitlyn rubbed her temples. "I probably should have run to warn Susana but I needed to find you."

"There'll be others to watch out for Susana." He took her hand. "Did Aerrol's arrest prevent you from accomplishing your own mission? Did you miss your opportunity?"

Silently, knowing she must be grinning like a fool but too suffused with happiness to care, she reached into her pocket with her free hand and a moment later displayed the Stone of Duadalne. As the stone dangled from the golden chain, light sparkled on tiny emerald and lavender tourmaline crystals embedded in the coal black surface.

"By the gods, you actually got it? How?" he asked.

"Our plan worked—the halls were deserted so I pretended to be leaving something in Ylain's rooms, walked further into the Queen's corridor, opened the door at the far end with one of the keys I stole from Ylain and followed the magic." She tried to keep her face serene. She had no intention of telling Kyler what she endured with the ghost king and with Nedd right before he arrested Aerrol. Kyler had enough worries.

Apparently Kyler wasn't fooled. Head tilted, he studied her face intently, green eyes narrowed. "Why do I suspect you're keeping something from me? Retrieving the Stone can't possibly have been so simple, not in this cursed place. I was sure you'd succeed though. Congratulations."

Restoring the Stone to her pocket, she said, "I never could have done it without you helping me to locate the right room. But, Kyler—"

He put his fingers gently on her lips. "I know what comes next. You must leave as soon as possible. You're in terrible danger now, with Ylain gone and Bradana exercising power openly."

Taking his fingers, she brushed a kiss on his palm. "Were you at the wedding?"

"The Queen specifically commanded me to stay away. I think she doesn't want the Ambassador from Shang to see a shapeshifter too closely." He shrugged. "There's competition between Azrimar and Shang when it comes to matters of magic. Not being invited doesn't bother me. On the contrary, her snub was a blessing, since I was here to meet you as the result."

"I had to see you again before I left Azrimar tonight, under cover of darkness." Caitlyn stood. "I planned to wait here, if you were at the wedding."

Kyler rose as she did and pulled her into his arms, bending to kiss her. Parting her lips slightly, she gave his questing tongue entry, enjoying the sensation as he plundered her mouth, twining his tongue with hers, deepening the kiss. His arms tightened as he held her, his cock pressing urgently against her body through their clothing. Humming in pleasure, she stroked her hands across the smooth, taut muscles of his back and then across his butt. He lifted her breast in one hand, fingers teasing through the fabric of her dress, till the sensitive nipple tightened into an aching bud. Grinding her hips against him, she enjoyed the way his manhood surged and throbbed in response to her.

"I ache for you," he whispered as they drew apart a few inches.

"I have the same longings," she said, meeting his eyes while she reached to stroke his jutting cock where it tented the folds of his kilt. "I'm not leaving Azrimar without becoming your mate in all ways. I'd never forgive myself if—if I didn't take this chance to be with you."

"Our making love today wouldn't be fair to you." Kyler broke their embrace, adjusting himself without much success, she was relieved to see. He paced across the room to the window before turning to give her an anguished glance. "I'd give anything to bring you safely to my home in the North and live there forever as mates. You know that?"

Hands clasped, waiting to see what he would say next, she nodded. "I do."

"Finding you—the woman who means more than life itself to me—and not being able to consummate the bond is torture. Not even Bradana could dream up anything so diabolical. Wanting you without hope of satisfying the desire drives the leopard insane and kills me a little more each day." His face was set in grim, hard lines, jaw clenched.

Not saying anything, she walked to him and laid a gentle hand on his chest, circled his nipple with the tip of one finger, toying with the fine hairs, lightly rasping the sensitive skin with her nails. She trailed her hand slowly over the hard muscles of his abdomen, edging under the waistband of his kilt. He took a deep breath and a shiver ran through him as her hand caressed his cock.

Watching him react to her seductive touches, Caitlyn could hardly bear the mix of desire and despair on his face, mirroring her own emotional storm. "I've been thinking about this ever since the last night we met at the stream. My heart holds no doubt," she said. "We don't need a ceremony in front of your people or mine. We're already bonded. Sharing our love with each other, now, today, before I leave, is something precious we can't deny ourselves."

Allowing her to caress him, he was silent for a minute, rubbing his hand reflexively over the lock on the golden collar, at the back of his neck. "And then what? What future is possible for us? None," he answered his own question bitterly before she could speak. He looped his arm around her waist, held her close. "How can I lie with you today, get you with child and then be forced to abandon you?" He rested one finger on her lips as she opened them to argue. "There will be a child, sweetheart, almost certainly. You're my mate. That's the way of things with shifters. How will your people treat you, if you return to them bearing a shapeshifter's child?"

"Babies are the natural order of life." Caitlyn couldn't repress a smile at the idea of having his child, bittersweet though the moment was. "My family, my people, will welcome me and the baby. They'll take their cue from me and be happy. And if Ordlathus held no welcome, I'd go north, find your Pack and give birth to our child there. You know I'm strong and resourceful. Never fear I'd take care of our son or daughter. Kellan would stand by me. I trust him."

He shook his head. "I trust *you*. Glad as I am to know your people would welcome you bearing a shifter child, I'm driven to cherish and protect what's mine and I can do neither for you." His fists clenched against her back for a moment, a sign of his frustration. "Much less for our child. Having my brother stand ready to welcome you into the Pack isn't enough."

Her heart ached even as she rejoiced in the priceless gift of his love for her but again the knowledge of time racing tweaked her nerves taut. "Please, set aside your worries? We only have these few hours, why waste them? I've got to be gone from the palace before Margred and Bradana somehow learn what I came for. I gave my oath to my goddess, to the people of Ordlathus before I ever met you. The Lady reminded me of my duty most forcefully last night. I may not linger. I'd have had to go already but nightfall is the safest time to flee."

"You've been honest with me since we became friends of the heart." He gave her a small smile. "I knew you couldn't stay."

Tears spilled from her eyes. "I came for one treasure, on behalf of my people. I never expected to find a second treasure for myself in the process." She stroked his cheek and he leaned into her hand, kissing her palm.

"I can't lie to you either," he told her. "My greedy heart wants to take what you offer, even if only for these few hours. I'd have the memory of making love to you, claiming you as my mate, to sustain me. The possibility we might have a baby born of our love, even if I never see our child, would keep me sane. The

knowledge might keep my heart intact; soothe the leopard in this dismal place."
He held her gaze; his eyes more cat than human.

"I want this as much as you do." Caitlyn insisted with absolute truth. "Your
determination and honor are part of what I love so much about you, stubborn
man." She feathered kisses along his jaw line. "I swear on the blood I shed for you
in the dreamspace, once my duty is discharged, I'll be taking action to resolve your
situation. I'll travel North, find your brother and your packmates, enlist their help,
bring what I need to do the proper spell casting and I *will* free you from Margred's
spell." Her voice shook with the intensity of that vow.

He shook his head.

"You doubt me?" Like a physical blow, Caitlyn felt the edge of disbelief mixed
with sharp disappointment he didn't accept her vow unquestioningly. She bit her lip,
at a loss what to say next. She didn't want to tell him what Belinu and Arduwina
said in the dreamspace last night because she didn't want to raise any false hope.

His next words reassured her heart. "It's not a question of doubt, not at all.
I see your love and your honesty bright and true in the air surrounding you. But
we both know I won't survive much longer. The queen doesn't let me run as a
leopard because she thinks it builds a store of magic power for her to use. You and
I understand in reality staying human all the time is killing me. My kind weren't
meant to walk as men twenty four hours a day. Margred doesn't care how much
she takes from me, nor does Bradana. Even if I told the queen of her error, she'd
have to release the collar for me to shift and she'll never do that."

Clenching her fists on his chest, she said, "You have to fight them, both
of them."

"My fierce champion." Enfolding her in a hug, he rocked her gently. "I've been
resisting their demands with renewed energy since you spilled your blood for me.
I have you to live for now, a reason to go on."

"Why are we wasting time talking?" Caitlyn went on tiptoes to kiss him
hungrily, linking her arms behind his neck to draw him into the embrace.

As they kissed, he took her hand, guided it past the waistband of his kilt and laid her fingers on his cock, hard and throbbing. Instinctively she closed her fist around him, marveling at the velvet feel of his skin, the raw strength and the heat there.

After kissing her thoroughly, Kyler disengaged, laughing as he removed her fingers from his cock. With a teasing grin, he pulled her dress over her head and threw it to the floor, a low whistle escaping him as she stood nearly naked in the golden sunlight of late afternoon. Caitlyn wore few undergarments, disliking the restriction of the bindings favored by the City women. Kyler hooked his thumbs in the lacy cotton drawers and she shimmied her hips to help him ease the garment from her body, stepping out of them while leaning one hand on his broad shoulder.

Reaching out to touch her breast, he looked at her with glowing eyes. "You're so beautiful, perfect."

She laughed self-consciously and blushed. "Not perfect, not even close."

"Perfect to me," he insisted nuzzling her neck with a combination of kisses and tiny bites that tingled. "Exactly right—we fit."

Probably just as well I never realized she wore next to nothing under her dresses. I had a hard enough time keeping my hands to myself. He twirled her slowly, as if they were at a ball. Caitlyn was so graceful, naked or clothed. "You have a tattoo?" he asked with delight, his leopard intrigued by the unexpected sight. Nestled in the hollow above the swelling curve of her backside was a small design in green and black, a swirling tree of life symbol. He bent to kiss the spot.

Giggling, she looked over her shoulder. "That tickles."

"Ah, I'm learning your vulnerabilities," he said with a chuckle. "Where else you might you be ticklish?"

"I dare you to find out." Hips swaying, she came closer until her ample breasts rubbed his bare chest, teasing him deliberately with the hardened points of her nipples.

He captured her lips, kissed her while she unfastened the kilt, expressing her pleasure at learning he wore nothing underneath either. The scent of her arousal pushed his passion to nearly unbearable heights, amplified by the leopard's savage triumph in finally claiming their mate. He crushed her to him, hands encircling her buttocks, then lifting her as if she had no more weight than a feather. She twined her legs around his waist, locking herself to him as they kissed. Two strides brought him to the bed. Holding her easily with one hand under the luscious curves of her butt, he threw the quilt aside so he could lay her on the cool sheets. Caitlyn scooted into the middle of the mattress and reached for him as he lowered himself to the bed beside her.

"I've dreamed of doing this since I first sat with you by the river," he said, holding her soft breasts in both hands, and kneading them. Lowering his head to get the right position, he worked first one breast, then the other, suckling, gently biting before soothing the erotic pain with his tongue, while rolling the other nipple in his fingers as the bud pebbled under his attention. Arching against him, Caitlyn slid her hand the length of his body, over the rippling muscles and smooth skin to his jutting cock. She ringed him with her fingers, unable to fully grip the girth, sighing appreciatively. Swirling her finger teasingly on the head, she rubbed her hand in the slick juices before caressing the length of his engorged manhood, varying the compression and the rhythm. She paid special attention to the ridge on the underside of his cock and then concentrated on the supersensitive edge where the shaft met the head. Under her skillful attention, his manhood throbbed, all the blood in his body pooled there. Groaning in pleasure he pressed against her as she massaged him.

"I want you inside me," she said, her voice low and seductive. "I ache for you. Please."

Control. The leopard and I must have control. She's human, not a shifter. He took a deep breath. "I want to be sure you're ready," he answered with a slight shake of the head. He kissed her again, nipping at her underlip. "If I'm only to be with you once, my beloved mate, I want the moments to be the most memorable sharing of passion you've ever experienced."

"For both of us," she answered. Now her hand strayed, his sac, touching the sensitive spot behind his balls, exploring every inch of his most private places with an endearingly shy possession.

"You're determined to drive me out of my mind in the best possible ways but two can play this game."

Licking along her closed lips, he sought the hot depths of her mouth. As he kissed her, Kyler stroked his hand across her body, gently parting the curls at the vee of her thighs, teasing along the soft folds hidden there. Delighted to find she was already wet, creaming for him, Kyler inserted one finger and rubbed and stroked, plundering her mouth insistently as he continued to work the sensitive bud of her clit. He inserted a second finger and she moaned. Still caressing his cock, she tightened her grip, nearly causing him to lose control. Skillfully he brought her to a shuddering climax. Before her trembling subsided, he transferred his attention to the vee between her legs, his tongue working its magic here, teasing at the pearl in her clit, tasting the cream, bringing her to a second climax even stronger than the first with just his tongue.

"Kyler," she said in between panting breaths as tremors racked her body, her hands fisted in his hair, "I want you, all of you, inside me now."

He kissed his way back up her body and to her lips, taking possession of her mouth fiercely. His cock nudged at her slick, wet folds. Reaching down with one hand, he guided himself as he slid into the hot, tight velvet of her embrace for the first time, penetrating and withdrawing in a controlled motion. Instinctively she moved in rhythm with him, drawing him deeper and deeper, trying to hold him inside her with clenched muscles, while he delighted in tormenting them both by nearly pulling out and plunging deeper in the next moment.

Laughing in sheer pleasure, Kyler lowered his head, nipping at her shoulder with his teeth, then biting down enough to break the skin, needing to mark her as his mate, continuing to pump in and nearly out of the warmth of her soft body, holding onto his control by a thread. Caitlyn arched her back, interior muscles contracting in response to his cock's motion. Aroused by the tightness of her channel, losing himself in the way her body molded itself to him, Kyler had never experienced anything as intense with any other woman, shifter, witch or human. And as long as he lived, there'd never be any other woman in his bed but his mate. Spurred by the thought, he plunged deeper. She cried out a little but as he kept moving, her body tightly caressing the length of him, she threw her head back, moaning his name. Kyler plunged balls deep into her and they finished together, his seed pulsing into her womb. Caitlyn bit him where his neck met his shoulders and the joy of being claimed by his mate flooded his heart. The leopard roared in triumph, deep in his soul. He shuddered, groaning with the ecstasy of a climax such as he'd never experienced before, completely entwined with his mate.

"Mine," he whispered, stroking her hair away from her perspiring face. "My beloved."

"I love you," she answered, breathing hard.

Bracing himself on his elbows, he surveyed Caitlyn, her hair spread out on his pillow, beautiful face flushed, lips swollen from his kisses. Giving the bite mark a quick swipe with his tongue to seal the wound, he said, "I hope I didn't hurt you?"

"And I can say the same," she answered, stroking her fingertips across the spot where her teeth had bruised him.

At Caitlyn's touch on the mark, his cock quickened again, buried inside her. He moved experimentally, shifting his hips and she responded, inner muscles tightening like steel bands, caging his cock in sensation, driving him crazy. He tried to pull away, to roll off.

She tightened her embrace. Brought her legs up to encircle him, hold him in place. "No, don't go."

"You must be sore—"

"I don't care. The two of us, together—I thought the ecstasy would never stop. I'll never have enough of you." She kissed him even as her hand was wandering to where their bodies joined. Paying special attention to his sensitive sac, she stroked his balls again, rolling them gently in her hand. He lost control and drove deeper inside her, pumping desperately to a second release that had him shivering with the pleasure she gave him. Again she matched him, her climax coming on top of his.

Reluctantly he slid from her body and rolled over, pillowing her head on his shoulder, holding her close, heart too full to speak. *What if I'd never met her? Never been blessed to know her love?* He kissed her cheek, inhaled deeply of her perfume and musk. The last ten years of hell were worth it, to end up with Caitlyn in his arms.

She allowed her hand to stray across his chest before she stroked his stomach, lazily following the trail of golden brown hair to his groin, toying with his semi erect cock. Reluctantly he moved a little away from her on the bed. "Insatiable mate."

"Hmmm," she said with a devilish smile and a gleam in her eyes. "You give every evidence of relishing my insatiability."

"We shapeshifters aren't like human men, you know. I'll be ready to take you again right now if you keep touching me." He tried to pull her wandering hand away from his already rising manhood.

She struggled a little in his arms. Instantly he released her but the next moment she'd rested her head on his thigh, licking his cock into full arousal while her hands massaged his balls and the sensitive area behind them. Laughing, she took him in her mouth, suckling and teasing the sensitive head with her agile tongue. She swallowed the first drops of his seed. Kyler groaned and pressed her head closer to him, urging her to continue. One slender hand fisted the base of his cock, squeezing and massaging in the rhythm he'd already discovered stripped him of control. She kept him firmly prisoner in her mouth as his hips bucked in response to her suction.

"If I didn't know you were human, I'd swear my mate was a wildcat." Grinning, Kyler took her by the shoulders and pulled her away from her fascination with his cock, rolling her over in the same motion and plunging deep into her slick depths, bringing them both to a surging climax more intense than any they had yet shared.

Spent and sated, they lay entwined on his wrinkled sheets, breathing hard.

A tear slipped down Caitlyn's cheek and he kissed the salty drop away as she said, "I can't bear to leave you."

"You must. You have to get away from Azrimar before Margred or Bradana realize what you mean to me." He withdrew from her body reluctantly, raising himself on one elbow, to gently wipe away the tears on her flushed cheeks. "Don't cry for me—your sorrow rips holes in my heart. You've given me more than I ever hoped to have, my precious mate. I swear to you, I'll endure whatever I must until you and my Packmates ride to Azrimar with a plan. All right?"

Caitlyn closed her eyes for a second. "I can't ask for more."

What else could either of them say? They'd stolen an hour or two, but the basic circumstances were unchanged.

Kyler kissed her hard, ending the embrace abruptly, unable to stop himself from taking possession of her lips a final time before sliding out of bed. Naked he walked across the room to his private bath, taking a few moments to wash before returning to scoop his kilt from the floor. Savoring the tender moment, he drew the covers over Caitlyn, tucking her in. "I want the scent of you on my sheets tonight to remind me of these hours we shared, when you've gone. No one will bother you in my quarters this afternoon. Rest as long as you need. Then you can make your escape from the city."

"Where are you going?" Sheet held modestly over her breasts, she scooted against the pillows.

He pulled on his boots, retrieved his tunic and military cloak from a nearby chair, taking care to pull them on and straighten the garments to hang properly. Combing his hands through his unruly hair took another second. Hand already on the door handle, he glanced over his shoulder to capture a final glimpse. "I'm going to perform my assigned duties, act as if nothing is different."

"When the world has changed," she whispered.

Smile for her. "Always remember I love you, Caitlyn of Ordlathus." And he left the room, closing the door behind him firmly.

CHAPTER SIXTEEN

Actually, he'd been summoned to a spell casting, but he wasn't burdening Caitlyn with the information. She'd worry and she needed to be on her way to Ordlathus tonight, not lingering here. He regretted not taking his brother's offer to leave a warrior close by, to accompany her on the long journey south, but too late now. And he selfishly wouldn't have wanted any other shifter to spend time in her company alone.

The young page Tabarus was waiting for him in the queen's foyer.

"Are you all right?" Kyler asked the boy, studying his face. Had he been crying?

"Yes, sir. We mustn't be late, the queen said to bring you right away." The page set off in the direction of the tower, not toward the normal spell casting chamber or to Margred's rooms.

Which was a relief as it meant she wouldn't be reopening the awkward conversation about having a child. Even a spell casting was preferable to that topic. Kyler studied the page's demeanor as they walked. "Something's the matter. Tell me."

Tabarus wiped his sleeve across his face. "The queen arrested the Duke. I saw the whole thing, in the foyer, after the wedding. She's condemned him to death and it's not right, sir. My family lives on his estate, outside the City, he's a fair master and he couldn't have done any of the bad things Princess Bradana was saying. My mother says he beggars himself to fix the City, when it's the queen who should pay, not our duke."

Kyler knelt on one knee to be at eye level with the boy. "Your loyalty to Aerrol does you great credit but also puts you in danger, understand? Margred and Bradana won't tolerate anyone speaking in his defense. It's safe to talk to me but no one else. Do you know if his sister was taken prisoner as well?"

"Not yet. Captain Nedd marched to arrest her but her room was empty. I hope she escaped," Tabarus said with a sudden burst of anger

"Escort me to the tower as you've been ordered and then walk out of the palace and go home to your family outside the City. The situation will get worse here for a while, I think. If anyone asks, tell them your mother is ill and you had permission from Ylain to go to her after your duties today were done." A dubious frown shadowed the boy's face. Kyler clapped him on the back. "Since Ylain is on the ocean sailing to Shang right now, no one can contradict you and you were known to be her favorite page. Promise me."

Sniffling a bit, Tabarus crossed his heart with one finger. "I promise. Even some of the soldiers were complaining about the duke not being given a trial, no chance to answer Bradana."

"Maybe something can be done for Aerrol," Kyler said, "But not right now." He stood, placing a hand on the boy's shoulder and squeezing gently. "I give you my word I'll see what may be possible after I recover from the spell the witches work tonight."

Tabarus left him at the entrance to the tower, which was guarded by Quarl and another man Kyler didn't recognize. After exchanging a brief greeting with the sergeant, he made his way up the long, winding stairs, the sound of his footsteps echoing in the space. He pondered what Margred and Bradana might have in mind. A private spell, no room in the chamber for all the adepts.

Bradana met him at the entrance, standing in the open doorway as if she'd been waiting for him. "Took you long enough to get here, shifter. We're nearly ready to begin. Go into the side chamber, drink the wine and disrobe."

Not answering her, Kyler walked into the small room she indicated. Throat closing, stomach roiling at the idea of choking down the potion yet again, Kyler contemplated the golden goblet of drugged wine. He shoved the cup away, spilling some of the dark liquid on the table, the drops staining the cloth like blood.

His oath called for him to give Margred magic to make her spells more powerful. Nothing was said ten years ago of his taking drugs. He fingered the black robe, lying neatly folded on the chair next to the table. Or of special garments. She wanted a shifter's magic and that's what he owed her, not all this extra. In the beginning there'd been none of this claptrap. When did they start wearing him down? He rolled his shoulders. *I thought I was resisting but I can see now, thanks to Caitlyn's influence, how far these two witches dragged me into their schemes. If Margred wants me to drink this concoction and stand before her half naked, she'll have to command me specifically. I'm not giving her an inch of leeway.*

"We're waiting," Bradana said as she crossed the threshold. "Why haven't you prepared as I ordered?"

"You can have my magic as I am or not at all," he replied.

"We'll see about such defiance." She hustled from the room, calling to Margred.

Not surprisingly, a moment later the collar constricted around his throat but stopped short of cutting off his breath. Either the queen was playing games with him or else she wasn't upset by his rebellion. A curious new warmth flared in his chest, close to his heart. Seeing no reason to remain in the room when he wasn't going to drink the wine or change clothes, Kyler prowled into the spell chamber, still puzzled why the collar wasn't choking him into unconsciousness. He wouldn't put it past Bradana to pour the drugged wine down his throat once he'd blacked out. She'd done it a time or two before, in the early days.

Both women were staring at him with wide eyes. He smothered a chuckle at their identical expressions of disbelief. "This shifter's not going to make everything easy for you anymore."

"Sister, use the collar to compel his obedience," Bradana said, gesturing in Kyler's direction. "He must drink the wine."

"I *am* using the damn thing, but the constriction spell isn't working properly." Eyebrows drawn together in a frown, Margred aimed the golden key at him.

There was a subtle constriction of the golden torque, an annoyance but nothing more. Maybe Belinu granted part of his prayer the other night after all. Whatever blocked the collar's spell, he was grateful and hoped the effect lasted. Kyler grinned, wishing he had the leopard's fangs to make his fierce pleasure at disconcerting them even more obvious. "Shall we get on with the spell you want to work tonight?"

"I need you to be properly prepared," Margred said, tapping one toe on the marble floor, hands on her hips. "Why have you chosen tonight of all nights to be difficult?"

"The question is, why did I comply with your demands so many times in the past?" he countered. "Our agreement is for you to draw upon my magic. Here I am." Buoyant with rekindled defiance, Kyler walked to the spell altar, which occupied nearly the entire chamber but was only half the size of the one in the room normally used for spell casting. The sand was golden, neatly raked. A rectangular object shrouded in black silk, embroidered with red characters in the language of Shang, lay on a small table outside the perimeter of the altar. He tweaked one edge of the cloth. "This must be the famous red jade tablet you traded poor Ylain's hand in marriage to obtain?"

Hands raised as if to shove him away, Bradana bustled to place herself between him and the tablet. "Don't touch it!"

"Attend to me, shifter," Margred said, the snap of command in her voice.

The inexorable pull of the spell tugged at him. Raising one eyebrow, he turned to face the queen.

Hands clasped, eyes narrowed, she gave him a severe look. "I don't need you to lie on the sands this evening as we're burning no special candles. The altar needs to stay clear for the Summoning, so I suppose it'll be acceptable if you remain clothed, but I'm going to need your blood to energize the tablet's magic. Take off your shirt and sit in the chair." She pointed to an elaborately carved mahogany chair off to the side. "Now."

He strove to resist but Margred was exercising the spell she'd laid on him a decade ago, and he was bound to obey, his feet taking him to the chair as if he was sleepwalking. As he marched, he took off the tunic, dropping it on the floor from nerveless fingers. Damn, Belinu only granted his prayer to a limited extent. He remained bound to obey her commands. Gritting his teeth, he fought to remain standing but his body betrayed his will and a moment later he was seated in the chair, spine straight, his arms stretched out along the flat red velvet pads, held as immobile as if Margred had chained him down.

He heard the sounds of men toiling up the stairs in the tower, with much out of breath cursing. Margred and Bradana exchanged wide eyed, excited glances, seemingly eager to greet the new arrivals. A moment later, a battered and bruised Duke Aerrol was manhandled through the door by red-faced, panting soldiers, Captain Nedd on their heels. The officer had a huge smile on his face as he saluted the queen.

"The prisoner as ordered, your majesty," he said, dusting himself off as if he'd personally wrestled Aerrol up the stairs.

"Excellent." Margred pointed to a set of shackles set in the wall opposite where Kyler was sitting. "Chain him over there and then you and your men clear out so the spell casting can begin."

"What the hell do you think you're doing?" Aerrol shouted, doggedly fighting his captors as they dragged him toward the restraints anchored in the tower's outer stone wall. "Have you lost your mind, Margred?"

"You've been condemned to death for treason," she said. "The sentence will be carried out tonight and at least your death will serve some good for the City by enhancing a supreme spell casting."

Kyler watched as the soldiers exchanged glances. The situation wasn't meeting with much favor among the common folk of Azrimar, judging by how Tabarus reacted earlier, and the discomfort of these men now. Margred and Bradana might be pushing their luck.

But the guards locked a cursing Aerrol into the wrist and ankle irons under Bradana's watchful eye and beat a hasty retreat from the room. Captain Nedd lingered, as if he wished to be invited to participate or at least observe.

"What are you staring at?" Aerrol said to the hovering officer. One eye was swollen, purpled, his left arm hung awkwardly, as if his shoulder might have been dislocated, but the duke stood proud and undaunted.

"Not so high and mighty now, are you, your grace?" Nedd uttered the honorific as a sneering insult. "Nothing but a condemned prisoner, waiting to die." He fingered the dagger at his belt. "Wish I was the one to end your life. Killing a duke would be something for a man to boast of."

"Not if you killed him while he stood defenseless in chains." Kyler raised his voice to be heard.

"Leave us, captain," Bradana said, gesturing toward the door. "Tell the guards below to admit no one."

Saluting, Nedd left the room with a swagger, casting a derisive glance sideways at Kyler, held motionless in his chair.

The door crashed shut. Margred locked the bolts herself, ensuring privacy for whatever she had planned.

Bradana disappeared into a small antechamber, emerging a moment later carrying a white wood tray, on which sat an array of small glass bowls, each filled with different colored sand. Barefoot, she stepped onto the spell altar and knelt in the middle, setting the tray beside her. Using a lacquered stick inlaid with mother of pearl, she drew a pattern in the golden surface of the altar. She sang, moving her hands in time with the music, as she poured different colored sands into the pattern she was creating. Head cocked to one side, the princess studied her work for a moment, before smoothing out part of the uncolored design with a handful of large black feathers and redrawing it.

The chant was nothing Kyler recognized but he found it jarring, discordant. If he was in leopard form, he'd be snarling a challenge. Paralyzed by Margred's spell, he could only sit and watch as the queen's sister enlarged her work to create a more elaborate pattern. She was using primarily purples and reds, with black lines she poured even more carefully than the colored ones. Occasionally she added a sullen yellow as a bold accent.

What magic was this? Nothing he'd ever seen in the City before. Kyler observed a disruption in the air directly above the altar, a dark shimmer at about seven feet off the ground. As if storm clouds were gathering, in colors to match her pattern.

He exchanged glances with Aerrol, across the chamber from him. The duke had tested his shackles to no avail but now he was motionless, intent on Bradana. Waiting for any chance to get free. As a warrior, Kyler approved. *If I can help him against these witches, I will. Tonight is going to bring an end this captivity or I'll die in the attempt.*

A glossy black porcelain bowl in one hand and her deadly sharp belt knife in the other, Margred came to his side. As she laid the implements on the table next to him, he said, "Not using the crystals tonight?"

Glancing over her shoulder at Bradana's work, the queen shook her head. "A new, more powerful magic my sister found in her research. The red jade tablet was the key we required." Bending closer to him, she gasped and shifted the lit candle on the table to give her better light. She pointed one index finger at him, frowning, lips compressed. "What's this? A new tattoo? How dare you place a magical symbol on your body without my permission? Your magic belongs to me, with no interference."

What the hell was she talking about? Genuinely puzzled, Kyler glanced at his chest. He blinked in surprise at the small, bright green symbol on his skin above his heart. The design was a series of dots and resembled nothing so much as the triple circle of Tiermalleia. Could it be the representation of his mate bond with Caitlyn, denoting the blood she'd shed to save his life? His heart swelled with pride and the leopard settled somewhat, both man and beast pleased to wear a physical mark representing what Caitlyn meant to them.

Margred let loose a small shriek. "And what's this bruise here?" The touch of her cold hands on the bite mark Caitlyn had left infuriated him. Before he could say anything, the queen's next words struck him like a blow. "I'll get to the bottom of this mystery, shifter, don't think I won't. I don't care what slut in my castle you've bedded today, as long as it doesn't happen again but the tattoo was a foolish decision indeed. You'd better hope this new mark of yours doesn't interfere with our spell casting tonight."

He kept his expression as blank as possible, while his mind raced. He had to shield Caitlyn. Thank the gods Margred didn't recognize the green mark as Tiermalleia's sign or she'd make the connection immediately because his mate was the only person from the South in the palace. Belinu grant Caitlyn escaped by now and was on her way home with the Stone.

Running the leather thong through her fingers as she pondered, the queen chewed her lip for a moment. "I detect no adverse power or influence from this tattoo, luckily for you. The bite mark is merely disgusting." Binding his upper arm tightly with the strip of knotted black leather, she tapped his vein with two fingers to make the vessel stand out more. "Make a fist; you know the routine by now. Your special brand of magic will complement the power Bradana and I plan to summon nicely, shifter."

He gritted his teeth as she made a tiny incision with the point of the knife and his rich dark blood spurted out into the bowl Margred had waiting.

Wrong, this is all wrong. Making a vow never to submit to blood drawing again, he was light headed before Margred decided she had enough, releasing the tie and uttering one potent command to stop the bleeding.

"Are we ready?" she asked Bradana.

"In a moment." Bradana assembled a small lacquered easel at the side of the altar circle and then placed the red jade tablet carefully on the thin shelf. She tugged the black silk covering off, dropping the shimmering cloth to the floor.

Kyler laughed. "The Emperor of Shang got the best of this bargain."

The jade was old, cracked and discolored. Whatever incantation or symbols had been carved into its surface were now nothing but meaningless bumps, worn away by time.

Keeping the bowl of his blood warm in her interlaced fingers, Margred hastened to join her sister. "How little you know of magic, shifter."

She poured the blood along the top of the tablet. At first nothing happened but then the faded red jade glowed steadily brighter until it was a fiery red, with black writing standing out from the surface, the complex symbols moving and rearranging themselves in new groupings as the magic from his vein permeated the talisman.

Nausea assaulted him. The movement of the markings on the tablet gave him a headache. "This tablet must be of the Shadow," he said, shifting his focus to avoid seeing the roiling symbols. "You've no right to use my magic in conjunction with shadowed spells."

"Rise and come here," Margred said, not deigning to answer his charge.

Fighting the command tooth and nail, Kyler at last stood in front of the tablet. Margred and Bradana had taken positions on either side. Now Margred lifted a long box from the table and flipped open the lid, revealing a curious weapon. The foot long handle was carved from highly polished black wood, a single piece masterfully depicting a man garbed as a warrior, dressed for battle in a uniform Kyler didn't recognize. The warrior figure provided the balance for the stone blade. Lavishly embellished with mosaic pieces of turquoise, seashells, malachite and other stones Kyler'd never seen before, the figure wore an elaborate helmet, shaped like a bird, wings spread wide. A grinning stone face peered from the open beak of this headgear. Carved in a kneeling position, the warrior's hands wrapped around the haft of the knife. The long, v-shaped blade was bound to the hilt with tough plant fiber, sealed with amber-colored resin. Made from a smoky black stone, the edges of the knife were honed razor sharp.

Despite the warrior on the handle, this was clearly not an honorable weapon meant for combat. Sacrificing innocent victims was the only explanation for its unusual design. He thought he heard the faint screams of the many souls who'd been killed with this blade crying out to him, even as the demons who drank spilled blood whispered in his head, trying to tempt him to take the hilt, wield the power. He realized Marged was attempting to hand him an instrument of pure evil. His leopard was barely under control, incensed by the Shadow clinging to this knife.

She held the box out to him. "Take it."

Heat flared over his heart where the symbol of Tiermalleia was tattooed. The warmth spread outward, washing through his body in a soothing wave. Hands raised, ready for combat, he was able to retreat from Margred, despite her command. "I refuse."

"You what?" Margred recoiled. "You've no power to refuse me, shifter. I command you to take this knife and execute Aerrol."

Her willpower and her magic buffeted him like gusts of wind from a winter storm. The black symbols on the red tablet continued their restless motion and three of them suddenly flew off the jade altogether, to dart at him like enraged hummingbirds. Stinging pain blazed whenever one of the living spells touched his bare skin. Yet he stood fast. "I won't kill for you, Margred," he said through gritted teeth.

"This is a supreme spell, fool, and a death is required. His death." Margred pointed at Aerrol with her free hand. "You gave your oath to obey me in matters of magic, now do as I say."

"This goes beyond mere magic. You've crossed the line into the darkness of the Shadow now and no shifter willingly abides anything to do with evil. I'm sworn to battle the Shadow in all its forms and that oath predates the one I made to you." Each word he spoke brought more of the angry symbols flying off the red jade to join the assault on him. The force of the attack drove Kyler to one knee, trying to fend them off as best he could, partially held in Margred's thrall. "The knife is an abomination, meant to feed demons."

Bradana grabbed the knife from the box Margred was holding, adjusting her fingers to ensure a tight grip on the shiny wooden hilt as she advanced on Kyler. "Either you kill Aerrol with this knife now, or you'll become the sacrifice, shifter. I'll be content either way but there must be a death while the jade is imbued with life force."

CHAPTER SEVENTEEN

Caitlyn held her grief in abeyance until the door closed behind Kyler but then she wept at the thought of leaving him in peril. Eventually the tears subsided and she drifted off to an exhausted sleep for a time. When she awoke with a shudder from a bad dream, she rose from the bed, bathed herself in his private bathroom, then dressed. She moved a bit gingerly, but welcomed the minor discomfort as a reminder of the pleasures she and Kyler shared. After checking her pocket to make sure the Stone was safe, she paused, studying her reflection in the mirror for a minute, hands resting on her abdomen.

We've created a new life, a mere spark as yet but ours.

"We'll rescue him, my child, I promise," she whispered. "Somehow. You're not going to grow up fatherless. He's not going to die without knowing you."

She cracked the door open an inch, making sure no one was in the corridor to see her leaving Kyler's quarters. Then she crept into the hall and walked away, keeping her pace even, heading toward the main portion of the palace. She met surprisingly few people on her way to the dormitory floor. The magic currents perpetually swirling in the palace's air were turbulent, unsettled.

When she strolled into the room she shared with Susana and Gretha, she found only the latter, lying in her bed moaning. As Caitlyn went to her own portion of the chamber, Gretha leaned her head noisily over the edge of the bed and threw up into a basin. Wiping her lips with a damp washcloth, the apprentice said, "Where have you been? Not only did you miss all the excitement when Duke Aerrol was arrested but Headmistress was calling for you after the wedding. She wanted you to do some healing on her bunions."

Feigning amazement, Caitlyn sat on her own bed. "Aerrol arrested? Whatever for? Was Susana arrested too?"

Gretha tottered into their shared bathroom, taking the basin with her. "The duke committed treason, or so it's said. I'm sure Susana left the castle."

She sounded dubious about the treason charges yet Gretha was a zealous member of Bradana's faction until now. Curious, Caitlyn rose and leaned on the wall next to the partially closed bathroom door. "Can I get you something to settle your stomach?"

Gretha wrenched the panel open, Caitlyn recoiling. "Isn't the drain of power sucking at you? Isn't the queen's spell affecting you at all?" the other girl said, holding her head in both hands. "I know you don't respond to the magic the way we do, but surely you must be feeling something?"

"What are you talking about? What kind of spell?" Heavy foreboding sank into Caitlyn's bones. "What is Queen Margred doing?"

"The headmistress told me Margred's working a supreme spell tonight, taking herself to the next level of magic. She's drawing power from all of us within the palace walls right now, to prepare." Gretha waved the clean basin. "Her claim on my magic is why I'm ill."

"A supreme spell? But why? Are the demons from the West attacking? Is there some natural catastrophe threatening?" Caitlyn opened her senses to the dreamspace as she spoke. She'd been so caught up in the afterglow of making love with Kyler, she failed to pay enough attention to what else happened in the palace. A dangerous mistake in Azrimar.

Gretha shook her head weakly as she staggered to her bed. "She said Margred merely hungers for the sheer power and has stopped caring what the price may be. The jade tablet she got from Shang holds great magic. If she does a supreme spell, she can tap into the power of the tablet and wield more magic than any Witch

Queen has ever commanded. But the headmistress fears, and I believe, this new effort tracks to the Shadow. "

Kyler said he was going on duty when he left me but he must have been trying to shield me from the truth of another spell casting. He's blocking me from awareness of his peril. Anger rising in her gut, Caitlyn said, "Doesn't a supreme spell require the taking of a life?"

Gretha wouldn't meet her eyes. "Yes."

"She plans to kill Kyler tonight, doesn't she?"

The other girl's silence was answer enough. Pacing the length of their tiny, shared bedroom, Caitlyn swore terrible oaths in her native tongue. Her roommate shrank against the wall, shock and fright on her face.

"This has to end—she goes too far," Caitlyn said, not speaking to Gretha, but to Powers greater than herself. "I can't walk away, I refuse."

"You can't do anything about it," Gretha said. "I always suspected you desired the man, maybe even slept with him, but you've got to face facts, he's doomed and you can't help him. The queen and Princess Bradana are locked in the tower spell chamber. Surely they've summoned the shifter by now. You can't get in and even if you could, you've no magic, let alone enough power to match them."

Caitlyn laughed, the fury coursing through her providing a wild strength. "Then I'll die in the attempt. I don't believe the goddess Tiermalleia will abandon me now. I've too much to fight for."

Ignoring Gretha's protest, she ran from the room, looping the Stone's chain over her neck as she went. Moving quickly, Caitlyn traversed the halls to the tower which housed the queen's private spell chamber. At the door to the stairs, guards were posted. Faces set in wrinkles of worry and pain, the men were bone white as the powers the Witch Queen summoned affected even the non-magic dwellers of the palace. Arms trembling from the effort, the two soldiers crossed spears in front of her.

"Sorry, lass, no apprentices were called for this ceremony," Quarl said, swallowing hard, face screwed up in a scowl of discomfort, one hand on his considerable gut as it rumbled loud enough to be heard. Burping, he grimaced again. "No one is allowed to disturb the queen tonight."

"Is Kyler with her?" Caitlyn asked.

The burly soldier's eyes held pity as he answered her question. "Aye, he was required to attend. He's been in the tower with them for some time. Duke Aerrol too." He reached out and touched her shoulder for a second. "Best you go now. Forget the shifter."

"This is so wrong," she said. Quarl helped her before so she hoped he'd listen to reason now. "You must realize Margred has left the boundaries of the Light. She goes to the Shadow and you'll all be dragged there with her. The City will lie open to the demons of the West by dawn if she isn't stopped."

Quarl shook his head. "Doesn't matter what we think. She's our Queen."

"She and her sister must be prevented from opening Azrimar to the Shadow," Caitlyn repeated.

"Even if what you say is true, the likes of you can't halt her plans," said the other guard with contempt. "We've all seen you can't even do true magic."

Retreating a step, Caitlyn raised her chin. She allowed a hint of her real power to slip through her shields, imbuing her voice with the authority she carried in Ordlathus as a hereditary priestess. "One final time, I ask you to allow me through the tower door. I don't seek to hurt you but Marged's scheming has gone too far and I must stand against the Shadow. Don't risk yourselves by attempting to stop me. "

The younger guard laughed. Eyes narrowed, Quarl studied her for a moment, rubbing his chin. Grabbing his fellow soldier by the arm, he yanked the man out of Caitlyn's path. Setting his own spear aside, the sergeant extracted the other guard's weapon from his grasp, allowing it to clatter to the floor.

"What are you doing? Queen Margred will kill us." Mouth gaping open, the soldier stood aside in disbelief as Quarl unlocked the door to the tower. "And if she doesn't, Captain Nedd will throw us in the dungeon to rot."

Quarl straightened, pocketing the key. "Perhaps, but some things are worse than death. Caitlyn's right; this endless sorcery and spell casting have to stop before we lose ourselves to the Shadow. I have my honor today but by tomorrow we might all be under the Shadow, lost men. " After opening the door, he crooked a finger at Caitlyn. "Go then and may whatever powers you believe in help us all."

She swept past them, taking the stairs at a run. The door slammed shut behind her as she sped around the first curve. Fear for Kyler fed fresh energy to her aching leg muscles and she hardly paused as she made her way up the long staircase to the spell chamber. The heavy door at the top of the stairs was also closed and locked from the inside, although there were no guards.

"No human guards," she whispered to herself. With her mind's eye, Caitlyn was aware of massive spells, laden with deadly energy and menace, writhing across the wooden panels.

Taking the last step, she stood on the small landing, attempting to catch her breath and slow her pulse. She raised her hands, palms flat, a few inches away from the door. Tendrils of green light flickered from her to the scarred wood. "You've no power over me, no ability to deny me entry. You weren't set as a barricade against one such as me." When the green light faded, she lowered her hands to touch the wood, as if petting a skittish horse. "I speak to the spirit of what you once were, tall, towering trees, sovereigns in your own place and time. We are akin, not you and she. In the Name of Tiermalleia, Lady of the Forests, I beseech you to allow me entry. The goddess sent me to prevent a great wrong."

She heard whispering in her head, several deep voices murmuring to each other. There were no words but she understood the gist of what they shared with her. She took one hand away from the door and fished in the pouch at her belt, locating the spell-inscribed knife she used to cut her herbs and plants. She laid the small weapon square in the center of the massive metal bands crisscrossing the door, and took her hand away again. Glowing, the golden knife stayed, suspended against the cold black, the runes on its blade flashing green. The green light bled off the knife into the black metal, creating fractures, like ice cracking. The wood flexed, breathed. The voices murmured louder.

Caitlyn took shelter as best she could, crouching on the stairs a second before the door burst apart with a crack of breaking wood and the shriek of metal rendered into scrap, lethal shards flying in all directions. Retracing her steps, she picked her knife out of the rubble and stepped across the threshold into the room.

The occupants of the spell chamber were frozen, staring at her. The queen stood next to the red jade tablet, which appeared to be dripping blood. Kyler's blood no doubt. The shifter was down on one knee, bruised and bleeding from a number of places. As Caitlyn watched, several of the black symbols from the tablet flew at him and where they struck his shoulders and back, flecks of blood appeared. His face reflected pain, anger, determination.

Bradana had her hand cruelly fisted in his long hair; some kind of ritual dagger clutched in her other hand. Kyler had a death grip on her wrist, keeping her from slitting his throat.

Almost as an afterthought Caitlyn realized Aerrol was chained to the wall across the room.

Standing as tall as she could, Caitlyn took another step into the room, abandoning her glamourie and her mental shields. In the next breath she unleashed the full power of who and what she was, undiminished even in this place hostile to her kind. Like a wave, power swept into her from the Lady Tiermalleia. Caitlyn knew she'd chosen the right path, this was the moment Arduwina had promised, the chance to save Kyler's life. A major battle with the Shadow lay ahead of her. Her gown changed from a worn green travel dress to a pure white, flowing robe. Faint lavender-and-green threads of light ran across the fabric like embroidery, spelling out sacred runes. The ties of her loose braid came undone and her hair floated in the energized air.

"Stop!" Caitlyn's voice rang out in the room like a bell as she pointed at the queen. "You cross a forbidden barrier if you take Kyler's life, if you do this spell tonight. Sacrificing Aerrol to your ambitions will be a further abomination. There'll be no return to the Light for you, Margred."

Kyler took advantage of the moment to shove Bradana violently against the table, which crashed to the floor. Fisted hands raised in a defensive posture, he rose to his feet, batting away the flying darts, which retreated in a disorganized cloud to the safety of the red jade.

Recovering her balance, Bradana scurried into position between Caitlyn and the tablet from Shang. "You've no right here. How did you get in?"

"You've no true powers," Margred said, eyes narrowed, contempt in her voice. "We let you stay in the palace only out of pity."

Caitlyn laughed. "I've no powers such as yours nor do I want them, witch queen. I possess my own magic. Try to deny the evidence—unlike you, I walk in the Light."

She came forward, raising her hands. Emerald green light played along her fingers, flashed across the room, circled her in intricate patterns, tried to reach out to Kyler. Bradana casually pushed the illuminated tendrils of light aside with a motion of her own hand, somehow extinguishing them. One by one Caitlyn's serpentine lights winked out.

"Am I to understand you came here for the shifter? You lust for him?" the queen asked in puzzlement.

"Why are you doing this spell tonight?" Caitlyn threw a question of her own in return. "What need do you have to cross the threshold into the realm of black magic?"

The Queen shook her head. "I don't know what you mean—I don't practice the black arts." She gestured at the restrained Duke across the chamber. "He's been condemned to death for his crimes; we merely carry out the sentence tonight so his death can serve some good. I've commanded the shifter to execute him."

"Which I refused to do," Kyler said, moving a step or two closer to Caitlyn.

She kept her gaze locked on the queen's face. "You condemned Aerrol on trumped up charges, based on evidence Bradana falsified. No good comes of sacrificing an innocent man, much less consecrating his execution to the Shadow."

Margred glanced at Bradana for a moment. "The supreme spell we're crafting tonight will imbue me with more power than any other Witch Queen has ever held. I'll be able to protect my city and my people so the spell, strengthened by the death of the traitor, will result in good. Not service to the Shadow."

"This is hardly white magic," Caitlyn said, allowing her scorn to seep into her voice. This woman was mired in delusion and denial. "The spell you describe has nothing of the Light about it." Taking a deep breath, Caitlyn pointed an accusatory hand at Margred, who shrank away as if fearing a physical assault. "You've been traveling a grayer, more dangerous path for years. Your city shows the effects of your choices, falling apart, crumbling. Your people suffer, with illness rampant in the population. Your enemies circle Azrimar's borders, becoming bolder as you care less and less. I think Ylain tried to stanch the consequences of your choices but then you sent her away. Or someone did, in your name." Tilting her head, she indicated Bradana. "Aerrol's only crime is trying to hold your city together for you."

"You're too clever for your own good," Bradana said, stroking a finger along the center groove of the curious stone blade she held. "You meddle in things above your station."

"To crown your foolishness, now you choose to give yourself and your city to the Shadow," Caitlyn said to the Queen, ignoring Bradana. "You invite evil inside the walls."

Forehead wrinkled in an unbecoming frown, Margred seemed puzzled, unsure. "No, I do what I must to protect my city and my people." She took a step away from Kyler and Caitlyn, glancing anxiously at her half-sister. "Bradana, tell her the truth." When her sister remained silent, the queen rushed into more explanations, as if she sought Caitlyn's approval. "Bradana and I researched the oldest scrolls, found the most powerful spells, and acquired important talismans, like the knife and the tablet. The items are ancient, not of the Light perhaps but not Shadow. I believe they predate the Light and the Shadow."

"So she tells you. Or so you foolishly want to believe. Good and evil have always existed, no matter what labels we give them." Caitlyn shook a finger at

Margred. "You became addicted to the magic. You craved more and more power under Bradana's tutelage. You went way beyond what was required to maintain the safety of your people. The pursuit of this knowledge became about you and what you could do, new skills to master. But at the foundation, this entire affair is about Bradana and what she wants. Examine her heart and see how far under the Shadow she is."

"No, she only counsels what is best for me, for the City," Margred denied. "I make my own decisions."

"She wants to *be* you," Caitlyn said. "But since she's baseborn and you're the elder, legitimate daughter, she's worked hard since your birth to make you her tool, her cat's paw. She rules through you. You do what she wants, without fail, if she makes a big enough fuss about her desire. I've been here for months now and I see the situation clearly. You're as much a slave to her magic as Kyler is a slave to your collar."

"Enough of this time-wasting debate." Screaming curses or spells, the words lost in a peal of thunder, Bradana hurled a bolt of pure energy at Caitlyn.

Raising her hand, she stopped the assault with ease, establishing a solid green shield of light that absorbed the black lightning into itself and winked out. In the next heartbeat Caitlyn launched a torrent of her own green and lavender fire across the room.

Hand on her forehead as if she suffered a migraine, Margred stumbled to her throne while Bradana and Caitlyn battled, throwing spells at each other.

She blocks even the most powerful spells I hurl at her. Caitlyn realized she and Bradana were equally matched.

The princess wheeled toward Kyler, who Caitlyn feared must be weakened by the loss of blood and the effects of fighting Margred's commands. Uttering a curse, Bradana flung jagged red and black bolts of power at him. Caitlyn shrieked, losing no time in sending a roiling cloud of her own to absorb the fire and protect her mate.

But Bradana wasn't paying attention to the effect of her strike against the defenseless Kyler. She was screaming orders at Margred.

The Witch Queen left her throne, scuttling forward to grapple with Caitlyn. Kyler moved to separate the two women, dragging Margred away as she struggled against his grip.

"We may not have the sacrifice yet but I can do the Summoning," Bradana said. She rapped on the red jade with the stone knife and each time she touched blade to stone, a musical note reverberated in the room.

The sound was deafening, echoing in the chamber. The oily cloud above the altar sands swirled faster with each note Bradana struck, until it was a tornado, wobbling drunkenly in the center of the circle, sucking in all the painted sands to reveal the bare stone floor.

Kyler flung Margred into her chair and fought the winds to reach Caitlyn, bracing her against the gale. She buried her face against his chest and they clung together until suddenly the wind stopped. Raising her head, Caitlyn saw the sand fall like rain into the altar circle and when the shower ceased, a man stood where the tornado had been.

At first glance the newcomer was a rather ordinary man, with sandy gray-blond hair loose on his shoulders and down his back, and silver eyes, bare chested save for an elaborately incised pectoral necklace made from a huge iridescent shell strung on a leather thong. A pair of tight fitting leather pants was his only clothing. His feet were bare, the toes adorned with gold rings, the nails painted in black with jagged yellow designs. He had a string of tiny bells around his right ankle, their sound jarringly cheerful as the man moved. The aura of cold evil projecting from him despite his smile made Caitlyn want to gag. Her vision blurred, showing her the man and the Shadow, of some kind of animal, a dog or a wolf perhaps. Was the animal his actual form? Was this the moment of true sight Arduwina promised? She clenched her hand on the Stone of Duadalne till the points pricked her palm.

"Tezacuatli," Bradana said, her voice hushed yet proud. She knelt, head bowed.

"Indeed, although perhaps you ought not to make so free with my name. Actually a rather ancient form of one of my names, to be specific. Been studying old spell sheets perhaps?" His voice was a pleasant baritone, the tone mild, mocking, amused. "All this fuss in my honor? Yet when I arrive anywhere there must be hot blood spilled, a heart removed." He tapped one bare toe on the stone floor. "Who is my host or hostess tonight? I am compelled to inform you that you've been sadly lacking. Not a good way to entice me to answer your petition."

Bradana rose. "I summoned you."

"Yes, as you were supposed to do, daughter of the West. Your mother was created from the sand of my desert to be exactly what the last King of Azrimar would find most desirable." The newcomer licked his lips. "And then of course he had to lose her because that's the jest of it all. My particular delight lies in confounding people's expectations of happiness. But you aren't ruler here, are you? Or at least, not yet. Now we know what you want, let's move on, shall we?" He spread his arms wide. "Who is my hostess?"

"I'm the Witch Queen of Azrimar." Rubbing her elbow from where she'd been slammed into the chair by Kyler, Margred stood in front of her throne.

"And you want all encompassing power, unleashed by a supreme spell, to defeat known and unknown enemies, live forever and never have to endure the messiness of lying naked with a man or the inconvenience of bearing a child. Am I right? You only want the power." He tilted his head and as the shadow beast mimicked the gesture, chills raced along Caitlyn's spine. A predator studying his prey. She thought she saw red fire burning behind the silver mirrors of the man's eyes and his alter's eyes blazed scarlet as Tezacuatli spoke to Margred.

The attention of the Shadow in human guise moved on before Margred could speak. He pointed at Kyler. "Brother! A fellow shifter, how marvelous. I haven't seen one of your kind in, oh centuries, not since one wandered into my western deserts and died. Well, to be fair, I might have killed him. It's been so long, one forgets. I mounted his skull on my wall in fact."

Reaching out with one hand, Kyler dragged Caitlyn behind him. "I'm no brother of yours, Shadow Man."

"But you want your freedom, you want the human woman I see hiding behind you, you want cubs and a happy old age. I can give you these prosaic dreams."

Caitlyn held her breath.

"There's nothing you have that I want," Kyler said, the leopard's growl making his voice deep.

The man chuckled. "And the serving girl wants only you. And your cock of course. A story old as time. "

He can't read me. I see his true nature but he can only see the surface of me, thank the goddess. Caitlyn tightened her grip on the Stone, suspended between her breasts on its golden chain.

"And the poor devil in shackles over there was intended to be my meat, wasn't he?" Tezacuatli walked to the edge of the altar circle closest to Aerrol, who straightened in his bonds and spat.

Desperate for insight into this interloper and how to deal with him, Caitlyn realized he was staying in a confined area of the tower. Maybe he couldn't leave the altar circle, might somehow be penned there until a sacrifice was made perhaps.

"Defiant. I approve. But you see," said the Shadow, moving so quickly he was a blur, "That's not how I take my meal. The sacrifice must have spent the last year living in luxury, all wishes fulfilled, must want to be me, with all my powers, must have come to this meeting willingly. And in this entire room of people, the description fits only you." Exactly when he'd grabbed the stone knife from Bradana, Caitlyn had no idea, but now Tezacuatli hurled it unerringly at Margred.

The queen screamed as the knife buried itself hilt deep in the upper chest and sliced laboriously at her torso as if an invisible assailant was wielding it. Clamping her hands on the hilt, trying to pull the blade loose, she fell to the floor, writhing and screaming as she fought for her life.

Horror made Caitlyn's stomach heave. *He's trying to cut her heart out.* She threw a bolt of her magic, sizzling with power, at the altar. Tezacuatli recoiled, mouth open in surprise, revealing black fangs. The power she'd thrown spread, becoming a curtain blocking the Shadow from view as the magic ringed the entire altar. Bradana worked frantically on a countermeasure, screaming curses and hurling bolt after bolt of purple and black to break Caitlyn's screen.

Caitlyn ran to Margred, Kyler on her heels. They knelt by the queen's side as she moaned, foaming at the mouth, convulsing on the floor. He braced to yank the knife free, but Caitlyn prevented him from doing so, shaking her head. "Although the blade's stopped moving since the Shadow can't see to command it, if you pull it out, she'll bleed to death in seconds."

"Either way, there's... nothing... you can do for me," Margred said in gasps, her voice burbly and awful to hear. She clawed at Caitlyn's arm with one hand, leaving the other clenched on the knife's black wood hilt. "You were right, about Bradana, about the Shadow—"

"When she dies, her power will feed him and he'll come at us," Caitlyn said to Kyler. "He's some kind of a shifter, an animal unfamiliar to me."

Eyes narrowed, he asked, "What did it look like?"

"Not feline. Dog maybe? Wolf? Hellhound perhaps."

"Margred, set me free of your spell," Kyler said, his face right next to the queen's glazed eyes. "I have to shift *now*."

She stared at him for a long minute, her lips working but uttering no words.

"When she dies you'll be free regardless," Caitlyn said, clutching his arm.

"We can't wait and we can't risk Bradana or the Shadow doing something to interfere with the spell's lapse."

Caitlyn heard music, a haunting melody, a wordless chant sung by the Shadow Man to accompaniment of a small drum, and then an animal howled an approximation of the same tune. The paired vocalization was the eeriest sound she'd ever heard, raising gooseflesh on her entire body. Rising and falling, the call went on and on, till she wanted to cover her ears and cower.

The chant energized Margred, mortally wounded or not. The queen released Caitlyn's arm before reaching into her own bodice and retrieving the golden key.

Kyler swiveled awkwardly and Caitlyn guided the queen's quivering hand to insert the key into the lock and turn it. A second later the golden collar fell on the floor. Margred closed her eyes although Caitlyn could tell a tiny thread of life-force remained.

Iridescence filled her peripheral vision as Kyler shifted.

Next moment, the leopard snarled in triumph and challenge. Kyler in this form was majestic, three times the size of an ordinary leopard, with fangs like knives. His green eyes glowed as he rubbed against Caitlyn once and then took a stance between her and the altar. The short fur along his spine stood up and his tail lashed as he waited for his enemy to appear.

As she realized there were long tears and gaping holes in the green sheet of blazing light, Caitlyn knew there wasn't much time. She took a moment to melt the hated collar and its key into slag before rising to her feet. There was nothing else to be done for Margred.

The green magic shredded with an audible ripping sound, whether the protective spell's failure was because the queen had died or because Bradana had succeeded in throwing enough power at it to overwhelm Caitlyn's incantation, she didn't know.

The terrible keening cry sounded in the tower again and as the last shimmers of green fell to the tower floor and disappeared like drying raindrops, Tezacuatli came into view. He'd shifted and the reality now matched the shadow Caitlyn had seen before. Standing on stubby legs, the animal wasn't as large as Kyler's leopard, but when the beast snarled, a set of impressive fangs were revealed. The coat was lush, soft, matching the gray-blond color of the man's hair. His tail was like a rat's, skinny and naked, and studded with spikes or quills. Most surprisingly, two white snakes lay heavily across his shoulders and coiled down around his front legs, heads raised and hissing defiance.

Not directly challenging Kyler at first, the shadow hound trotted forward rather casually, stepping primly over the edge of the spell altar, claws clicking on the bare floor, then circling Bradana, sniffing her skirts. After this surprising inspection, the beast raised its head, ears pointed forward, red eyes glowing. He sat on his haunches for a moment, tongue lolling as if he was amused by a private joke.

Dangerous. To have such confidence in the face of the leopard meant he was extremely powerful. Caitlyn had grave misgivings about the creature's insouciant attitude.

The great cat slunk low to the ground, head tilted, growling deep in his throat. From her position behind him, Caitlyn could see the powerful muscles in his haunches tensing to pounce. Only the tip of his tail twitched.

Then so fast he was nothing but a blur, Kyler launched himself at the hellhound, who met him in midair, sinking his fangs into the leopard's flank even as Kyler ripped deep gashes in his enemy's body. Snarling, growling, the two shifters fell to the floor, entwined in a ball of bloody fur. The leopard's powerful hind legs raked at the hellhound's belly while for his part, the Shadow had a grip on Kyler's throat. Each of the snakes latched onto Kyler's body, striking again and again.

Free Aerrol. Kyler's voice rang in her head. *He's too exposed.*

Amazed he had attention to spare for talking to her, Caitlyn retreated a few steps, as if terrified by the animalistic battle in front of her, which truthfully she was, and sidled away. Bradana was riveted on the fight, hands poised as if to launch magic at Kyler if she could get a clear shot. The princess moved as the combatants shifted ground, all her attention on them, waiting for an opening to assist the Shadow in defeating Kyler.

Moving slowly so as not to attract Bradana's attention, Caitlyn circled the tower wall to where the duke was chained. He flicked his attention between the fight, Bradana's actions and Caitlyn's advance toward him. Aerrol fairly radiated impatience, muscles tensed, jaw clenched, pulling against the restraints.

He wouldn't to be much help in a battle of magic but she knew Kyler was right, they couldn't leave him where he'd be easy to kill. As she drew near, she saw the manacles were made of iron and her heart sank. "I can't break these with a spell. Did Margred have a key?"

"There's a lever to release the chains," he said, his voice low. "Hurry."

She located the switch he was talking about, on the other side of him. Anxious to watch over Kyler, to send power his way if he needed it, she scooted past Aerrol and flipped the lever. The manacles snicked into the recesses in the wall and the duke fell awkwardly to his knees, catching himself with his good arm.

Caitlyn helped him stand.

"Weapon?" His voice was raspy and she was horrified at how battered and bruised he was.

She fumbled her gardening knife out of her pocket and passed it to him. Aerrol weighed the blade in his hand, grimacing, but then got a firm grasp on the hilt. "Better than nothing."

Stumbling, they made their way slowly to the area of the tower by the stairs, where Aerrol stopped, leaning on the throne. "This is far enough." He coughed. "Your shifter has the upper hand on our Shadow visitor."

Caitlyn realized the fight had moved into the sand of the spell altar. At this moment the two animals separated, stalking each other, hellhound and cat poised to exploit any opening the other gave. She was surprised and frightened Kyler hadn't been able to defeat the smaller, less muscular creature by now but then, this was a battle of magic and size didn't always directly relate. Tezacuatli was the equivalent of Belinu or Harlann in power, and even Kyler couldn't defeat a god. She studied the enemy more closely and a chill ran along her spine as she realized the Shadow must be playing with Kyler, amusing himself.

The leopard sprang suddenly, pinning the Tezacuatli under his paws, ready to tear the enemy's throat out. There was a flash of black lightning and a huge bird fluttered upward. The leopard made an impossible leap, coming down with a mouth full of tail feathers, which he spit out in disgust. An eerie laugh echoed from the dark recesses of the tower's roof.

Caitlyn darted forward to snatch a handful of the feathers. *I know his name, even if it is an old name he didn't seem too worried about, and now I have a piece of his physical presence. Perhaps the two together will be enough to let me command him.*

"Give me those!" Appearing to have similar thoughts, Bradana launched herself at Caitlyn and the two women fell to the sand, fighting over the feathers, pulling each other's hair, kicking and cursing.

With a roar, Kyler catapulted himself into the air, landing on Bradana, claws out, slashing her horribly, carrying the woman away from Caitlyn with his momentum, rolling onto the floor. The easel holding the red jade collapsed as they crashed into it and the tablet broke into fragments when it hit the floor, burning with a dull red smoke. With a triumphant snarl awful to hear, the leopard sank his fangs deep into Bradana's throat and tore it out. A moment later the leopard threw its head back, muzzle covered in Bradana's blood and yowled its victory over the hated enemy.

Kyler rose as the man a heartbeat later and kicked the woman's body away from him. He ran across the sand to Caitlyn. "Are you all right?"

She rose, leaning on him. "Fine. You?"

"Heads up, he's coming back," Aerrol shouted. He dropped the knife and snatched one of the torches from its holder.

Caitlyn retreated to the table next to the throne, grabbing the knotted leather thong lying there. Quickly she used it to tie the feathers together in a crude approximation of a man. Sweeping up the sharp silver knife stained with Kyler's blood, she took a deep breath, girding herself for the coming battle. Spinning to face the spell altar, she gasped in horror, for their Shadow visitor had transformed himself yet again.

"This has all been amusing," Tezacuatli said from his position on the altar sand. Taller than the humans, he was now a heavily muscled warrior, his long hair braided, wearing an elaborate feather-plumed helmet similar to the one depicted on the sacrificial knife's handle. Two stripes crossed his cheeks, in black and the dark yellow color Bradana had used in her sand painting. He carried a sword of the same black stone as the knife, adorned with white feathers matching the ones on his helmet. The shell pectoral had morphed into a polished disk of the stone material and now served as a breastplate. Oozing from the surface of the mirrorlike armor, tendrils of acrid smoke drifted into the air behind him, forming the image of the hellhound, complete with the snake duo, still hissing defiance.

Tezacuatli pointed the sword at Kyler. "Pleasant as it was to spar with a fellow shifter, I've no more time to amuse myself. You fight well, warrior. I could use one like you."

Kyler spat. "Go to hell. I'll never serve the Shadow."

"No, I suppose not." Tezacuatli strode over to Bradana's lifeless corpse. "Disappointing." He assessed Margred's equally crumpled form, on the floor by the throne, then wheeled to face Caitlyn, Kyler and Aerrol again. "Did you know the one power denied to me is reviving the dead? Immense gifts are mine; nothing is beyond me save this one trivial thing." He heaved a theatrical sigh. "You've left me without a pawn to rule this place in my name." Pointing the feathered sword at the duke, Tezacuatli said, "You'll have to do."

Caitlyn stepped forward, holding the mannequin she'd created from the bird form's tail feathers in one hand, Margred's knife in the other. "By the power of the goddess Tiermalleia, I order you to be gone from this place and trouble us no more, Tezacuatli." She stabbed the knife into the 'chest' of her makeshift doll and threw the bundle onto the floor.

He recoiled, stumbling a step or two, sword raised as if fending off an attacker. The snakes on the hellhound apparition hissed, revealing fangs dripping with venom. The shadow beast snarled and the eyes flashed red fire as the man collapsed to his knees, head lowered, free hand clenched over his heart. But a moment later, Tezacuatli was on his feet again, laughing boisterously. "Fooled you all, didn't I? You've an interesting amount of power, girl, but nothing capable of standing against mine. I have many names more significant than the one my pawn so foolishly gave away and the blackwing hunter isn't my true alter. But I admire the effort. Quick thinking." His face grew serious, the eyes gleaming in an uncanny mix of silver and red. "I believe I'll take you with me into the West, to provide amusement for as long as you last. Your shifter will have to die first and my pawn will have to submit to me, but then you and I'll go." A thin strand of the gray smoke wound its way through the air toward Caitlyn.

Kyler shifted to leopard form, placing himself in front of her, spine arched, fangs bared. Aerrol drew near, holding a torch in one hand for a weapon.

As Tezacuatli strode across the sand toward them, Caitlyn depressed the small emerald button on the chain holding the Stone of Duadalne, freeing the rock from the necklace. Holding the Stone in both hands, she closed her eyes, took a deep breath and sent the goddess a prayer. As she reopened her eyes, she kissed the rock and said, "I command you to reveal your power and obliterate the Shadow now threatening us."

As Kyler snarled, visibly bracing himself to make a suicidal attack on the approaching enemy, Caitlyn reached out to touch him, locking her fingers in the soft folds of fur at his neck. "Wait." She gave Aerrol a quick sideways glance. "Hang onto my shoulder and don't let go."

There was a chiming sound from the Stone as it split, three jagged green lines running down its sides, like a cracking egg. Pure white light speared out from the interior of the Stone as it continued to open in her hand. When the Stone had fully deployed, Caitlyn couldn't help but gasp at the iridescent white gemstone lining the inside. More beautiful than any opal she'd ever seen, this hidden layer displayed green, blue, purple and red fire in a translucent medium so pure it seemed to be water. Rainbows played on the walls as the white light spread, pulsing in all directions from its source in her hands. Her eyes watered at the intensity of the illumination. She and the two men stood in a small circle of vibrant color, as if encased inside the expanding gemstone, gazing out through the clear walls. As the circle of white light spread, everything it touched vaporized, exploding in clouds of red, black and purple, which rapidly leached away under the influence of the Stone's energy. Margred's corpse became a skeleton, flaring solid black against the white background, before it melted to ash and disappeared. The throne, the tables, the torchieres—all the objects in the room were destroyed. As the light reached the spell altar, the rainbows concentrated, blasting the surface again and again, in a blinding series of strikes.

Tezacuatli leaped into the air as the light rose below him like a living thing seeking prey. He shifted into the gigantic black avian form. "You may have won for today," he said, his voice hoarse as he flapped in a lazy circle, ascending the tower, "But I am the West and to truly vanquish me you'd need the help of the East, which you don't have. The world is out of balance in my favor. Despair is your reward for this day's work, humans."

"We have the North and the South allied together, with Azrimar safe in the center now," Caitlyn cried. "You've no business here, no one who serves you. Be gone to your home and leave us in peace. By the power of Duadalne, I order you out of our lands for all time."

The strange high pitched howling she'd heard before echoed through the tower, raising gooseflesh all along her arms. The white light mushroomed upward in the tower, completely filling the space wall to wall. There was an earsplitting noise from high above them and huge stones fell, threatening to crush them before the power of Duadalne blasted the blocks into harmless gray dust, rapidly absorbed in the incandescence.

"He must have breached the upper wall, by the ventilation slits," Aerrol shouted, hanging onto Caitlyn with a death grip, trying to shield her as best he could. He'd dropped the torch at some point. The leopard crowded close, curled around her body as if determined to take any blow that might fall before she could be harmed.

Next moment there was a tremendous explosion and the white light blew the roof of the tower to smithereens, becoming a solid column of illumination reaching to the heavens, rushing past the moon overhead. Fascinated, awed, Caitlyn threw her head back and wondered how far the opalescent light would travel—back to the Stone's place of origin?

Kyler shifted to human form, taking her in his arms to kiss her, breaking her awed concentration on the light. "Enough, the Stone is going to expend all its power needlessly and the Shadow is fled."

She took a deep breath to extricate herself from the intense pleasure of commanding the power at her fingertips. *Borrowed power, not mine. Tiermalleia's.* She focused on the stone in her hand, cupping her fingers to try to reassemble the pieces. Panic assaulted her for a moment and the nursery rhyme about not being able to mend a broken egg danced incongruously through her head. But the Stone was reforming, green light stitching a seam in the fissures like a needle pulling thread through cloth as she brought the jagged edges close to each other, until with an audible snap, the Stone was whole and the light extinguished itself. For a second, all the lines in her hands glowed with the white light—the lifeline the heartline, every crease—and then she felt the power seep into her. A gift? Feeling so shaken she could hardly stand, she sagged against Kyler.

In the space of one heartbeat, she and the two men were standing in the dark, no roof above their heads, only the moonlight and the stars to provide illumination. She managed to snap the Stone onto its gold chain before her legs gave out, Kyler catching her as she collapsed. Holding her in his arms as if he'd never let her go, he kissed her. Arms around his neck, she reveled in his passionate caress until the cold wind howling through the broken walls above them reminded her of their circumstances.

"You did it," Kyler said, admiration and awe in his voice. "You banished the Shadow."

"With your help and the gift of the Stone. He isn't destroyed, merely exiled to his proper place." Caitlyn nestled closer to Kyler. "I hope I've done enough."

"It has to be, for we can do no more," Kyler said.

"All those years my cousin was so duped by Bradana." Aerrol shook his head. "I wish now I'd tried harder to talk sense to Margred, make my case for less magic, more earthly defense. Azrimar was so near to being lost tonight, but for the two of you."

Caitlyn shook her head. "She probably wouldn't have listened. Tezacuatli told us Bradana's mother was his creation, remember? So Bradana was at least half Shadow from the day she was born. You've nothing to reproach yourself with."

"And now you're king," Kyler said. He held out his hand. "Allow me to be the first to congratulate you, on behalf of the Packs of the North."

Wincing, Aerrol shook hands. "I haven't absorbed my new status in yet."

"Put me down, please, Kyler. I can stand," Caitlyn said

As he complied, steadying her, she reached out to Aerrol. "Let me heal your shoulder at least, your majesty."

"I'd appreciate the gesture, but how can you have any power left?" Despite the question, Aerrol turned to give her access to his dislocated shoulder. "No offense, but who could have guessed before today, based on your modest demeanor and appearance, that you were a sorceress of such incredible power?"

"Ah now you perceive my disguise, sir." She laughed a bit shakily. "But the magic wielded tonight wasn't mine." She lifted the necklace away from her chest, the embedded flakes of gemstone catching the moonlight. "The Stone of Duadalne holds the power of the goddess Tiermalleia, which is as boundless as Nature. Your ancestors stole this talisman from mine and I was sent here to retrieve it. Tiermalleia gave me permission to use the Stone if circumstances required." *Would I have dared otherwise? Would the Stone have opened for me?*

"And now she's taking the Stone home to Ordlathus," Kyler said, challenge in his tone.

Aerrol grimaced a bit under Caitlyn's ministrations, as she directed her own healing power at his badly damaged joint. "Clearly the thing belongs to her, not my people. I'd be the last person to object, after what the two of you did tonight on my behalf, for my City."

Kyler walked over to the remnants of the spell altar. He whistled. "Come see this."

When Caitlyn finished with Aerrol, she joined Kyler. The entire circle of the altar had been fused by the power of the Stone's light, becoming one giant piece of opalescent glass, shot through with the purple, red and green fire. "Amazing."

"I don't suppose I can persuade the two of you to stay in Azrimar? Help me get my kingdom organized after the chaos Margred created?" Aerrol pulled his sleeve down.

"I think you'll find you have a great deal of support waiting for you, among the army, the people, most of the nobles," Kyler said as he and Caitlyn walked behind the new king toward the blasted door. "You don't need us. I've been a prisoner here for far too long."

Aerrol clasped his shoulder briefly. "I argued with Margred over her treatment of you as well."

"I know. I appreciate the fact." Kyler helped Caitlyn step past the debris.

"I'm sure most of the adepts will enthusiastically proclaim you king as well," Caitlyn said, moving cautiously as she descended the stairs, holding tightly to Kyler's hand, vertigo assaulting her. Did she actually run up this treacherous open staircase earlier tonight? "By the end even some of Bradana's most ardent adherents were appalled at her trip into the Shadow. And your mother's well respected. She can lead the witches until you wed."

Aerrol laughed. "A fate not even on my mind today. I know the two of you are all about roses and moonbeams but after this experience I may never wed. What if I wake up after my wedding night to find my bride was a construct of the Shadow?"

"Send me word and I'll come check her magic for you," Caitlyn said with a laugh.

"Before the wedding," Kyler added.

They'd reached the bottom of the stairs. Aerrol pounded on the door and a moment later the massive portal swung open, revealing Quarl peering cautiously around the edge, spear at the ready, a squad of soldiers behind him and a crowd of nobles, witches and servants behind them, all white-faced and anxious. The crowd fell silent.

Lowering the spear, straightening to attention, Quarl saluted. "What are your orders, sir?"

Kyler stepped forward before Aerrol could speak, projecting his voice to all corners of the corridor. "Behold the new King of Azrimar, crowned by the gods themselves. Three cheers for your new ruler!"

As the cheers rang out, louder and louder, Aerrol raised his arms for quiet. "People of Azrimar, tonight a great battle has been fought between the Light and the Shadow, a battle which claimed the lives of both my cousins and left the throne to me. I make you my solemn pledge, never again will this City spend time and treasure on pursuit of magic to the exclusion of all else." His proclamation was greeted with more cheers. "Magic is our shield and our sword by birthright, but must be kept in balance."

Caitlyn recognized his mother and sister in the crowd, Nadelma and her staff, many of the others she'd come to know during her time in the City. Yet she had no desire in her heart to do anything but escape with Kyler.

As Aerrol continued, naming his mother to lead the City's witches and setting forth his immediate plans for consolidating his power, each fresh announcement greeted with rousing cheers, Kyler leaned over to Caitlyn and whispered in her ear. "I wish him well, but none of this has anything to do with us now. I want nothing from this place, only to leave it without delay."

"I have a horse in the stables," Caitlyn said. "And I must reclaim my trunk."

Taking her by the hand, Kyler led her off to the side, behind the line of soldiers, and into the corridor. At the last moment, she glanced back and waved one hand, which Aerrol acknowledged with a tilt of his head and a smile.

"We can be on the road in an hour," Kyler said, his voice bursting with happiness.

"I see I must be the practical one. Clothing for you perhaps?" she asked, gesturing at his bare chest. "We can make a quick stop in your quarters. We might need those coins you boasted of the other day. It's a long trip to Duadalne and we have to be there well before the eclipse."

"True enough, my practical mate." He kissed her. "I'll run beside you as a leopard. Finally."

"Are you sure you're strong enough yet? It is a journey of several weeks after all." She was genuinely concerned. "Perhaps we should take a second horse—"

He laughed, picking her up and swinging her in a big circle, holding her tight in his undeniably strong arms. "Shifting to the leopard and back heals all wounds, restores my strength. Margred and her sister never understood anything about shifters beyond the magic we carry in our blood and bones. They cast the spell deliberately so I couldn't shift, driving me to the edge of insanity, but it was all worth it tonight."

"We do have to go to my home in Ordlathus, to restore the Stone of Duadalne to its rightful place in the center of the great stone circle," Caitlyn said as he set her on her feet. "But then we'll be free to travel North, find your people. I've nothing to keep me in the South. I need to be wherever you are."

"A vow which satisfies me. And pleases the leopard." He stopped her for a minute, framed her face gently with his big hands, kissing her before touching her stomach hesitantly. "I can scent you're carrying our child, Caitlyn. Will you mind having the baby in my homeland? Raising him—or her—there?"

She laughed. "Not just this one child, my lord! I trust we'll have many children over the years and savor the pleasure involved in the process of creating them."

"You're indeed much more than you seem," he teased, as they resumed their progress toward his chambers.

"To your great good fortune, cat." she answered archly. "You'll never be bored, I assure you."

"A cat can ask for nothing more," he purred.

***

Thank you for reading THE CAPTIVE SHIFTER! I really hope you enjoyed the adventure (and of course I'd love a review if you have time and the inclination to write one – even a few sentences would be wonderful. Authors relish reader feedback).

If you'd like to stay up to date on all my new releases, please sign up for my newsletter http://wordpress.us7.list-manage1.com/subscribe?u=2a337b96e2ee1ee 1250004b9d&id=7462393c9e

ALSO BY VERONICA SCOTT

ABOUT THE AUTHOR

Best Selling Science Fiction, Fantasy & Paranormal Romance author, as well as the "SciFi Encounters" columnist for the USA Today Happy Ever After blog, Veronica Scott grew up in a house with a library as its heart. Dad loved science fiction, Mom loved ancient history and Veronica thought there needed to be more romance in everything. When she ran out of books to read, she started writing her own stories.

Seven time winner of the SFR Galaxy Award, as well as a National Excellence in Romance Fiction Award, Veronica is also the proud recipient of a NASA Exceptional Service Medal relating to her former day job, not her romances! She recently was honored to read the part of Star Trek Crew Member in the audiobook production of Harlan Ellison's "The City On the Edge of Forever."

Blog: http://veronicascott.wordpress.com/
Email: veronica.scott.author@gmail.com

www.ingramcontent.com/pod-product-compliance
Lightning Source LLC
Chambersburg PA
CBHW061150170626
46809CB00003B/1041